D1285112

CARTOON NETWORK

STEVEN UNIVERSE

JUST RIGHT

kaboom!

Ross Richie CEO & Founder
Joy Huffman CFO
Matt Gagnon Editor-in-Chief
Filip Sablik President, Publishing & Marketing
Stephen Christy President, Development
Lance Kreiter Vice President, Licensing & Merchandising
Phil Barbaro Vice President, Finance & Human Resources
Arune Singh Vice President, Marketing
Bryce Carlson Vice President, Editorial & Creative Strategy
Scott Newman Manager, Production Design
Kate Henning Manager, Operations
Spencer Simpson Manager, Sales
Sierra Hahn Executive Editor
Jeanine Schaefer Executive Editor
Dafna Pleban Senior Editor
Shannon Watters Senior Editor
Eric Harburn Senior Editor
Whitney Leopard Editor
Cameron Chittock Editor
Chris Rosa Editor
Matthew Levine Editor
Sophie Philips-Roberts Assistant Editor
Gavin Gronenthal Assistant Editor
Michael Moccio Assistant Editor
Gwen Waller Assistant Editor
Amanda LaFranco Executive Assistant
Jillian Crab Design Coordinator
Michelle Ankley Design Coordinator
Kara Leopard Production Designer
Marie Krupina Production Designer
Grace Park Production Design Assistant
Chelsea Roberts Production Design Assistant
Samantha Knapp Production Design Assistant
Elizabeth Loughridge Accounting Coordinator
Stephanie Hocutt Social Media Coordinator
José Meza Event Coordinator
Holly Aitchison Digital Sales Coordinator
Megan Christopher Operations Assistant
Morgan Perry Direct Market Representative
Cat O'Grady Marketing Assistant
Breanna Sarpy Executive Assistant

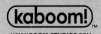

WWW.BOOM-STUDIOS.COM

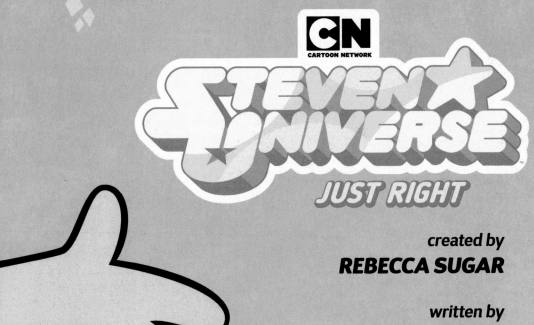

STEVEN UNIVERSE
JUST RIGHT

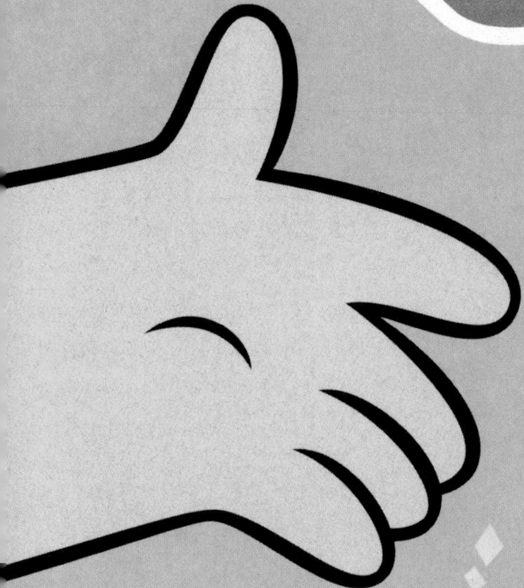

created by
REBECCA SUGAR

written by
GRACE KRAFT

chapter thirteen
illustrated by
KATIE JONES

chapter fourteen, fifteen, and sixteen
illustrated by
RII ABREGO

colors by
WHITNEY COGAR

letters by
MIKE FIORENTINO

cover by
MISSY PEÑA

series designer
GRACE PARK

collection designer
JILLIAN CRAB

assistant editor
MICHAEL MOCCIO

editor
MATTHEW LEVINE

Special thanks to
Marisa Marionakis, Janet No, Becky M. Yang,
Conrad Montgomery, Jackie Buscarino and
the wonderful folks at Cartoon Network.

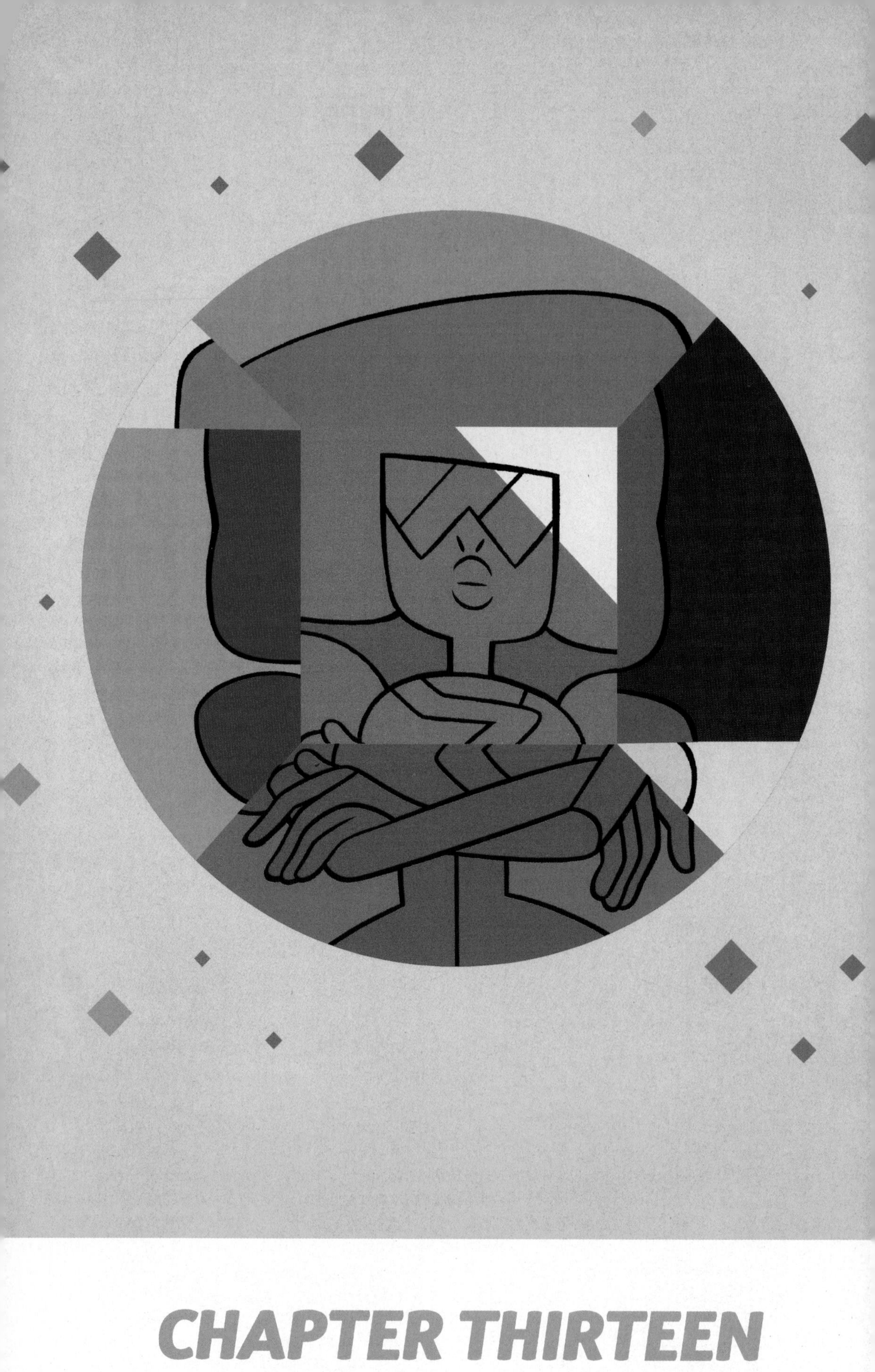

CHAPTER THIRTEEN

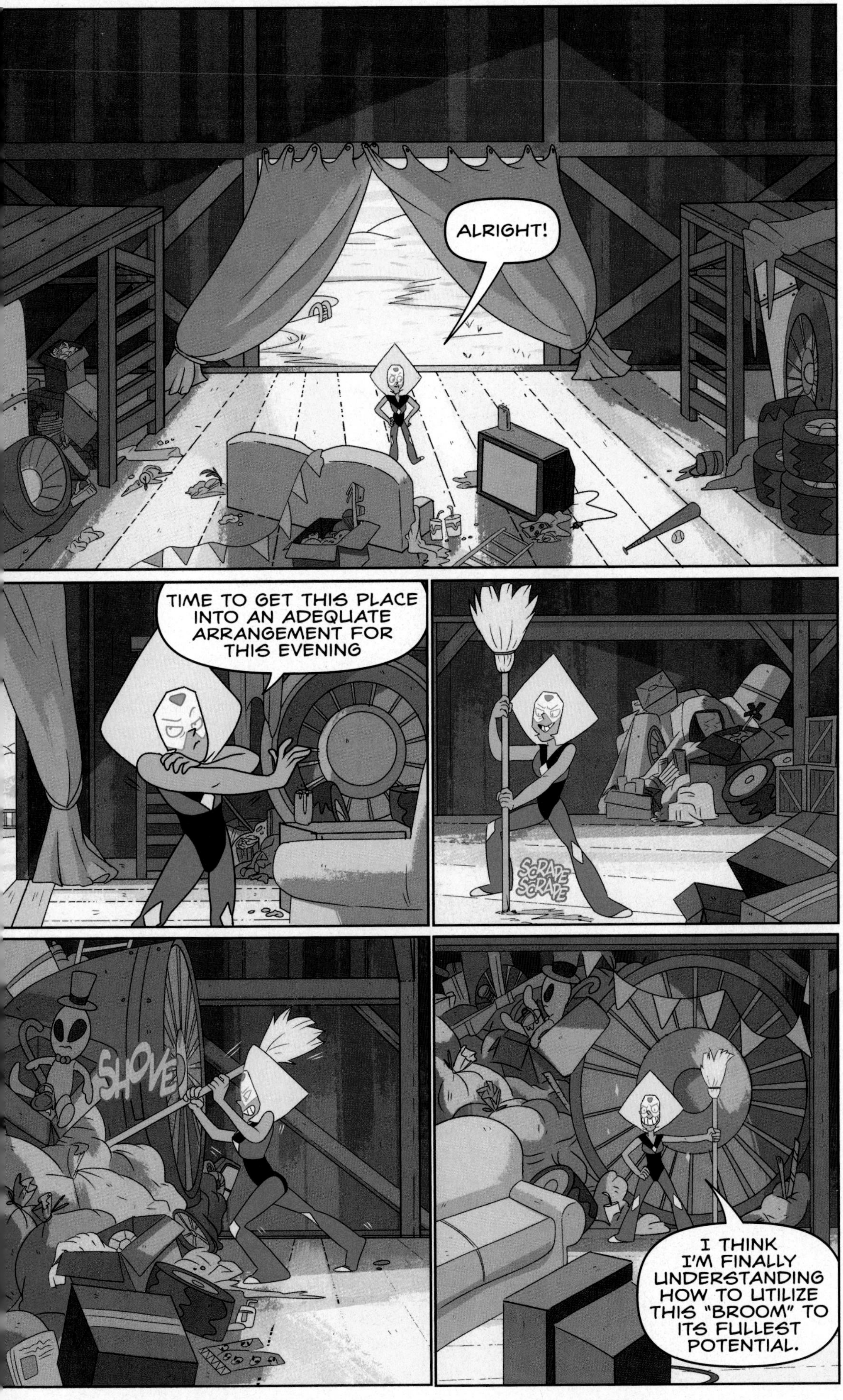
ALRIGHT!
TIME TO GET THIS PLACE INTO AN ADEQUATE ARRANGEMENT FOR THIS EVENING
SCRAPE SCRAPE
SHOVE
I THINK I'M FINALLY UNDERSTANDING HOW TO UTILIZE THIS "BROOM" TO ITS FULLEST POTENTIAL.

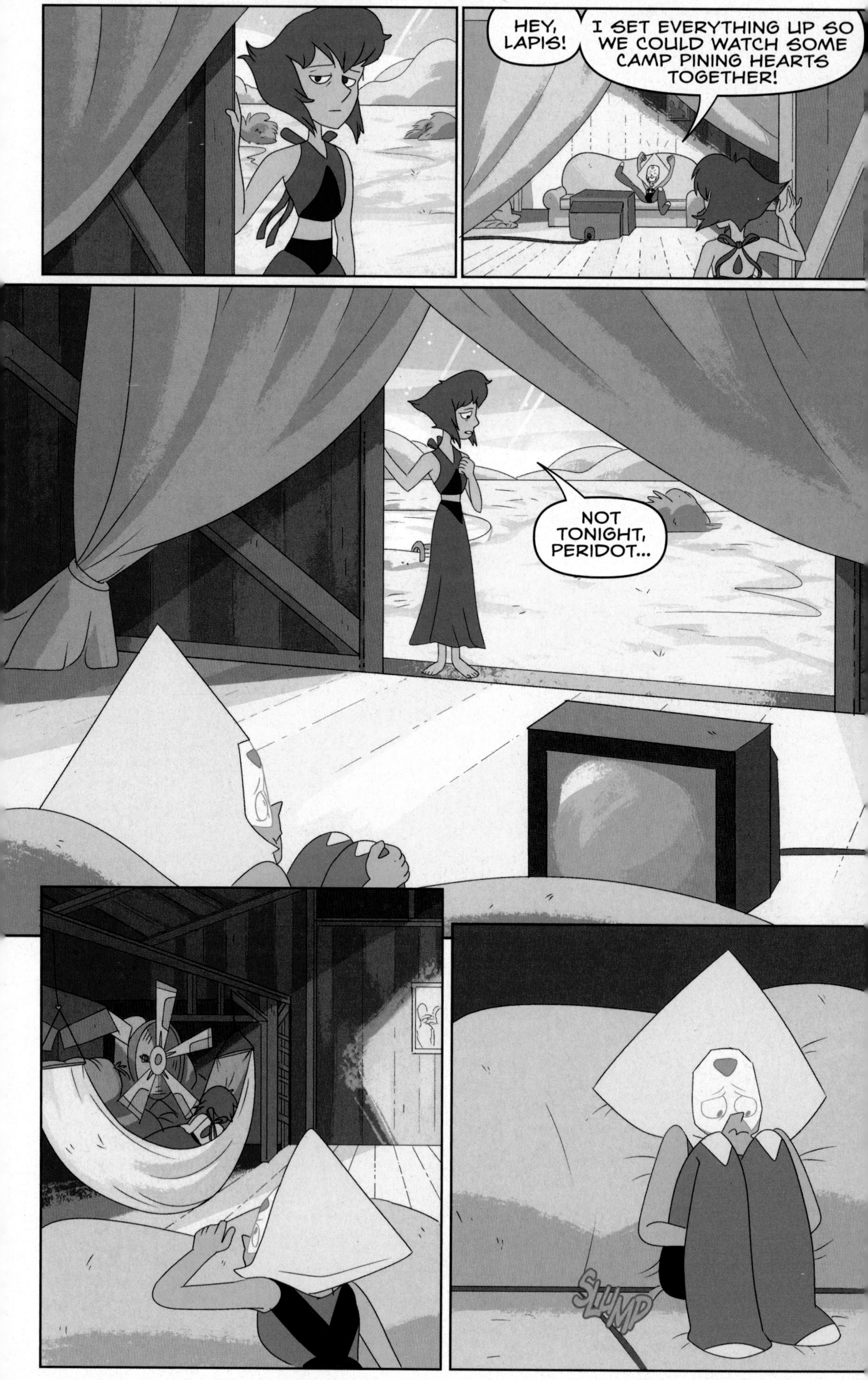
HEY, LAPIS!
I SET EVERYTHING UP SO WE COULD WATCH SOME CAMP PINING HEARTS TOGETHER!
NOT TONIGHT, PERIDOT...
SLUMP

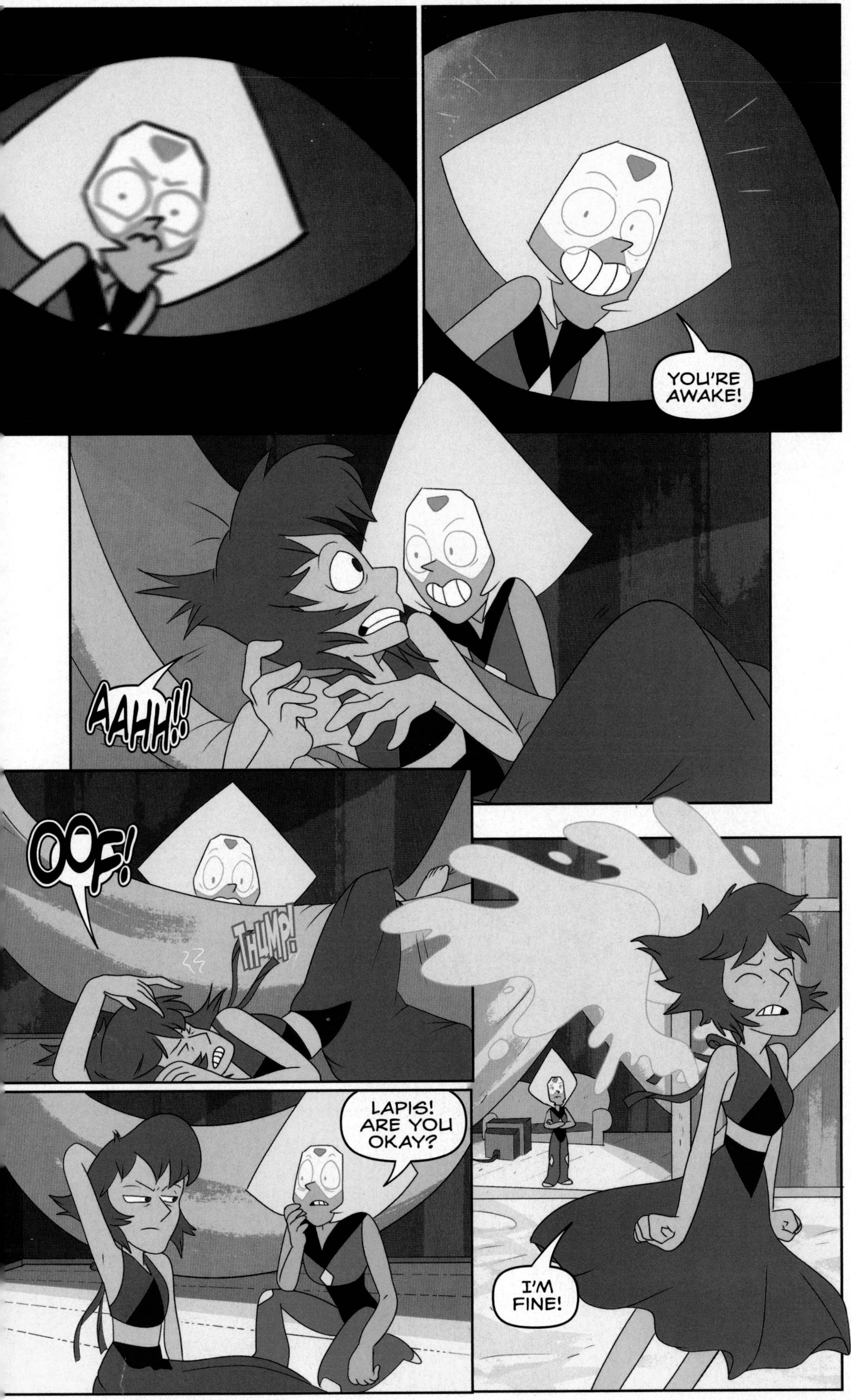
YOU'RE AWAKE!
AAHH!!
OOF!
THUMP!
LAPIS! ARE YOU OKAY?
I'M FINE!

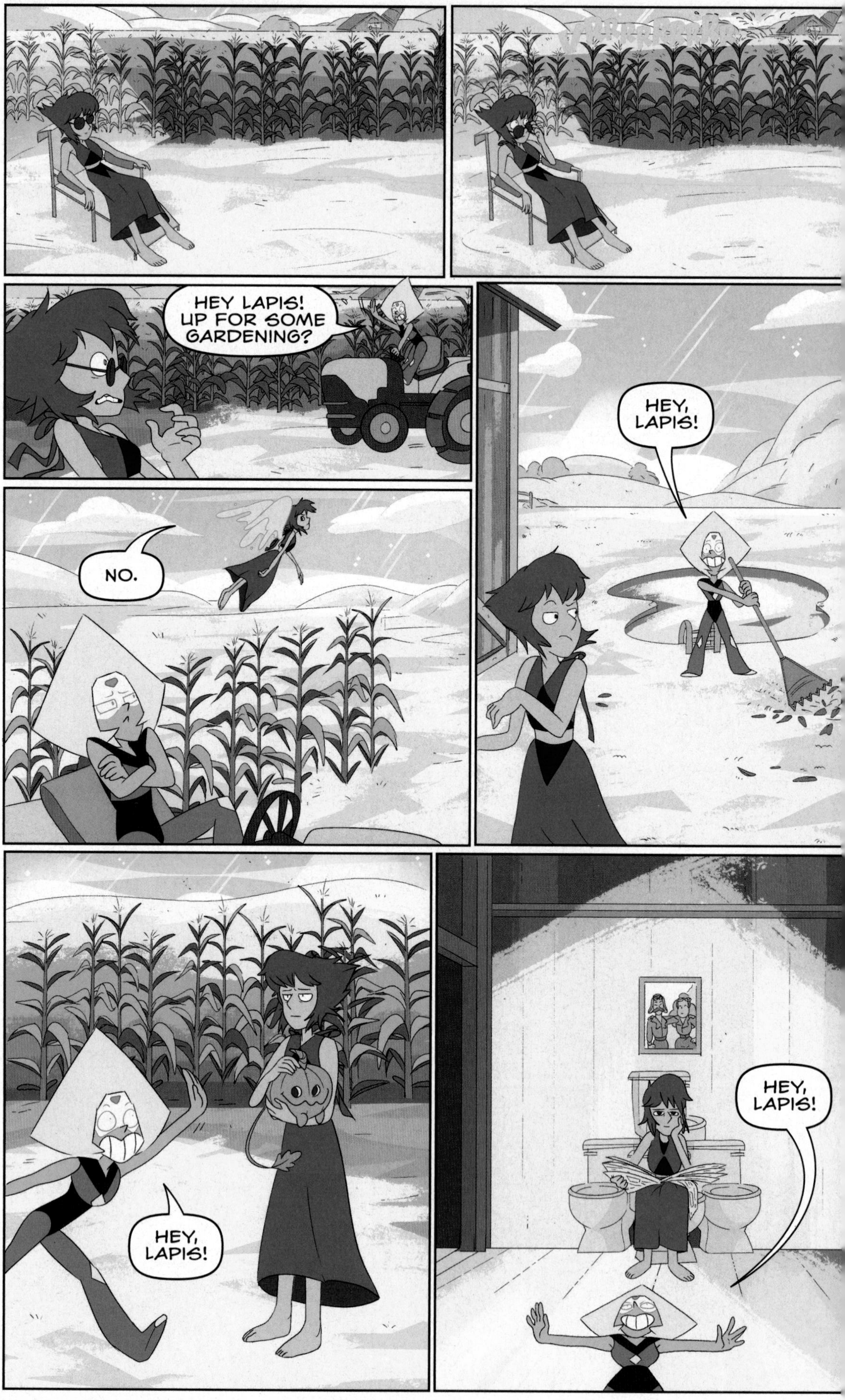
HEY LAPIS! UP FOR SOME GARDENING?
NO.
HEY, LAPIS!
HEY, LAPIS!
HEY, LAPIS!

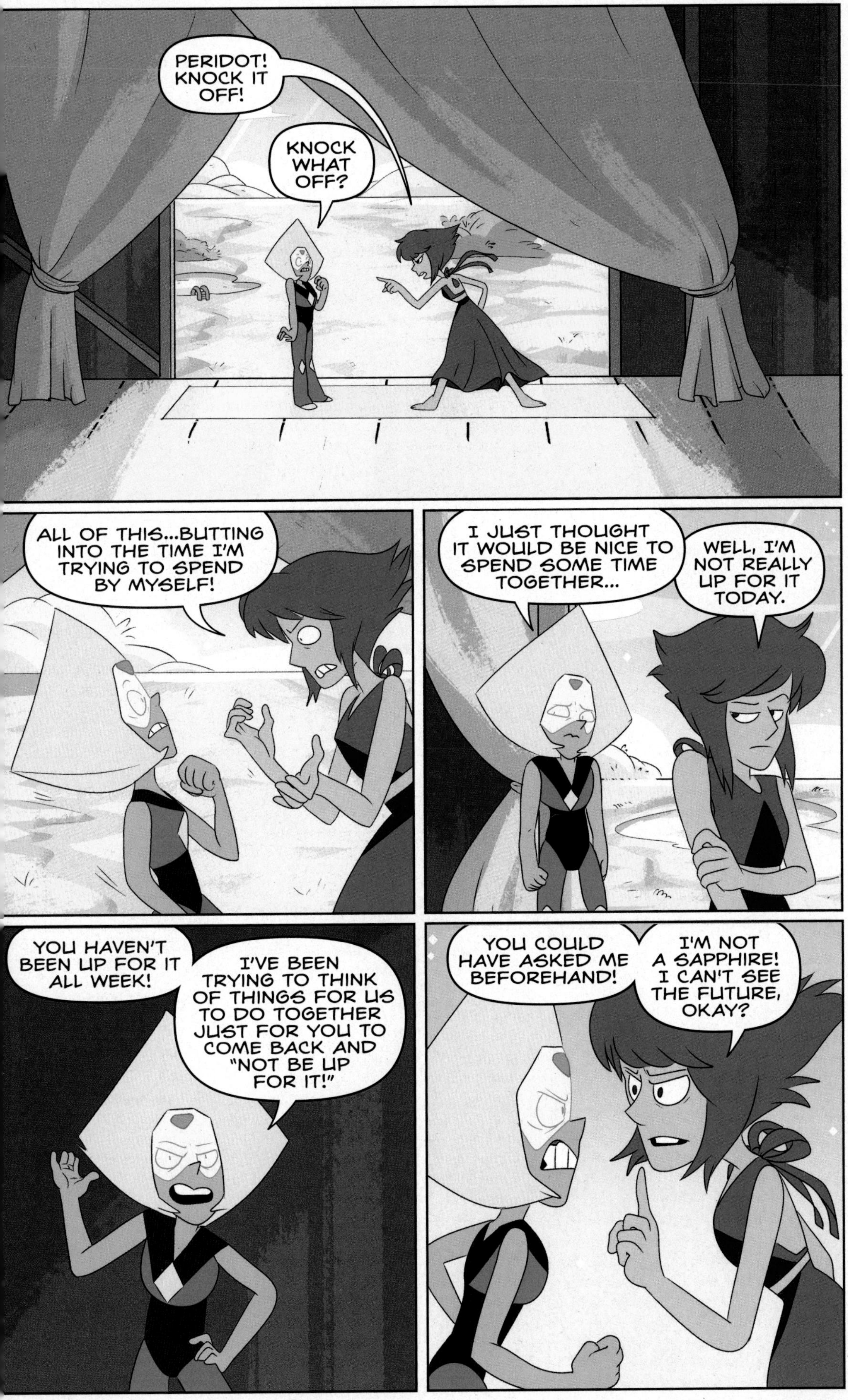
PERIDOT! KNOCK IT OFF!
KNOCK WHAT OFF?
ALL OF THIS...BUTTING INTO THE TIME I'M TRYING TO SPEND BY MYSELF!
I JUST THOUGHT IT WOULD BE NICE TO SPEND SOME TIME TOGETHER...
WELL, I'M NOT REALLY UP FOR IT TODAY.
YOU HAVEN'T BEEN UP FOR IT ALL WEEK!
I'VE BEEN TRYING TO THINK OF THINGS FOR US TO DO TOGETHER JUST FOR YOU TO COME BACK AND "NOT BE UP FOR IT!"
YOU COULD HAVE ASKED ME BEFOREHAND!
I'M NOT A SAPPHIRE! I CAN'T SEE THE FUTURE, OKAY?

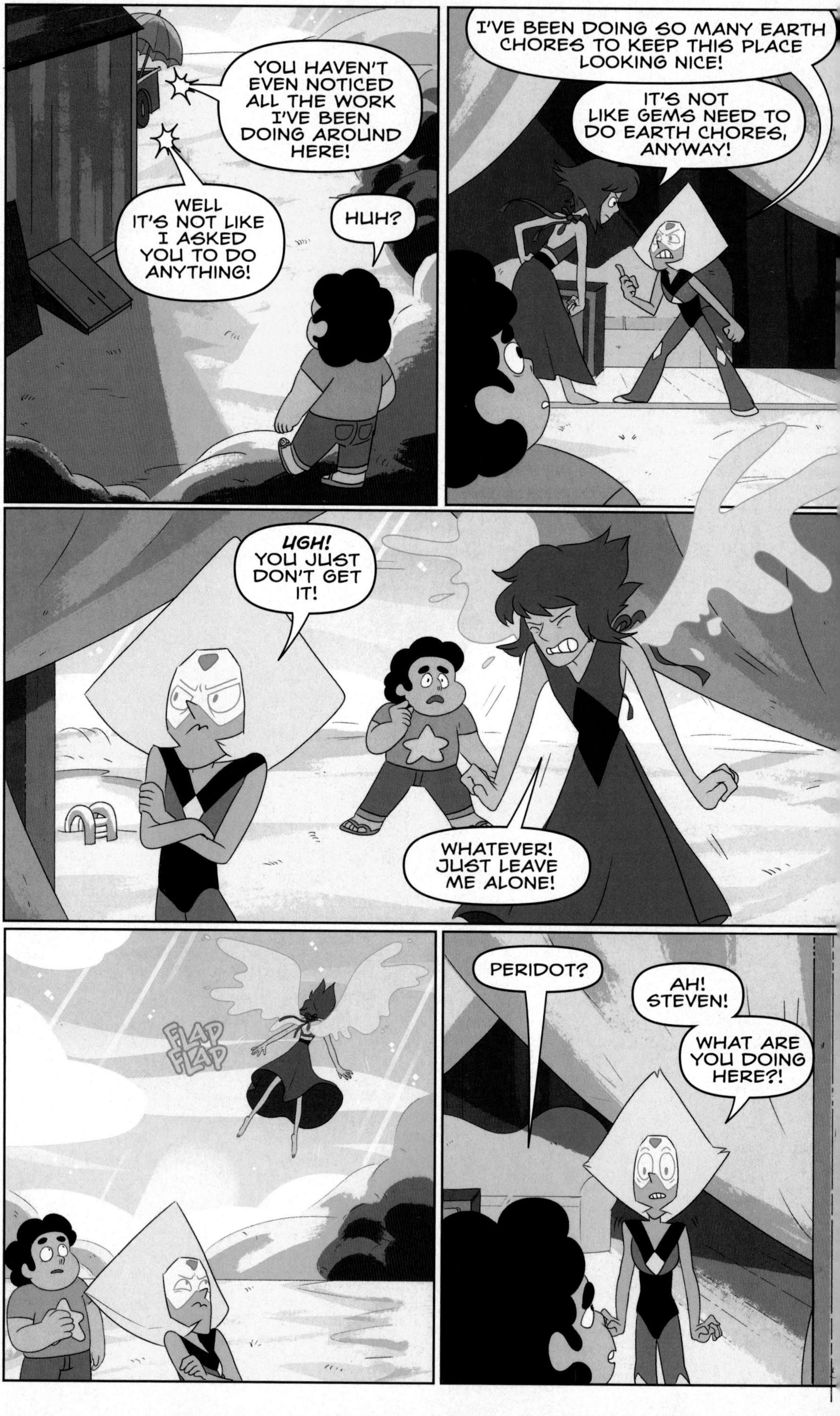
YOU HAVEN'T EVEN NOTICED ALL THE WORK I'VE BEEN DOING AROUND HERE!
WELL IT'S NOT LIKE I ASKED YOU TO DO ANYTHING!
HUH?
I'VE BEEN DOING SO MANY EARTH CHORES TO KEEP THIS PLACE LOOKING NICE!
IT'S NOT LIKE GEMS NEED TO DO EARTH CHORES, ANYWAY!
UGH! YOU JUST DON'T GET IT!
WHATEVER! JUST LEAVE ME ALONE!
FLAP FLAP
PERIDOT?
AH! STEVEN!
WHAT ARE YOU DOING HERE?!

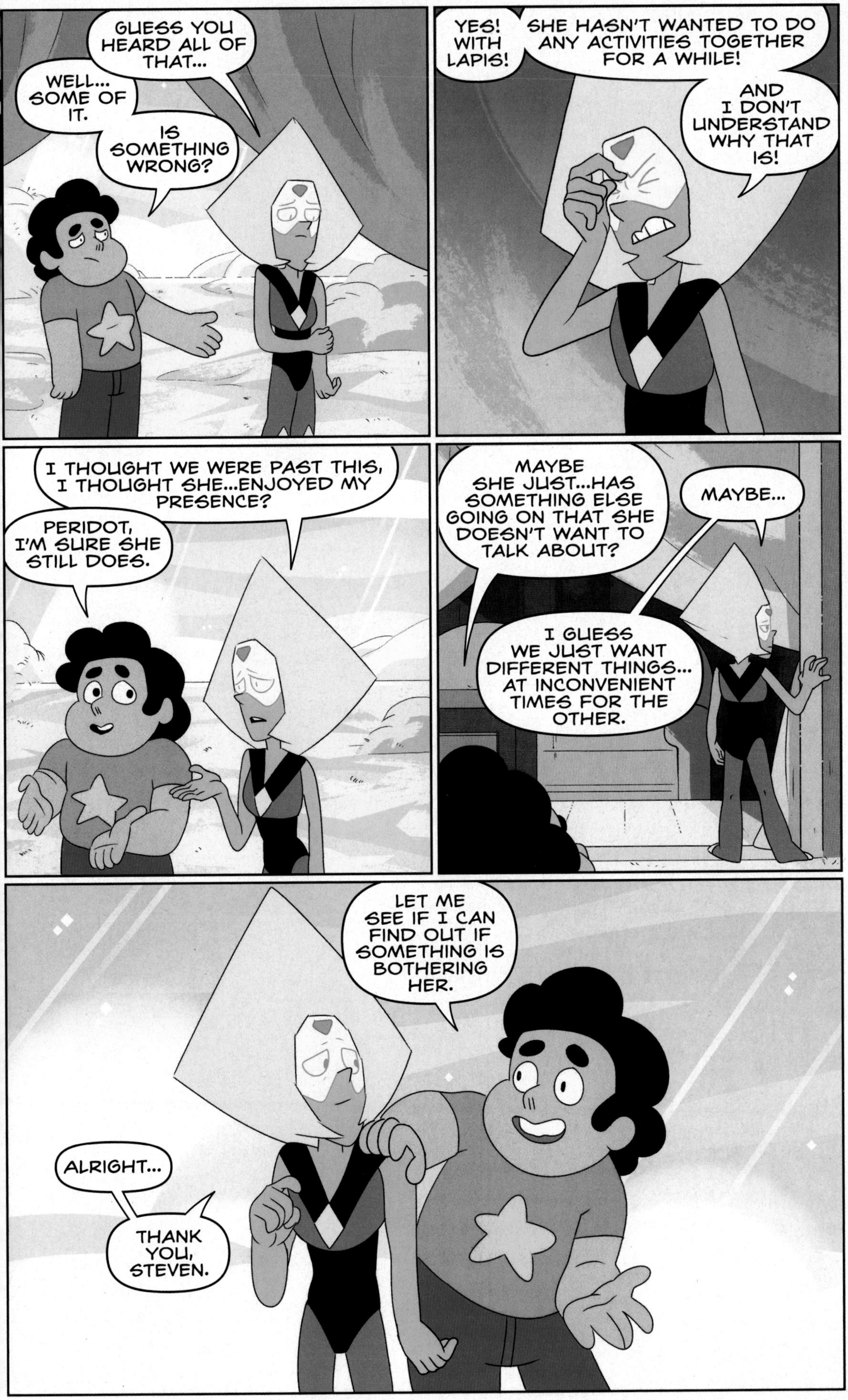
GUESS YOU HEARD ALL OF THAT...
WELL... SOME OF IT.
IS SOMETHING WRONG?
YES! WITH LAPIS!
SHE HASN'T WANTED TO DO ANY ACTIVITIES TOGETHER FOR A WHILE!
AND I DON'T UNDERSTAND WHY THAT IS!
I THOUGHT WE WERE PAST THIS, I THOUGHT SHE...ENJOYED MY PRESENCE?
PERIDOT, I'M SURE SHE STILL DOES.
MAYBE SHE JUST...HAS SOMETHING ELSE GOING ON THAT SHE DOESN'T WANT TO TALK ABOUT?
MAYBE...
I GUESS WE JUST WANT DIFFERENT THINGS... AT INCONVENIENT TIMES FOR THE OTHER.
LET ME SEE IF I CAN FIND OUT IF SOMETHING IS BOTHERING HER.
ALRIGHT...
THANK YOU, STEVEN.

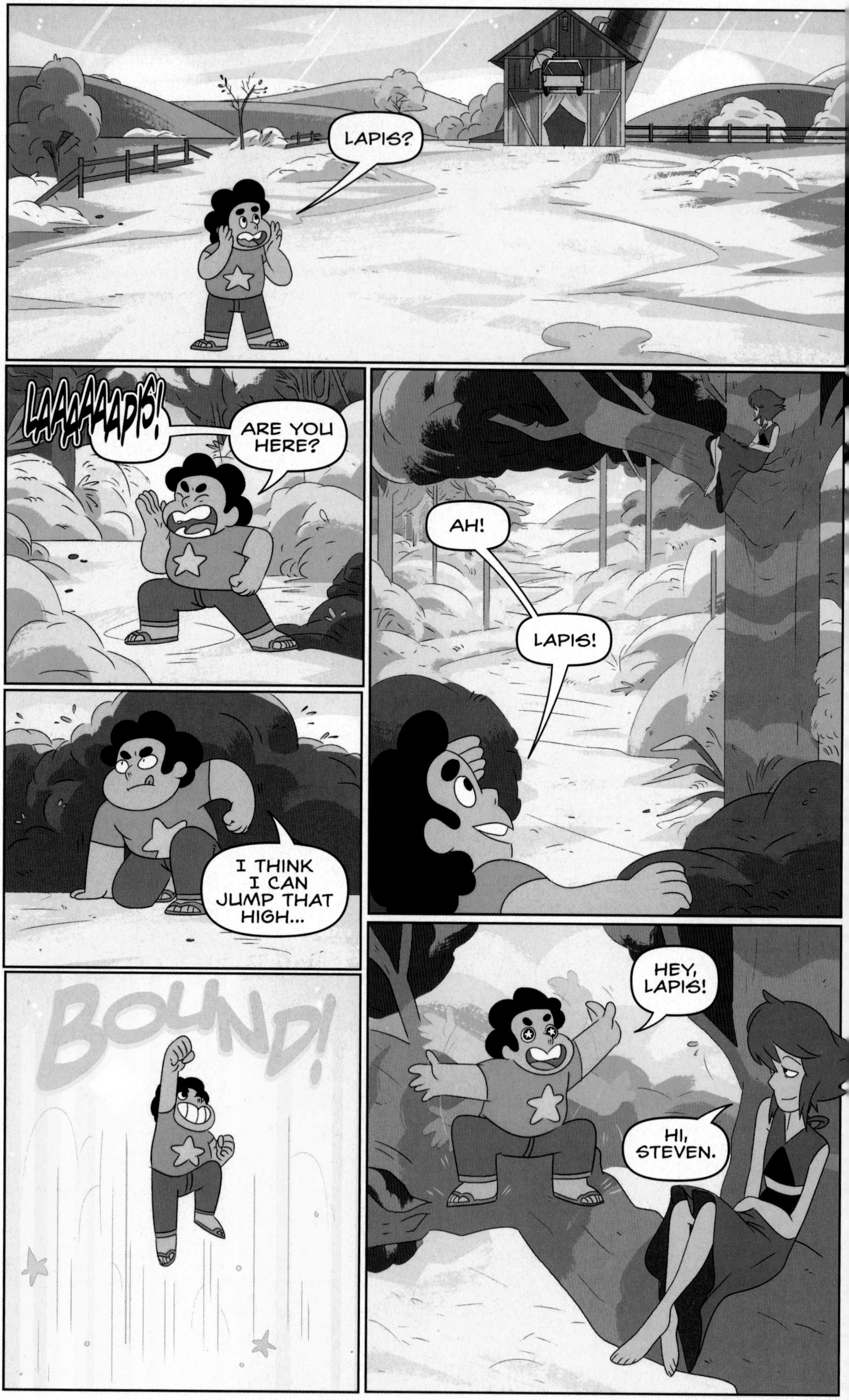
LAPIS?
LAAAAAAPIS!
ARE YOU HERE?
I THINK I CAN JUMP THAT HIGH...
AH!
LAPIS!
BOUND!
HEY, LAPIS!
HI, STEVEN.

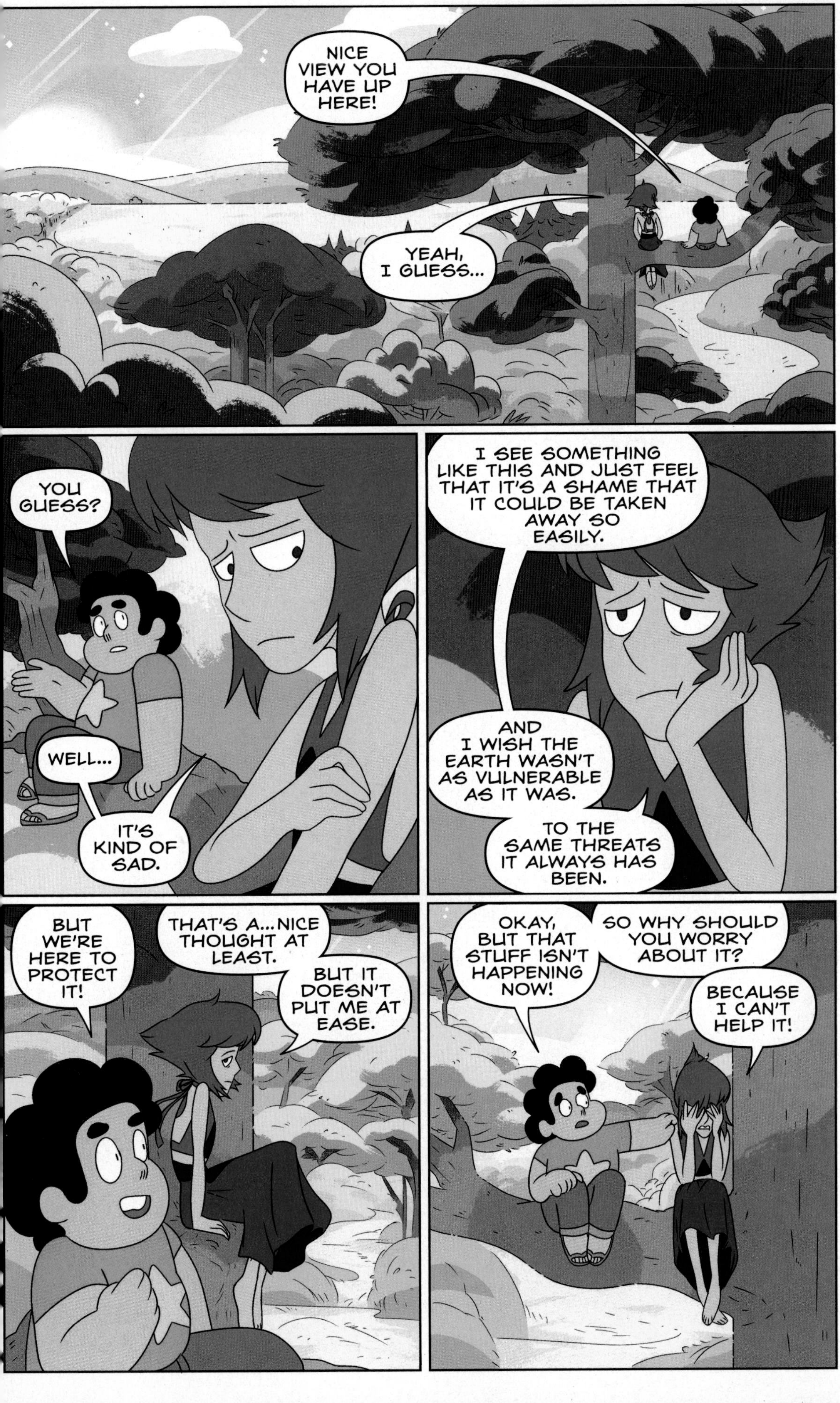
NICE VIEW YOU HAVE UP HERE!
YEAH, I GUESS...
YOU GUESS?
WELL...
IT'S KIND OF SAD.
I SEE SOMETHING LIKE THIS AND JUST FEEL THAT IT'S A SHAME THAT IT COULD BE TAKEN AWAY SO EASILY.
AND I WISH THE EARTH WASN'T AS VULNERABLE AS IT WAS.
TO THE SAME THREATS IT ALWAYS HAS BEEN.
BUT WE'RE HERE TO PROTECT IT!
THAT'S A...NICE THOUGHT AT LEAST.
BUT IT DOESN'T PUT ME AT EASE.
OKAY, BUT THAT STUFF ISN'T HAPPENING NOW!
SO WHY SHOULD YOU WORRY ABOUT IT?
BECAUSE I CAN'T HELP IT!

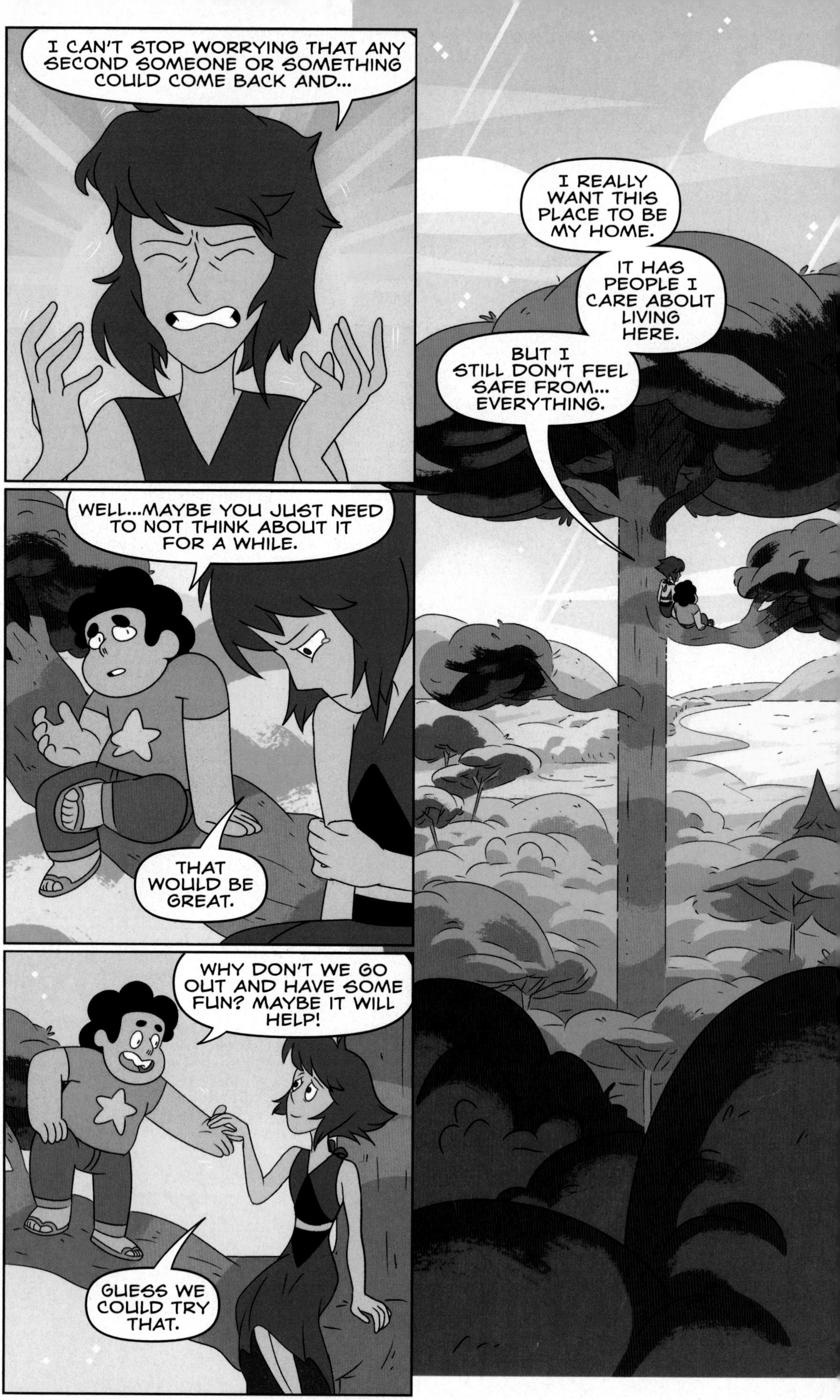
I CAN'T STOP WORRYING THAT ANY SECOND SOMEONE OR SOMETHING COULD COME BACK AND...
WELL...MAYBE YOU JUST NEED TO NOT THINK ABOUT IT FOR A WHILE.
THAT WOULD BE GREAT.
WHY DON'T WE GO OUT AND HAVE SOME FUN? MAYBE IT WILL HELP!
GUESS WE COULD TRY THAT.
I REALLY WANT THIS PLACE TO BE MY HOME.
IT HAS PEOPLE I CARE ABOUT LIVING HERE.
BUT I STILL DON'T FEEL SAFE FROM... EVERYTHING.

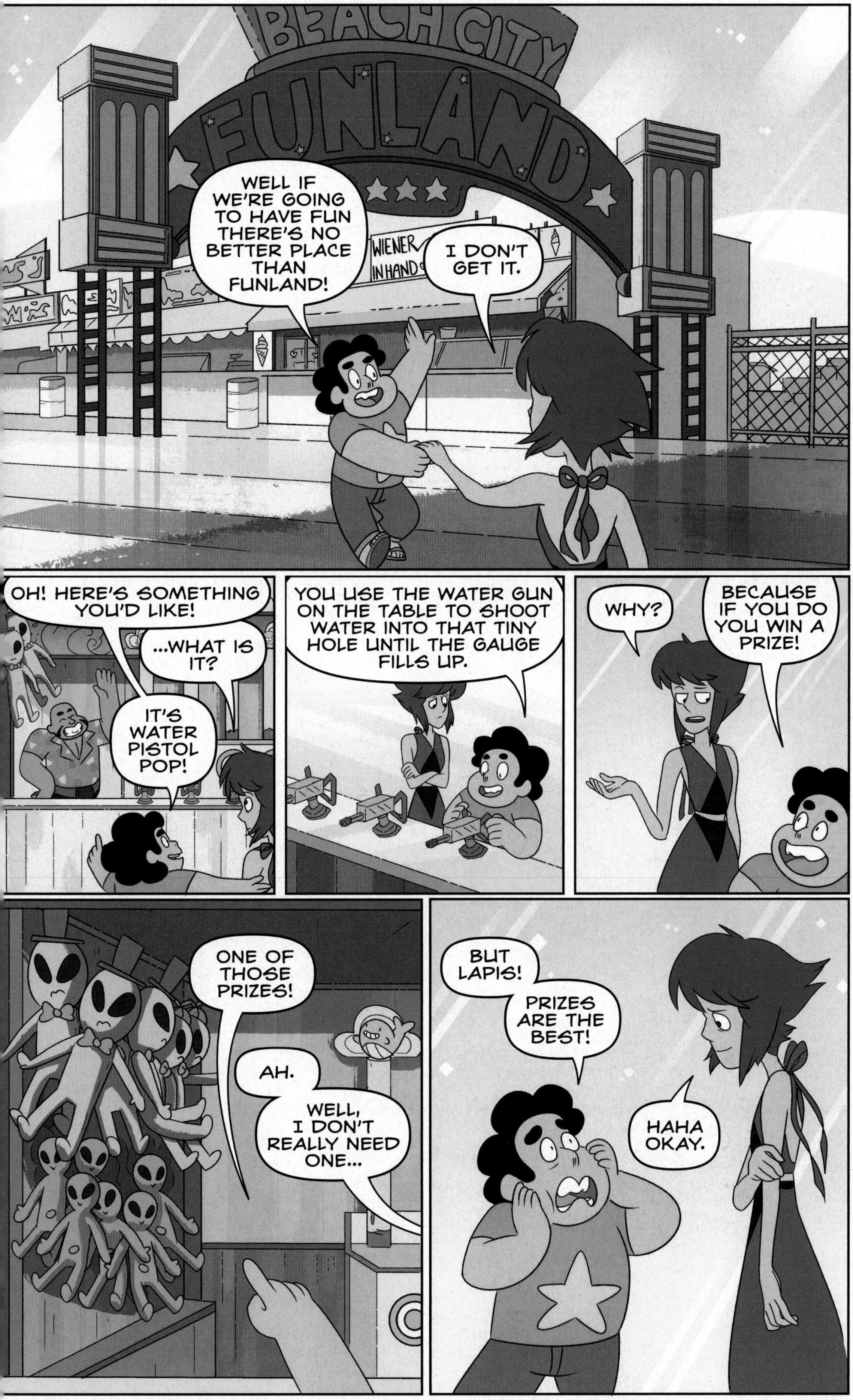
BEACH CITY
FUNLAND
WELL IF WE'RE GOING TO HAVE FUN THERE'S NO BETTER PLACE THAN FUNLAND!
WIENER IN HAND
I DON'T GET IT.
OH! HERE'S SOMETHING YOU'D LIKE!
...WHAT IS IT?
IT'S WATER PISTOL POP!
YOU USE THE WATER GUN ON THE TABLE TO SHOOT WATER INTO THAT TINY HOLE UNTIL THE GAUGE FILLS UP.
WHY?
BECAUSE IF YOU DO YOU WIN A PRIZE!
ONE OF THOSE PRIZES!
AH.
WELL, I DON'T REALLY NEED ONE...
BUT LAPIS!
PRIZES ARE THE BEST!
HAHA OKAY.

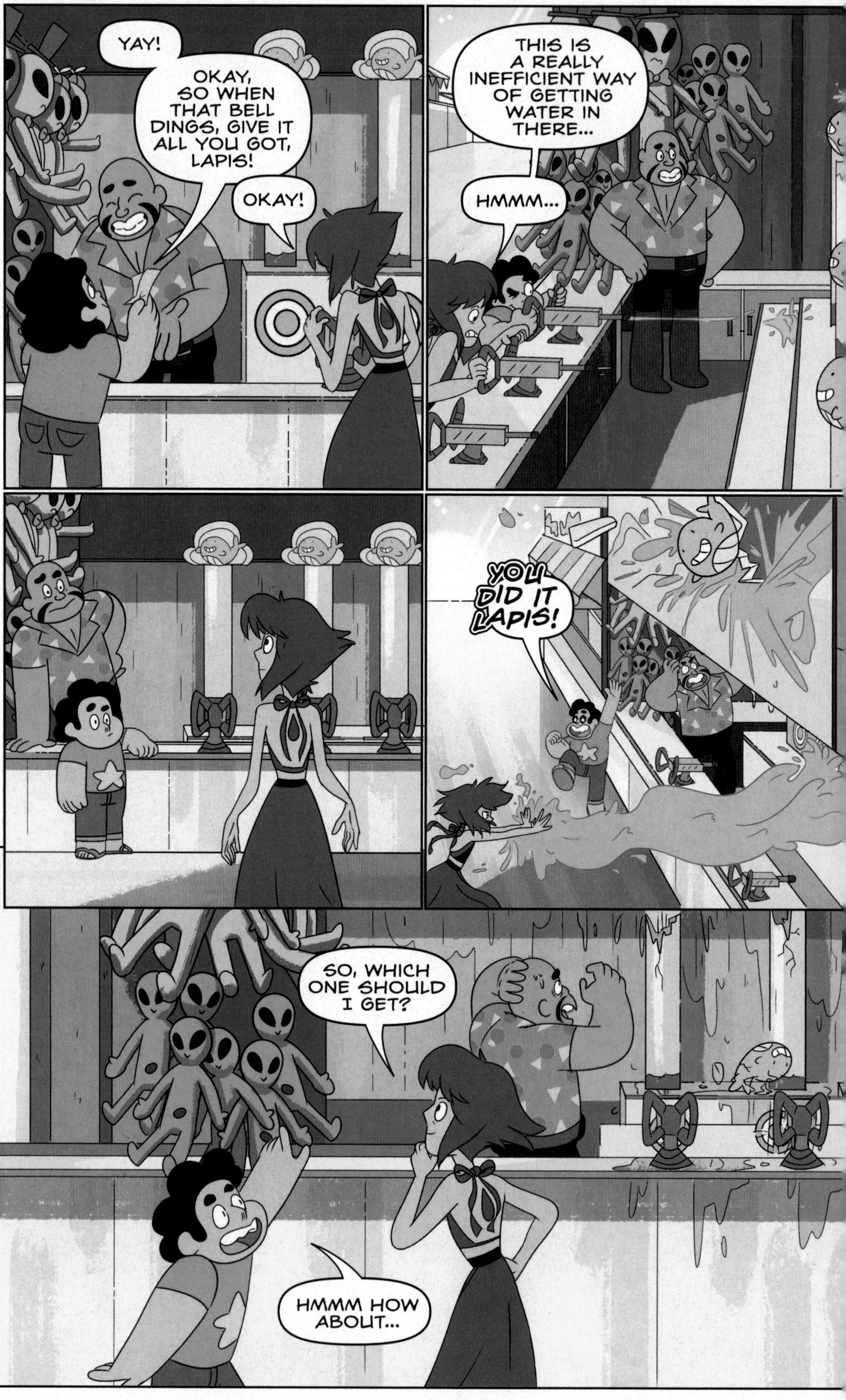
YAY!
OKAY, SO WHEN THAT BELL DINGS, GIVE IT ALL YOU GOT, LAPIS!
OKAY!
THIS IS A REALLY INEFFICIENT WAY OF GETTING WATER IN THERE...
HMMM...
YOU DID IT LAPIS!
SO, WHICH ONE SHOULD I GET?
HMMM HOW ABOUT...

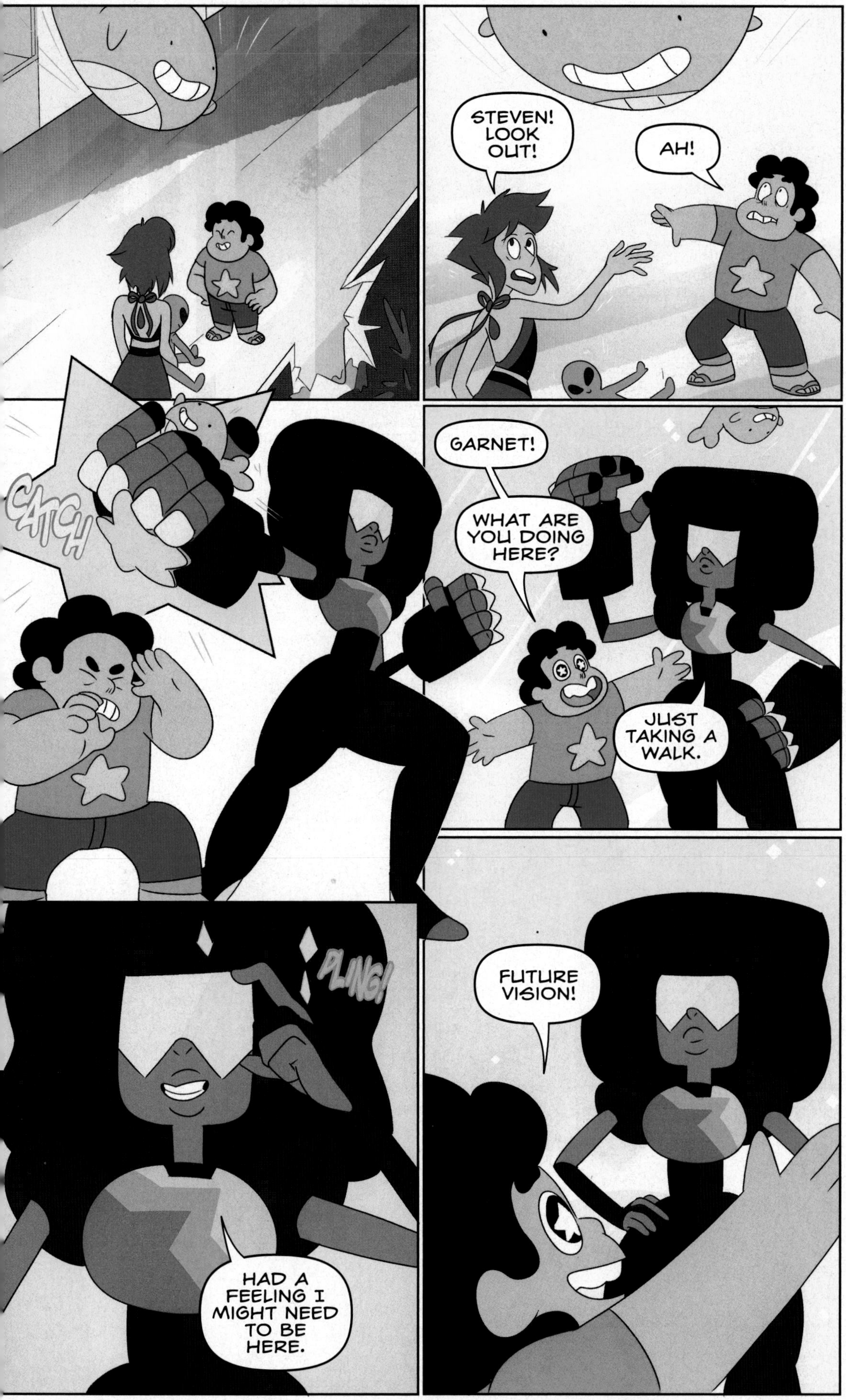
STEVEN! LOOK OUT!
AH!
CATCH
GARNET!
WHAT ARE YOU DOING HERE?
JUST TAKING A WALK.
PLING!
HAD A FEELING I MIGHT NEED TO BE HERE.
FUTURE VISION!

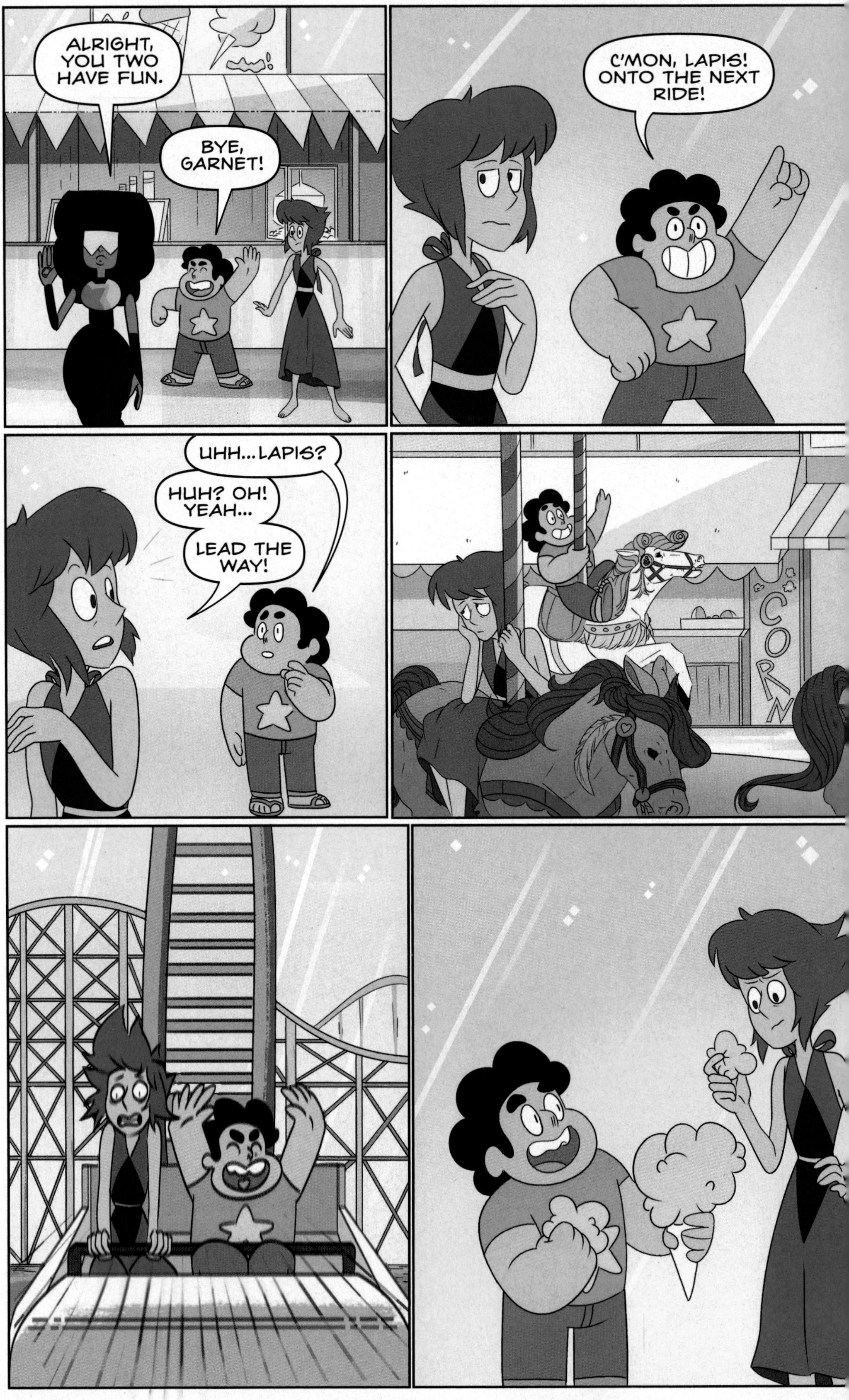
ALRIGHT, YOU TWO HAVE FUN.
BYE, GARNET!
C'MON, LAPIS! ONTO THE NEXT RIDE!
UHH...LAPIS?
HUH? OH! YEAH...
LEAD THE WAY!
CORN

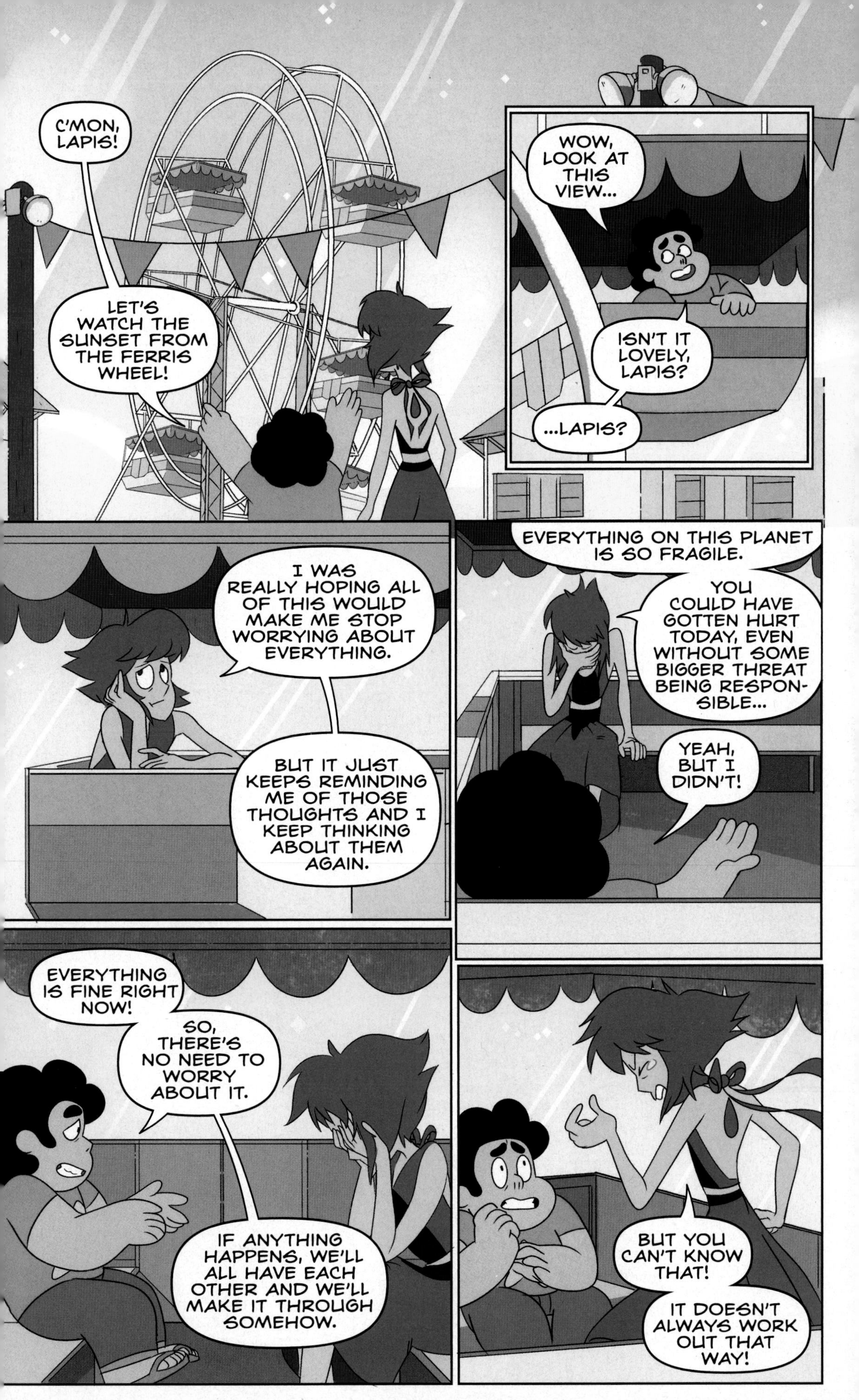
C'MON, LAPIS!
LET'S WATCH THE SUNSET FROM THE FERRIS WHEEL!
WOW, LOOK AT THIS VIEW...
ISN'T IT LOVELY, LAPIS?
...LAPIS?
I WAS REALLY HOPING ALL OF THIS WOULD MAKE ME STOP WORRYING ABOUT EVERYTHING.
BUT IT JUST KEEPS REMINDING ME OF THOSE THOUGHTS AND I KEEP THINKING ABOUT THEM AGAIN.
EVERYTHING ON THIS PLANET IS SO FRAGILE.
YOU COULD HAVE GOTTEN HURT TODAY, EVEN WITHOUT SOME BIGGER THREAT BEING RESPON-SIBLE...
YEAH, BUT I DIDN'T!
EVERYTHING IS FINE RIGHT NOW!
SO, THERE'S NO NEED TO WORRY ABOUT IT.
IF ANYTHING HAPPENS, WE'LL ALL HAVE EACH OTHER AND WE'LL MAKE IT THROUGH SOMEHOW.
BUT YOU CAN'T KNOW THAT!
IT DOESN'T ALWAYS WORK OUT THAT WAY!

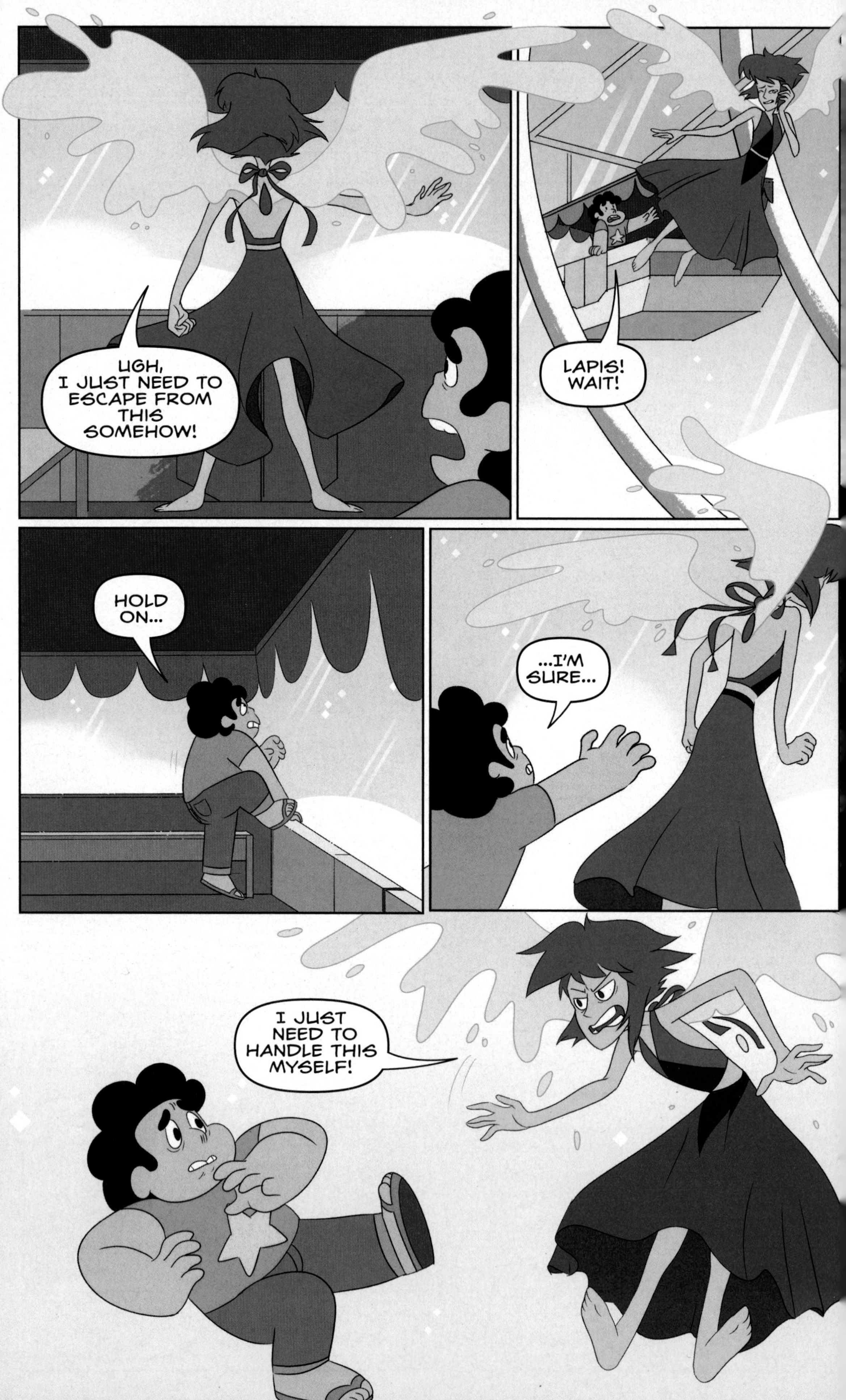
UGH, I JUST NEED TO ESCAPE FROM THIS SOMEHOW!
LAPIS! WAIT!
HOLD ON...
...I'M SURE...
I JUST NEED TO HANDLE THIS MYSELF!

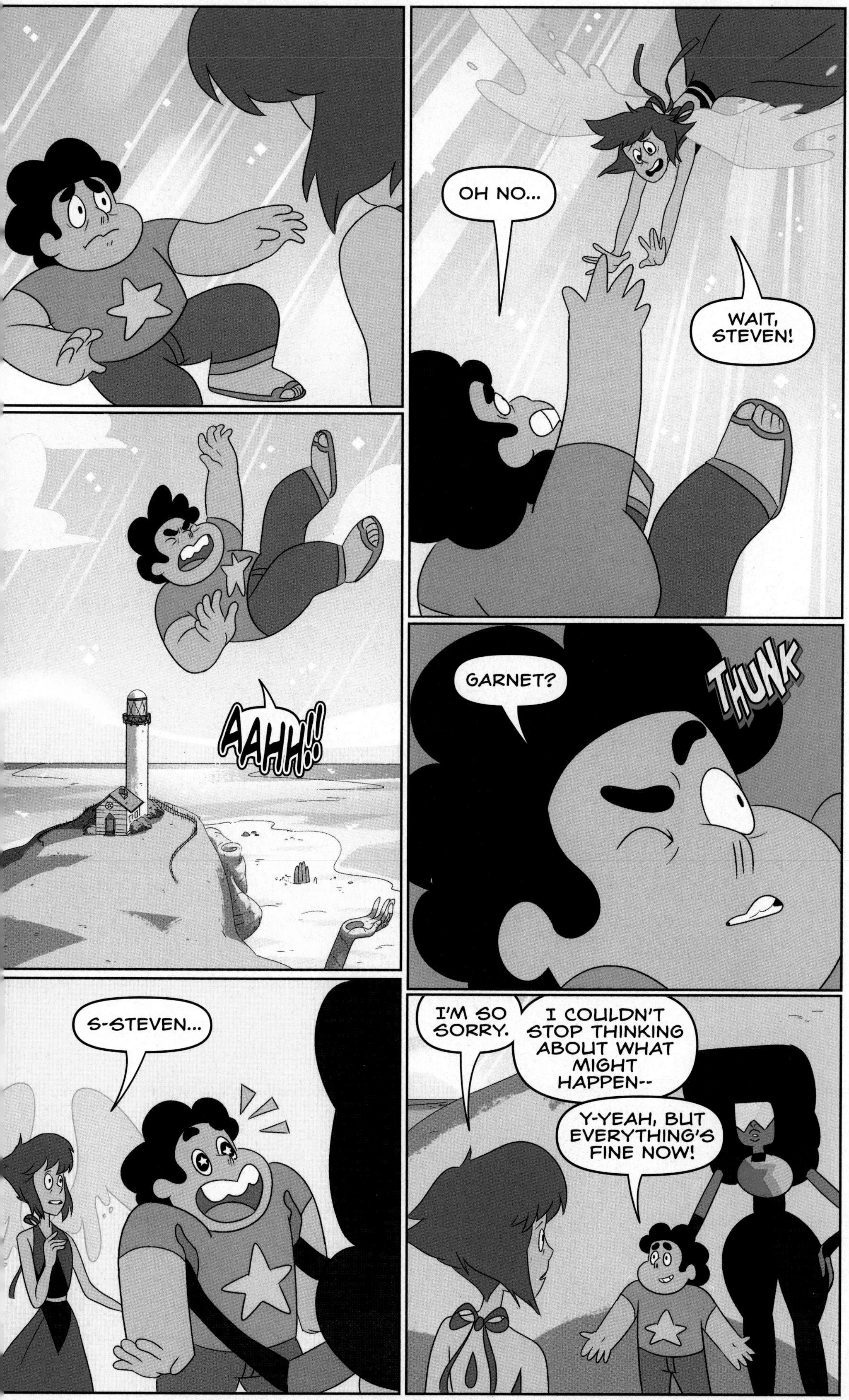
OH NO...
WAIT, STEVEN!
AAHH!!
GARNET?
THUNK
S-STEVEN...
I'M SO SORRY.
I COULDN'T STOP THINKING ABOUT WHAT MIGHT HAPPEN--
Y-YEAH, BUT EVERYTHING'S FINE NOW!

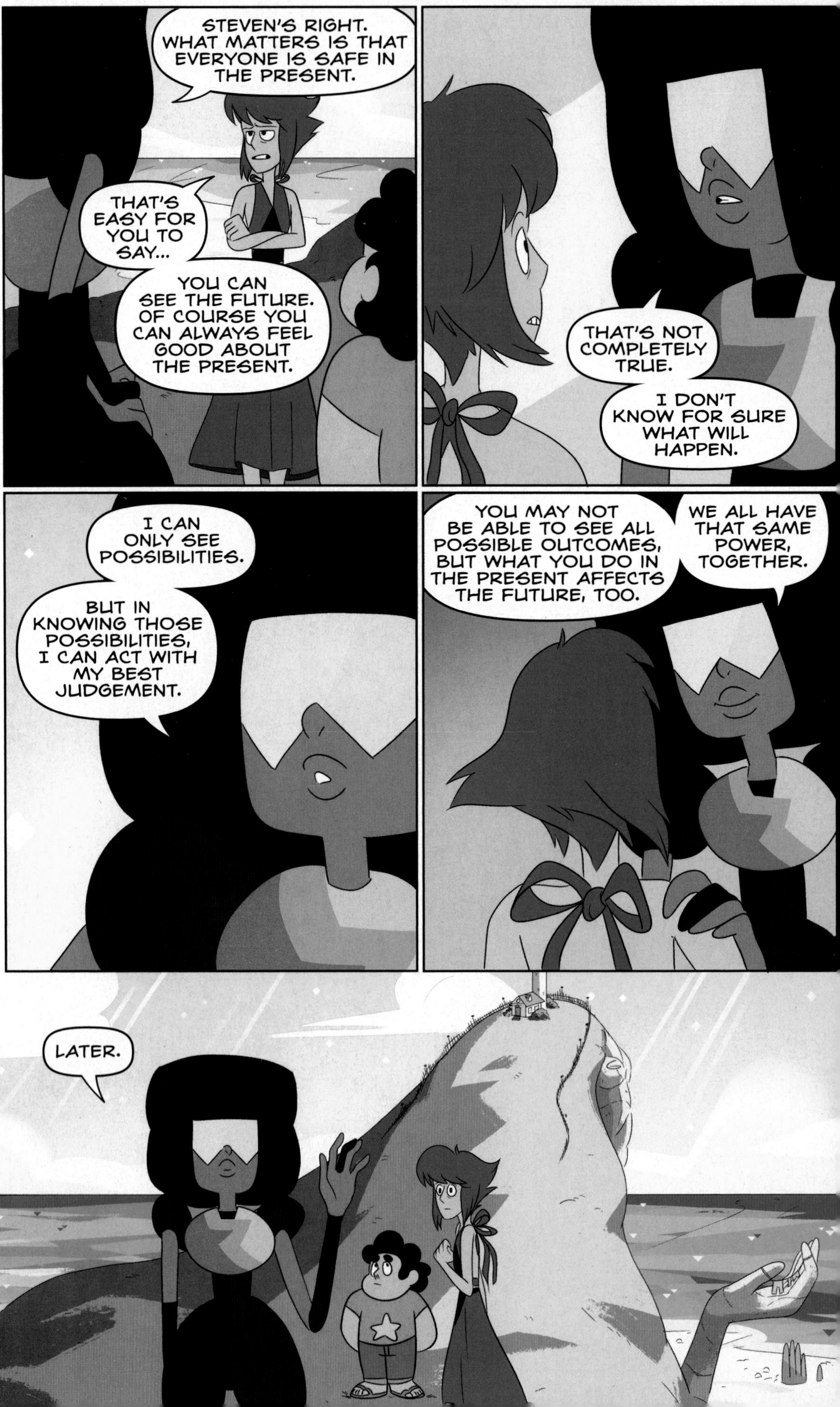
STEVEN'S RIGHT. WHAT MATTERS IS THAT EVERYONE IS SAFE IN THE PRESENT.
THAT'S EASY FOR YOU TO SAY...
YOU CAN SEE THE FUTURE. OF COURSE YOU CAN ALWAYS FEEL GOOD ABOUT THE PRESENT.
THAT'S NOT COMPLETELY TRUE.
I DON'T KNOW FOR SURE WHAT WILL HAPPEN.
I CAN ONLY SEE POSSIBILITIES.
BUT IN KNOWING THOSE POSSIBILITIES, I CAN ACT WITH MY BEST JUDGEMENT.
YOU MAY NOT BE ABLE TO SEE ALL POSSIBLE OUTCOMES, BUT WHAT YOU DO IN THE PRESENT AFFECTS THE FUTURE, TOO.
WE ALL HAVE THAT SAME POWER, TOGETHER.
LATER.

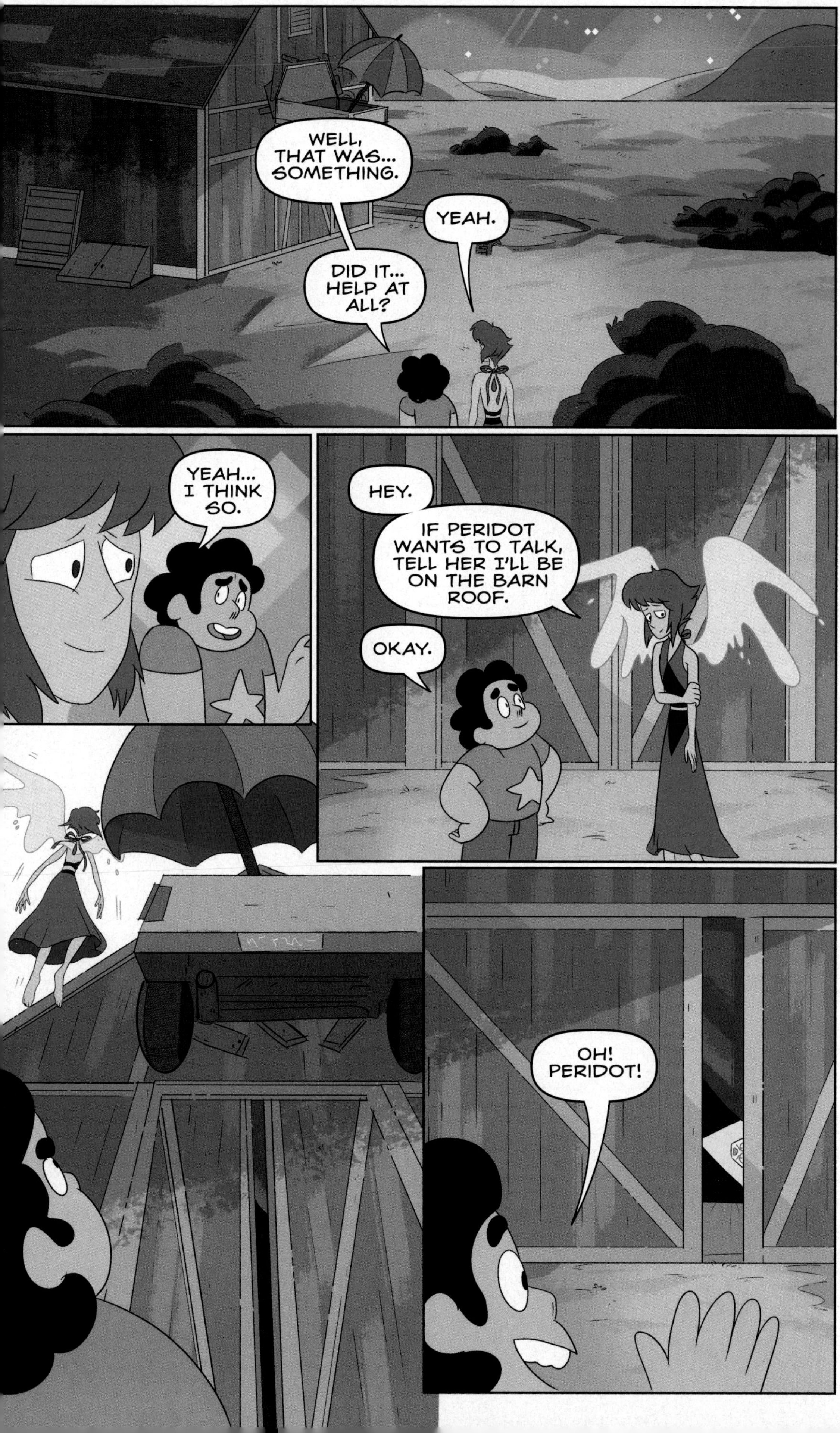
WELL, THAT WAS... SOMETHING.
YEAH.
DID IT... HELP AT ALL?
YEAH... I THINK SO.
HEY.
IF PERIDOT WANTS TO TALK, TELL HER I'LL BE ON THE BARN ROOF.
OKAY.
OH! PERIDOT!

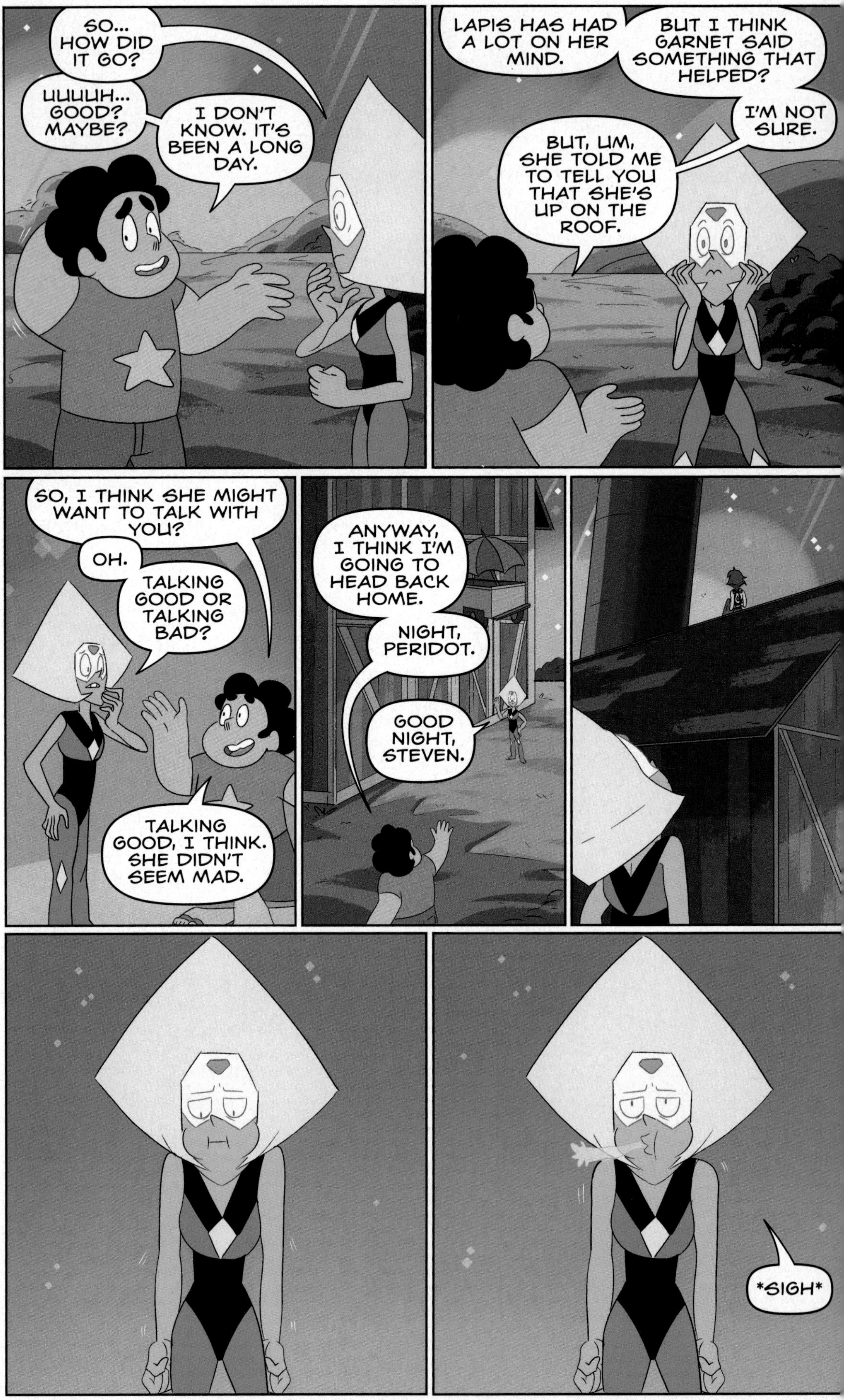

SO... HOW DID IT GO?
UUUUH... GOOD? MAYBE?
I DON'T KNOW. IT'S BEEN A LONG DAY.
LAPIS HAS HAD A LOT ON HER MIND.
BUT I THINK GARNET SAID SOMETHING THAT HELPED?
I'M NOT SURE.
BUT, UM, SHE TOLD ME TO TELL YOU THAT SHE'S UP ON THE ROOF.
SO, I THINK SHE MIGHT WANT TO TALK WITH YOU?
OH.
TALKING GOOD OR TALKING BAD?
TALKING GOOD, I THINK. SHE DIDN'T SEEM MAD.
ANYWAY, I THINK I'M GOING TO HEAD BACK HOME.
NIGHT, PERIDOT.
GOOD NIGHT, STEVEN.
SIGH

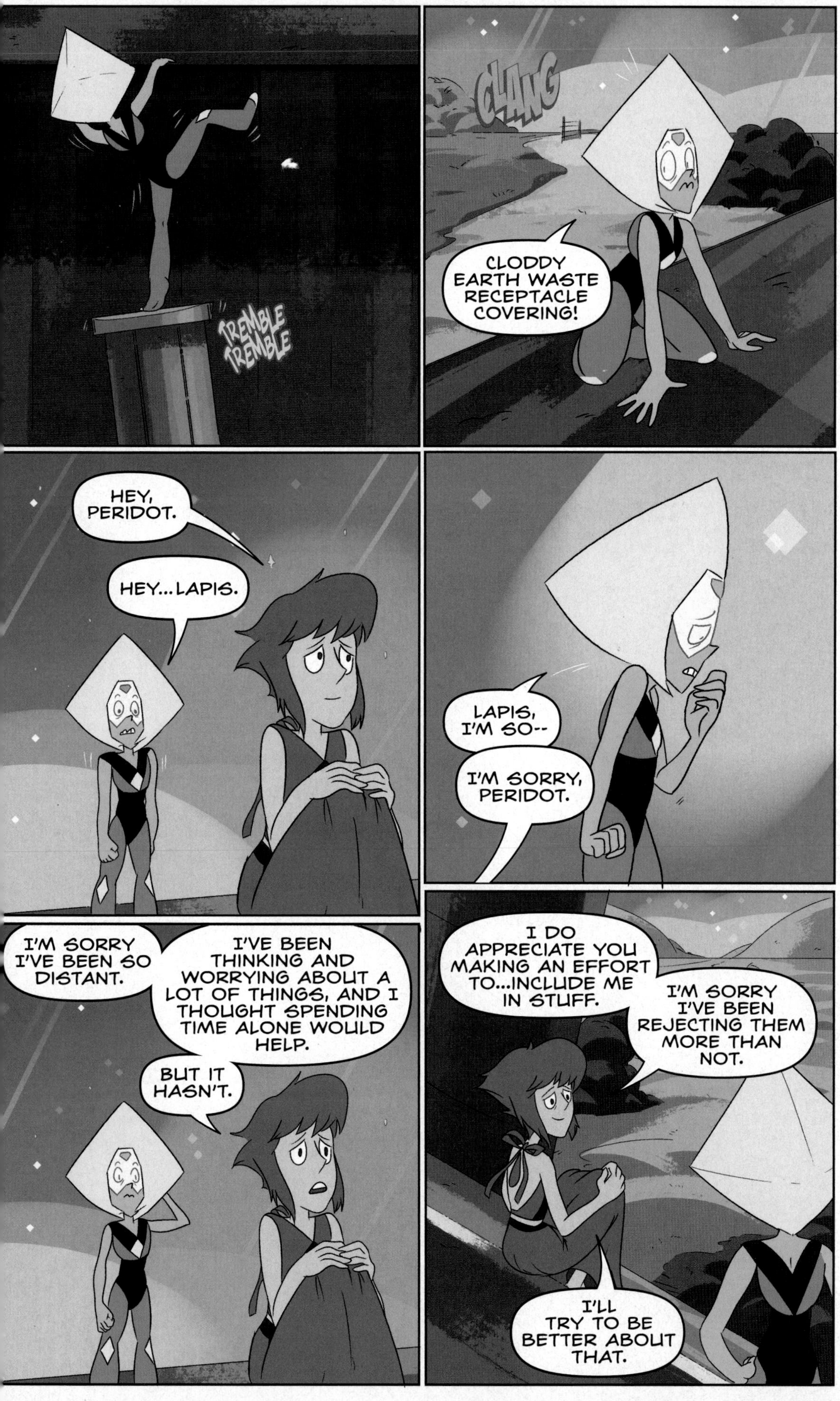
TREMBLE TREMBLE
CLANG
CLODDY EARTH WASTE RECEPTACLE COVERING!
HEY, PERIDOT.
HEY...LAPIS.
LAPIS, I'M SO--
I'M SORRY, PERIDOT.
I'M SORRY I'VE BEEN SO DISTANT.
I'VE BEEN THINKING AND WORRYING ABOUT A LOT OF THINGS, AND I THOUGHT SPENDING TIME ALONE WOULD HELP.
BUT IT HASN'T.
I DO APPRECIATE YOU MAKING AN EFFORT TO...INCLUDE ME IN STUFF.
I'M SORRY I'VE BEEN REJECTING THEM MORE THAN NOT.
I'LL TRY TO BE BETTER ABOUT THAT.

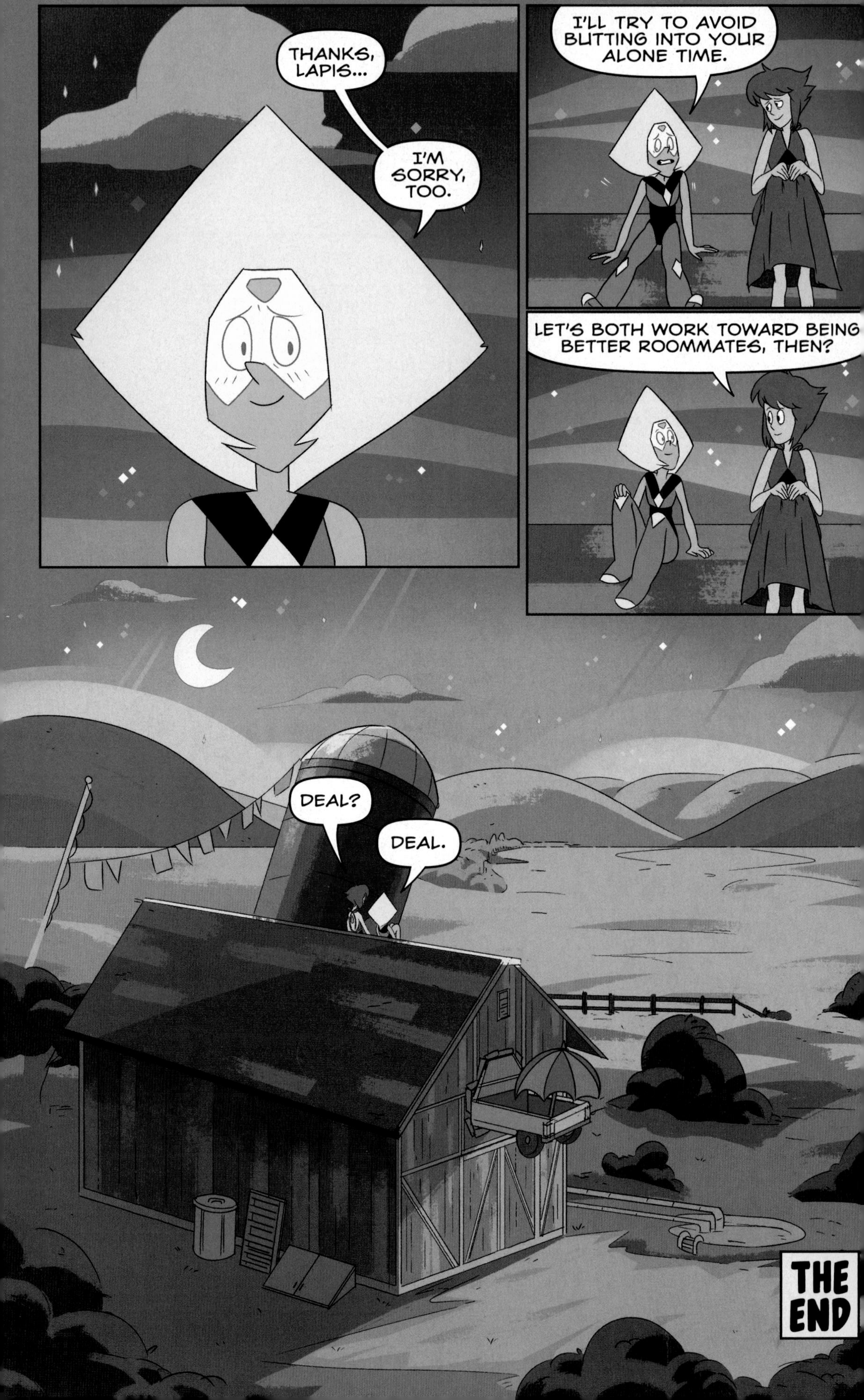
THANKS, LAPIS...
I'M SORRY, TOO.
I'LL TRY TO AVOID BUTTING INTO YOUR ALONE TIME.
LET'S BOTH WORK TOWARD BEING BETTER ROOMMATES, THEN?
DEAL?
DEAL.
THE END

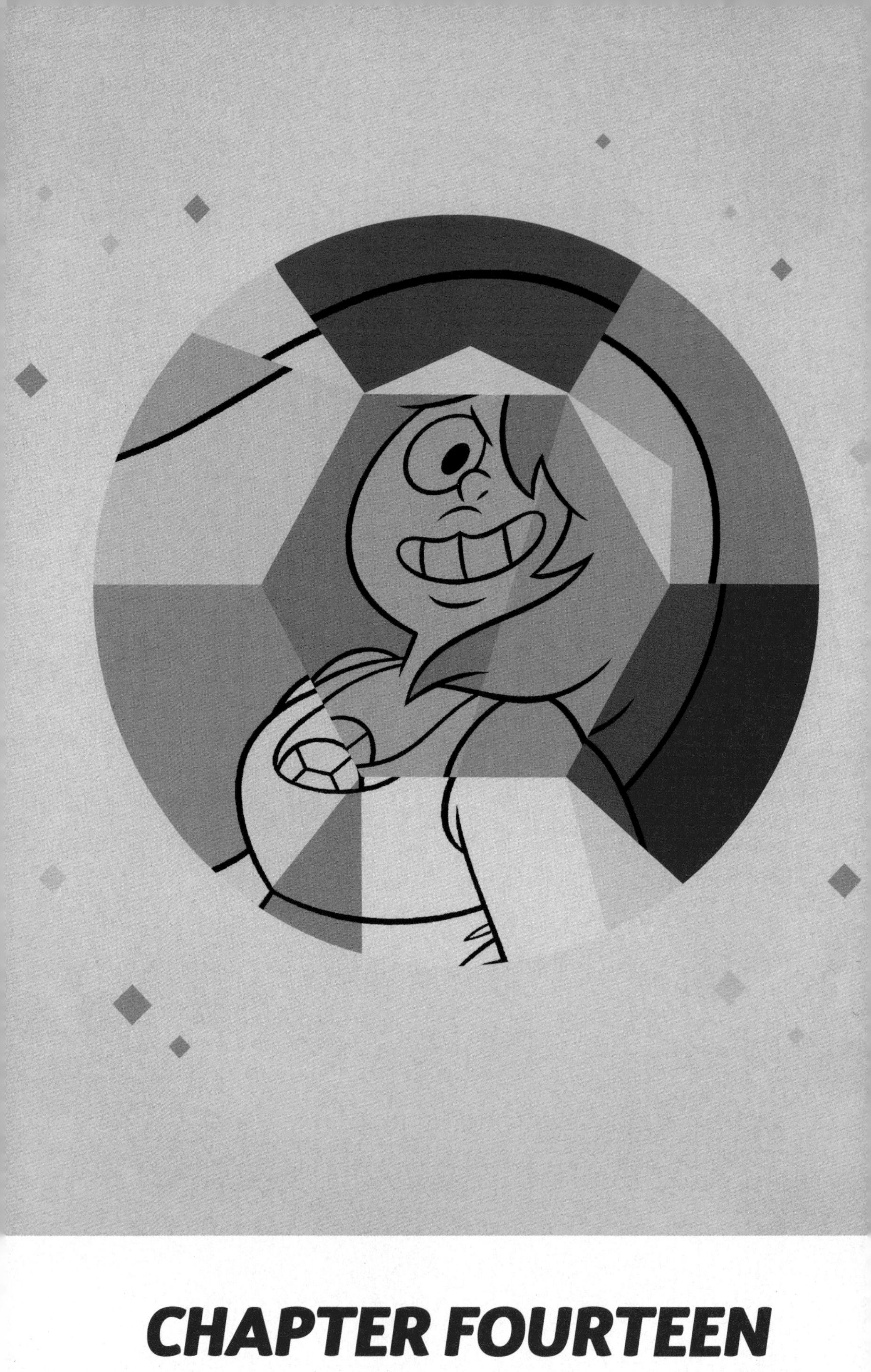

CHAPTER FOURTEEN

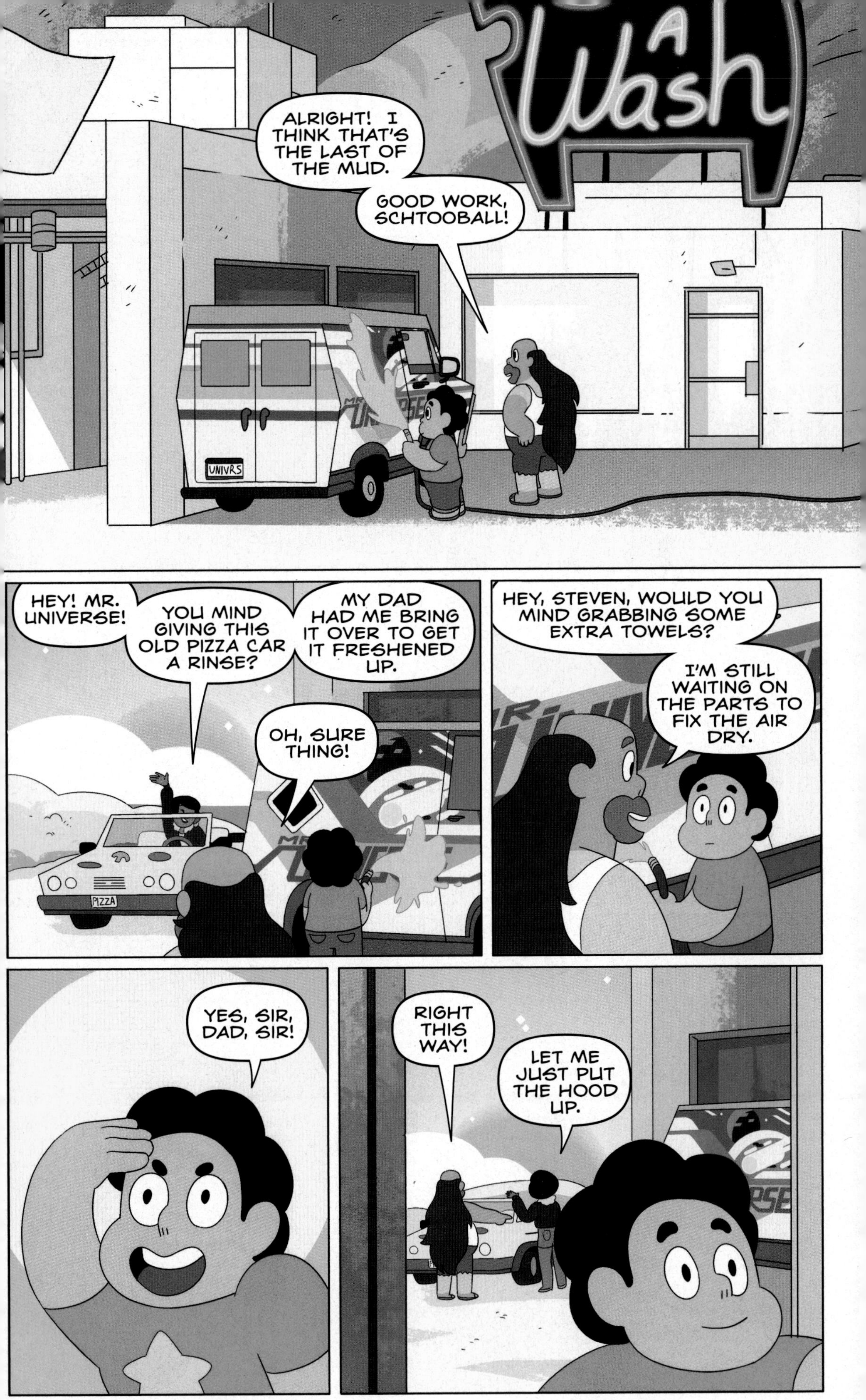

A Wash
ALRIGHT! I THINK THAT'S THE LAST OF THE MUD.
GOOD WORK, SCHTOOBALL!
UNIVRS
MR. UNIVERSE
HEY! MR. UNIVERSE!
YOU MIND GIVING THIS OLD PIZZA CAR A RINSE?
MY DAD HAD ME BRING IT OVER TO GET IT FRESHENED UP.
OH, SURE THING!
PIZZA
HEY, STEVEN, WOULD YOU MIND GRABBING SOME EXTRA TOWELS?
I'M STILL WAITING ON THE PARTS TO FIX THE AIR DRY.
YES, SIR, DAD, SIR!
RIGHT THIS WAY!
LET ME JUST PUT THE HOOD UP.

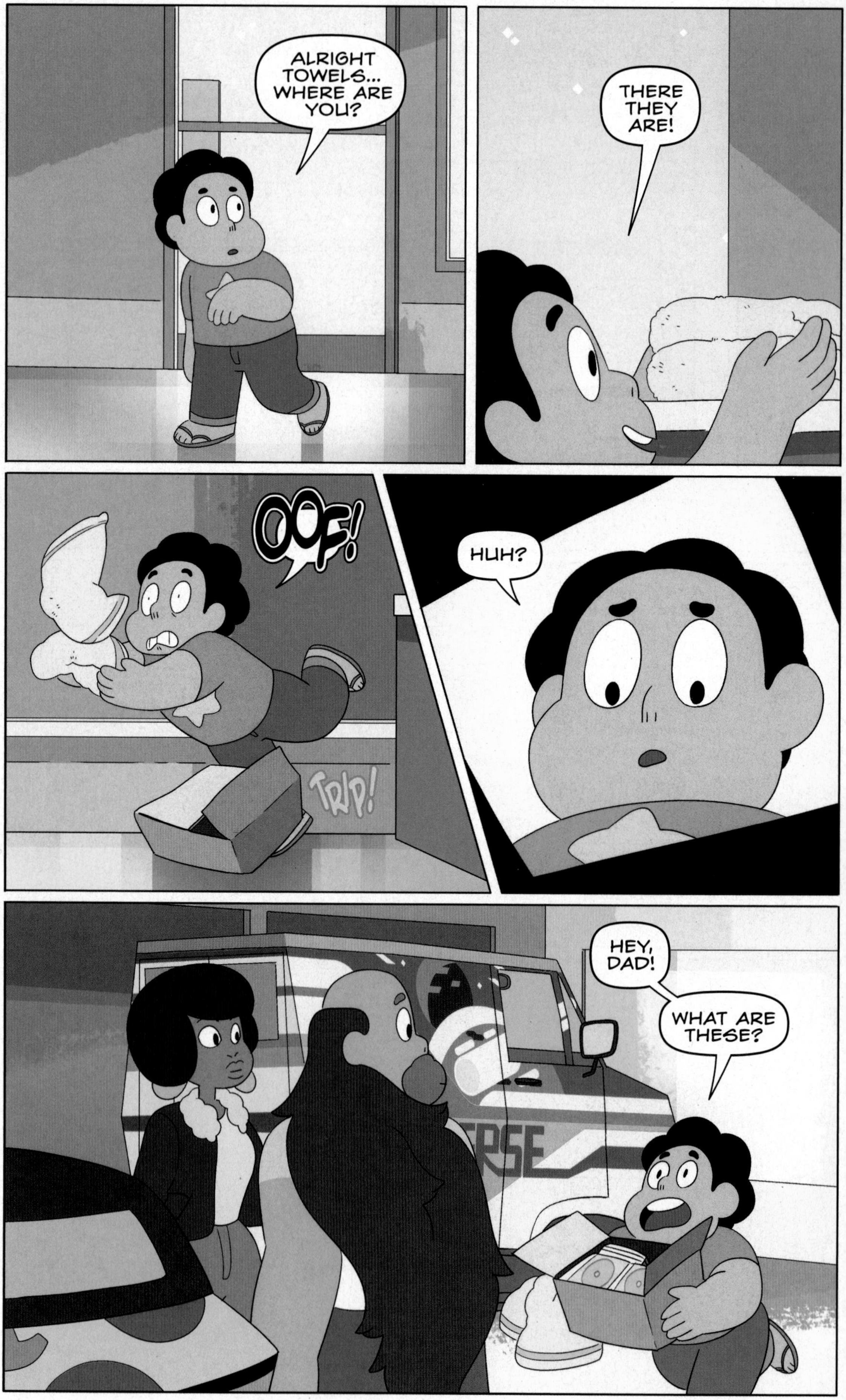
ALRIGHT TOWELS... WHERE ARE YOU?
THERE THEY ARE!
OOF!
TRIP!
HUH?
HEY, DAD!
WHAT ARE THESE?

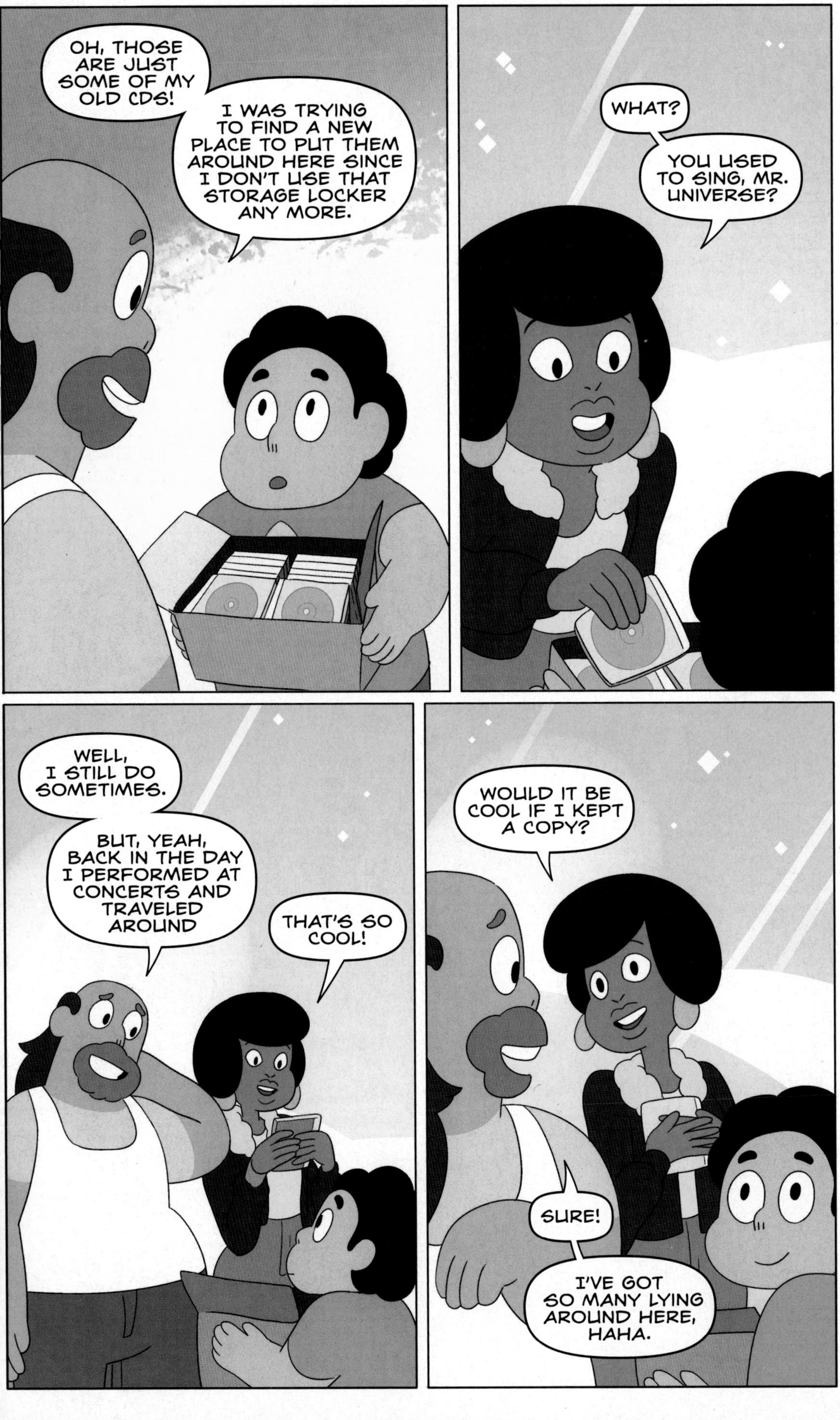
OH, THOSE ARE JUST SOME OF MY OLD CDS!
I WAS TRYING TO FIND A NEW PLACE TO PUT THEM AROUND HERE SINCE I DON'T USE THAT STORAGE LOCKER ANY MORE.
WHAT?
YOU USED TO SING, MR. UNIVERSE?
WELL, I STILL DO SOMETIMES.
BUT, YEAH, BACK IN THE DAY I PERFORMED AT CONCERTS AND TRAVELED AROUND
THAT'S SO COOL!
WOULD IT BE COOL IF I KEPT A COPY?
SURE!
I'VE GOT SO MANY LYING AROUND HERE, HAHA.

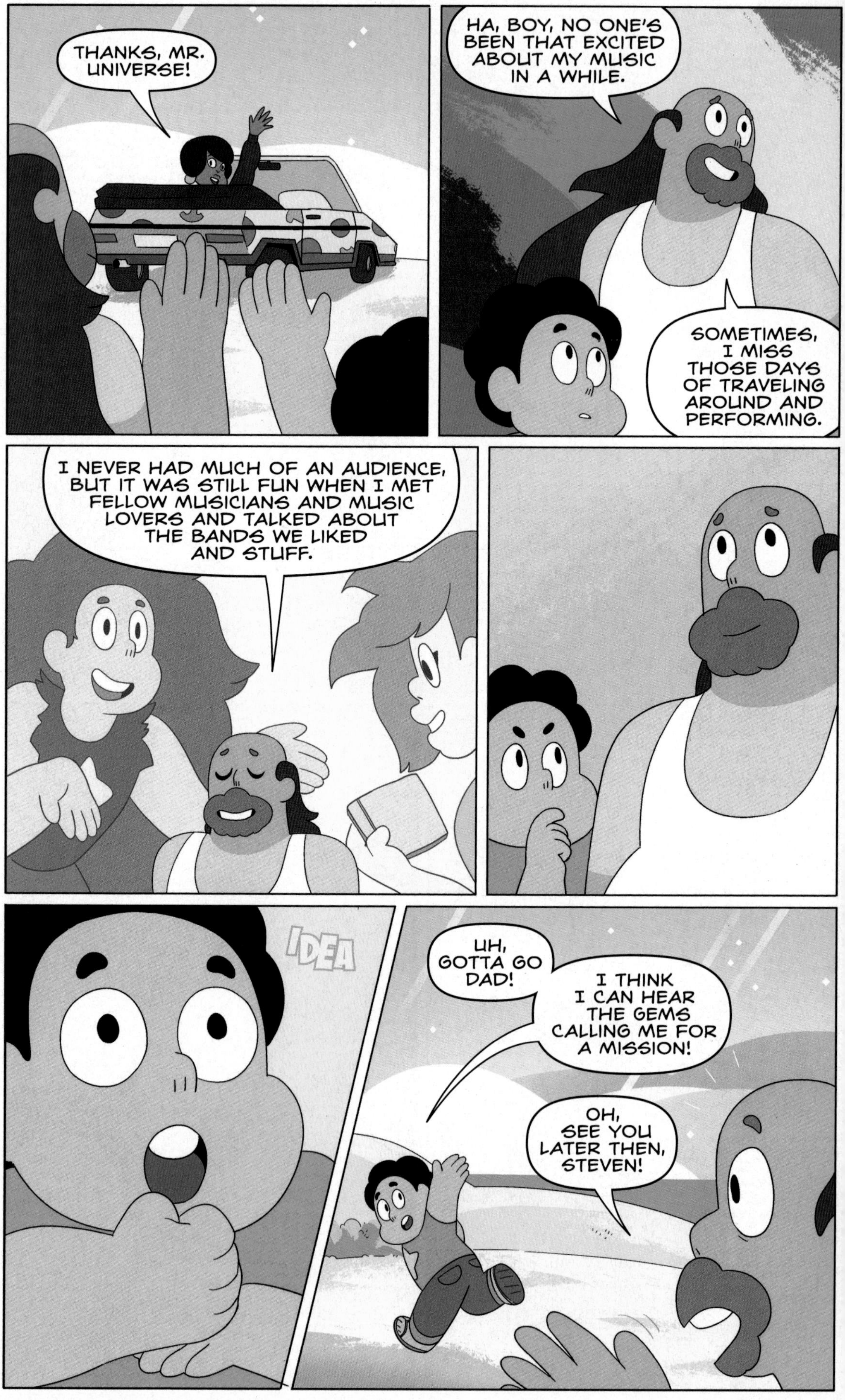
THANKS, MR. UNIVERSE!
HA, BOY, NO ONE'S BEEN THAT EXCITED ABOUT MY MUSIC IN A WHILE.
SOMETIMES, I MISS THOSE DAYS OF TRAVELING AROUND AND PERFORMING.
I NEVER HAD MUCH OF AN AUDIENCE, BUT IT WAS STILL FUN WHEN I MET FELLOW MUSICIANS AND MUSIC LOVERS AND TALKED ABOUT THE BANDS WE LIKED AND STUFF.
IDEA
UH, GOTTA GO DAD!
I THINK I CAN HEAR THE GEMS CALLING ME FOR A MISSION!
OH, SEE YOU LATER THEN, STEVEN!

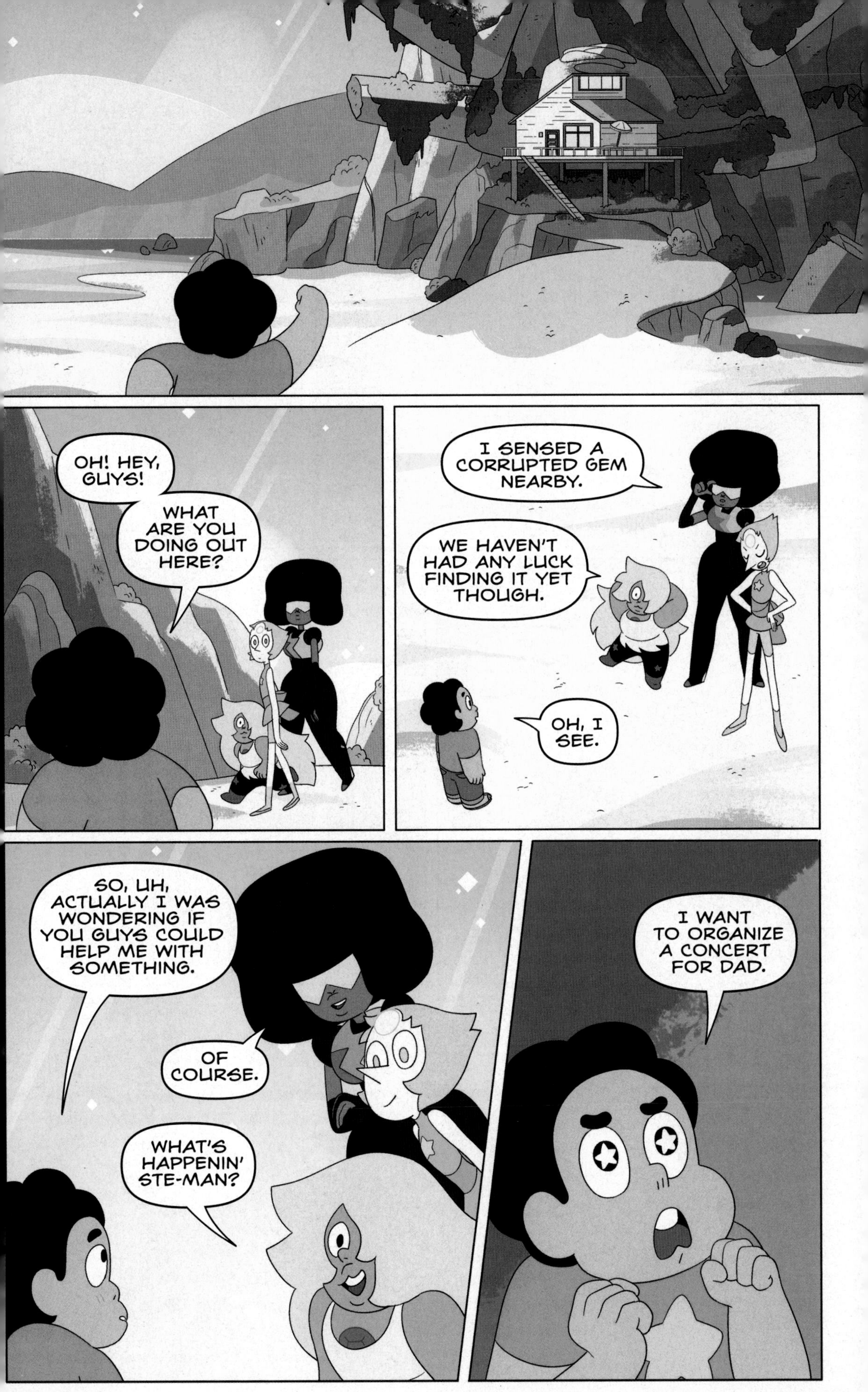
OH! HEY, GUYS!
WHAT ARE YOU DOING OUT HERE?
I SENSED A CORRUPTED GEM NEARBY.
WE HAVEN'T HAD ANY LUCK FINDING IT YET THOUGH.
OH, I SEE.
SO, UH, ACTUALLY I WAS WONDERING IF YOU GUYS COULD HELP ME WITH SOMETHING.
OF COURSE.
WHAT'S HAPPENIN' STE-MAN?
I WANT TO ORGANIZE A CONCERT FOR DAD.

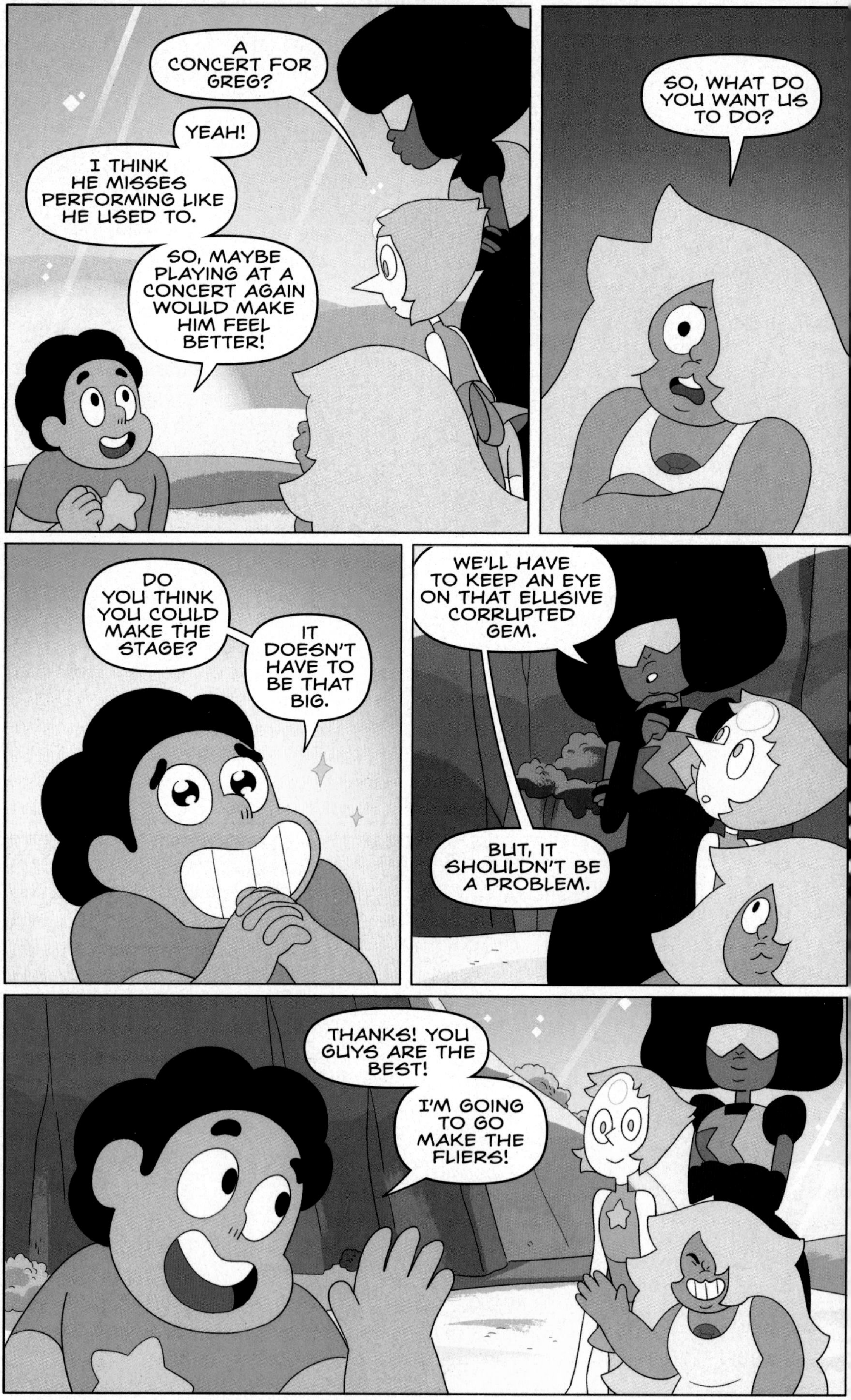
A CONCERT FOR GREG?
YEAH!
I THINK HE MISSES PERFORMING LIKE HE USED TO.
SO, MAYBE PLAYING AT A CONCERT AGAIN WOULD MAKE HIM FEEL BETTER!
SO, WHAT DO YOU WANT US TO DO?
DO YOU THINK YOU COULD MAKE THE STAGE?
IT DOESN'T HAVE TO BE THAT BIG.
WE'LL HAVE TO KEEP AN EYE ON THAT ELUSIVE CORRUPTED GEM.
BUT, IT SHOULDN'T BE A PROBLEM.
THANKS! YOU GUYS ARE THE BEST!
I'M GOING TO GO MAKE THE FLIERS!

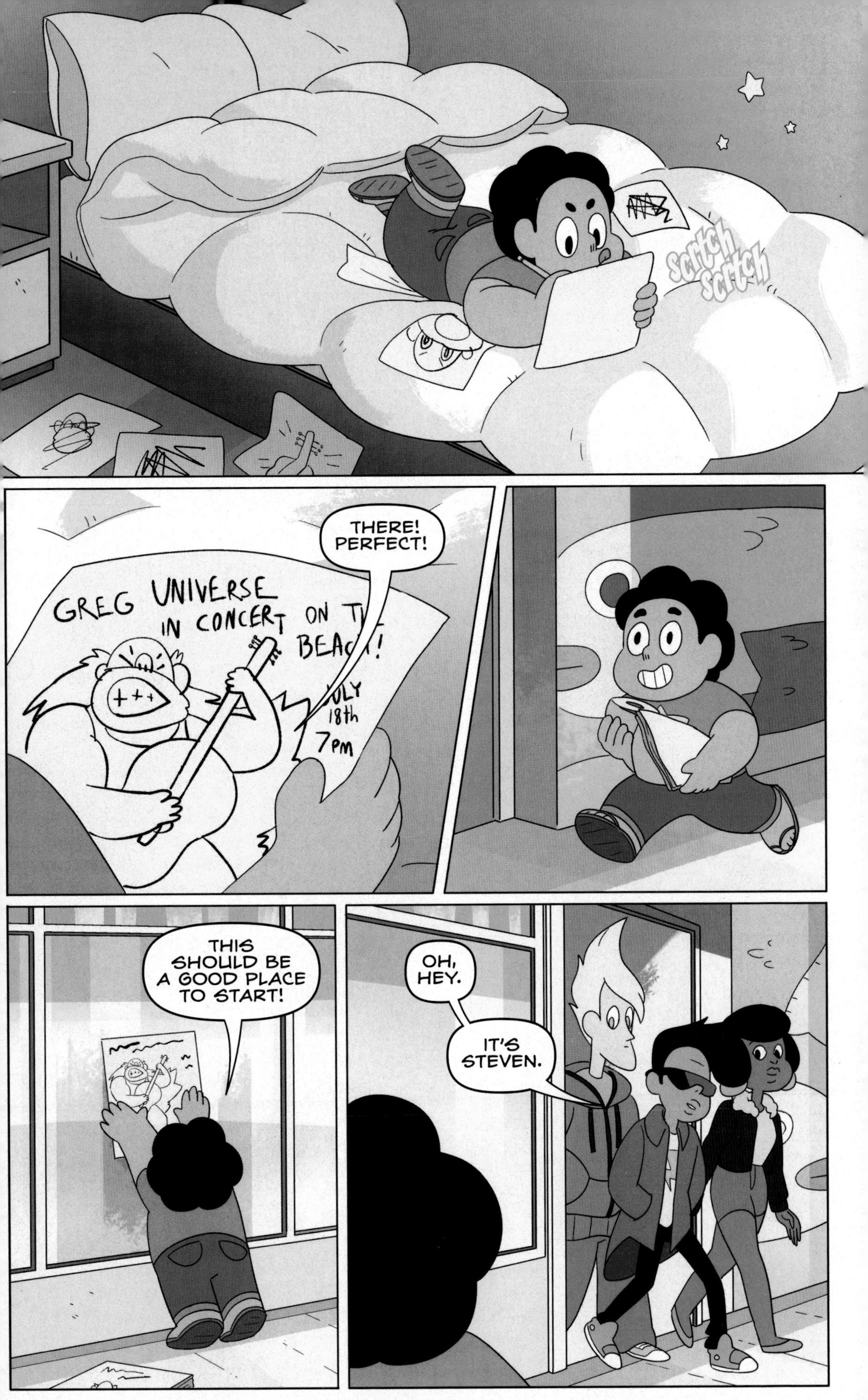
SCRTCH SCRTCH
GREG UNIVERSE IN CONCERT ON TH BEACH! JULY 18th 7PM
THERE! PERFECT!
THIS SHOULD BE A GOOD PLACE TO START!
OH, HEY.
IT'S STEVEN.

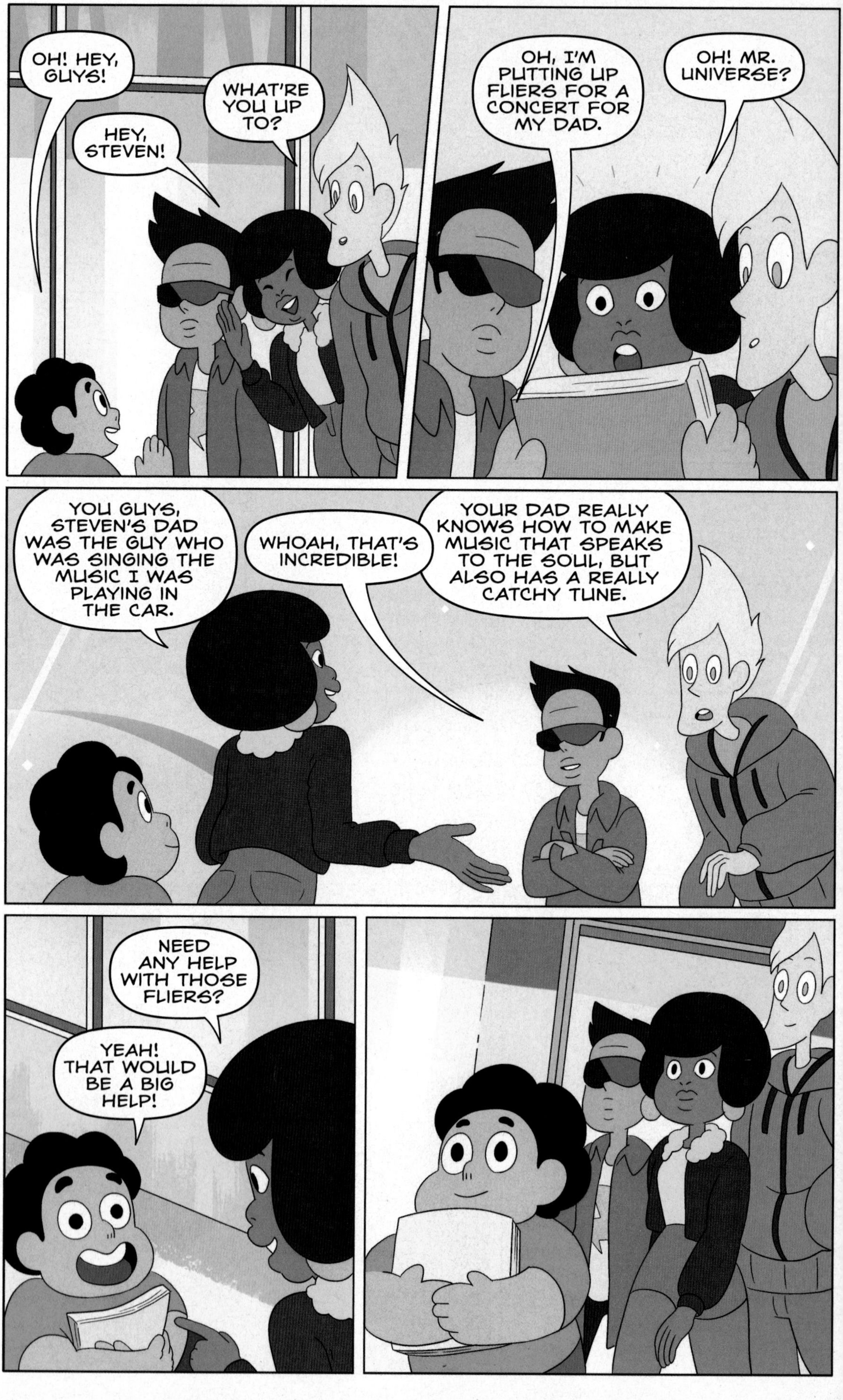
OH! HEY, GUYS!
HEY, STEVEN!
WHAT'RE YOU UP TO?
OH, I'M PUTTING UP FLIERS FOR A CONCERT FOR MY DAD.
OH! MR. UNIVERSE?
YOU GUYS, STEVEN'S DAD WAS THE GUY WHO WAS SINGING THE MUSIC I WAS PLAYING IN THE CAR.
WHOAH, THAT'S INCREDIBLE!
YOUR DAD REALLY KNOWS HOW TO MAKE MUSIC THAT SPEAKS TO THE SOUL, BUT ALSO HAS A REALLY CATCHY TUNE.
NEED ANY HELP WITH THOSE FLIERS?
YEAH! THAT WOULD BE A BIG HELP!

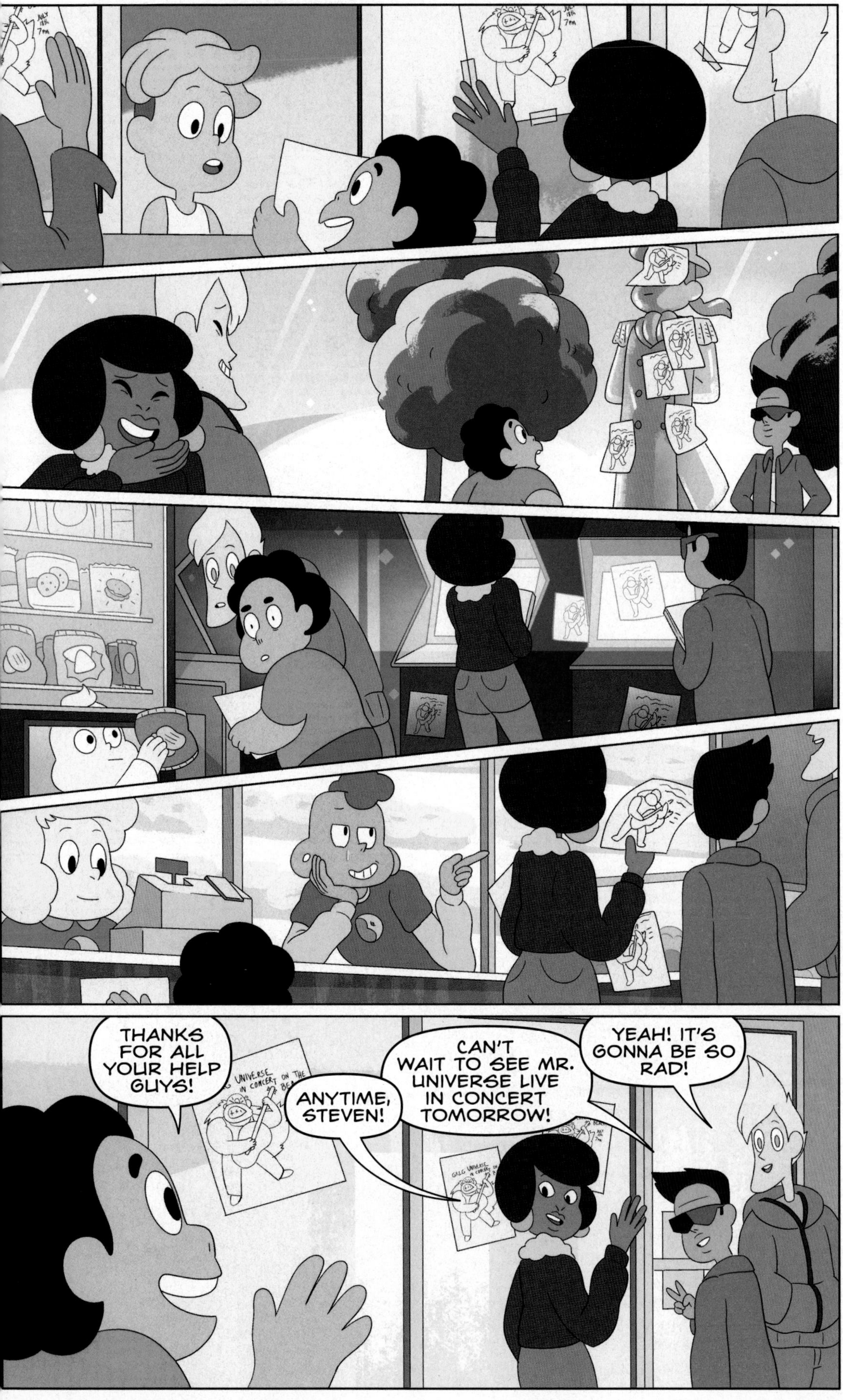
THANKS FOR ALL YOUR HELP GUYS!
ANYTIME, STEVEN!
CAN'T WAIT TO SEE MR. UNIVERSE LIVE IN CONCERT TOMORROW!
YEAH! IT'S GONNA BE SO RAD!

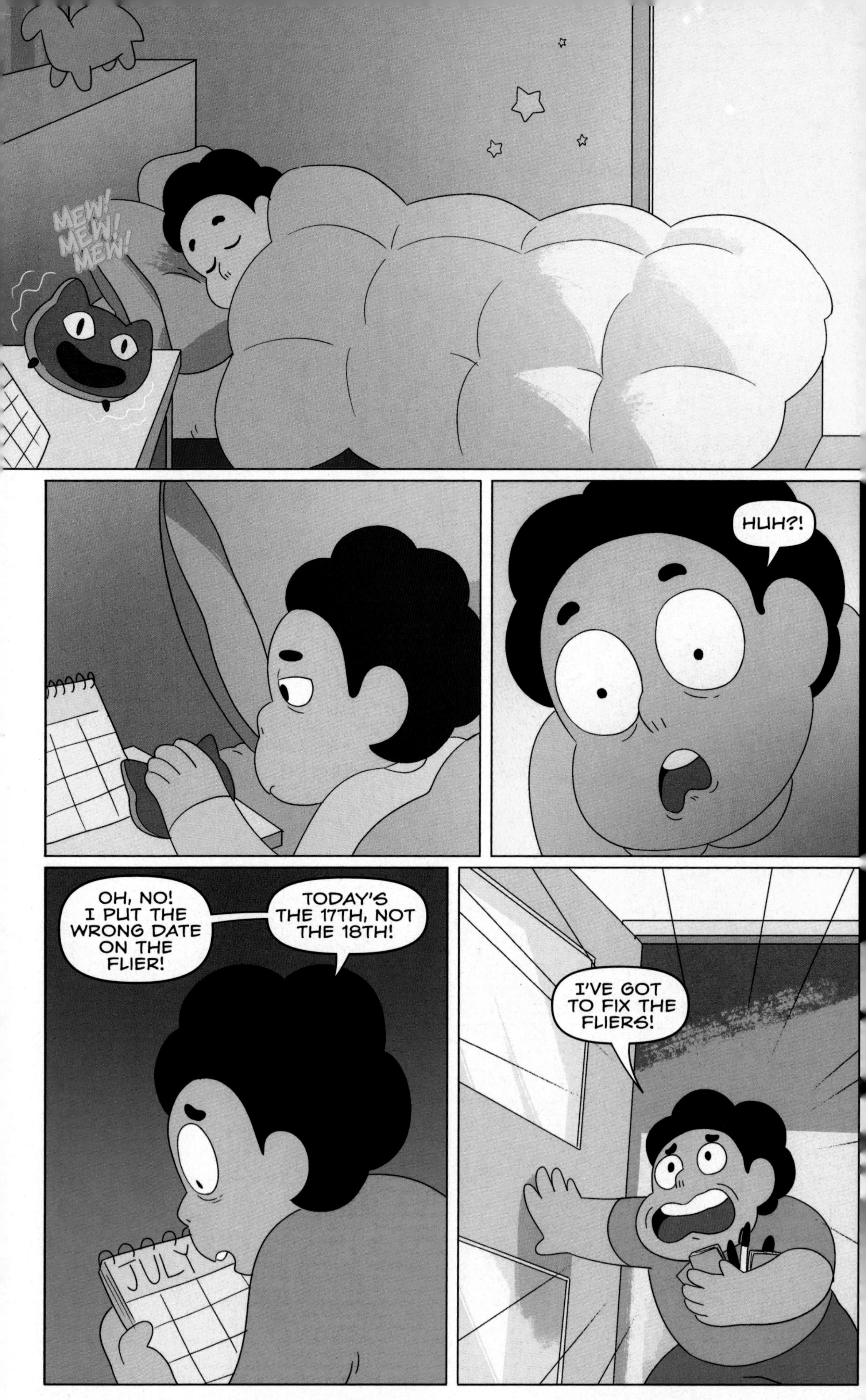
MEW! MEW! MEW!
HUH?!
OH, NO! I PUT THE WRONG DATE ON THE FLIER!
TODAY'S THE 17TH, NOT THE 18TH!
JULY
I'VE GOT TO FIX THE FLIERS!

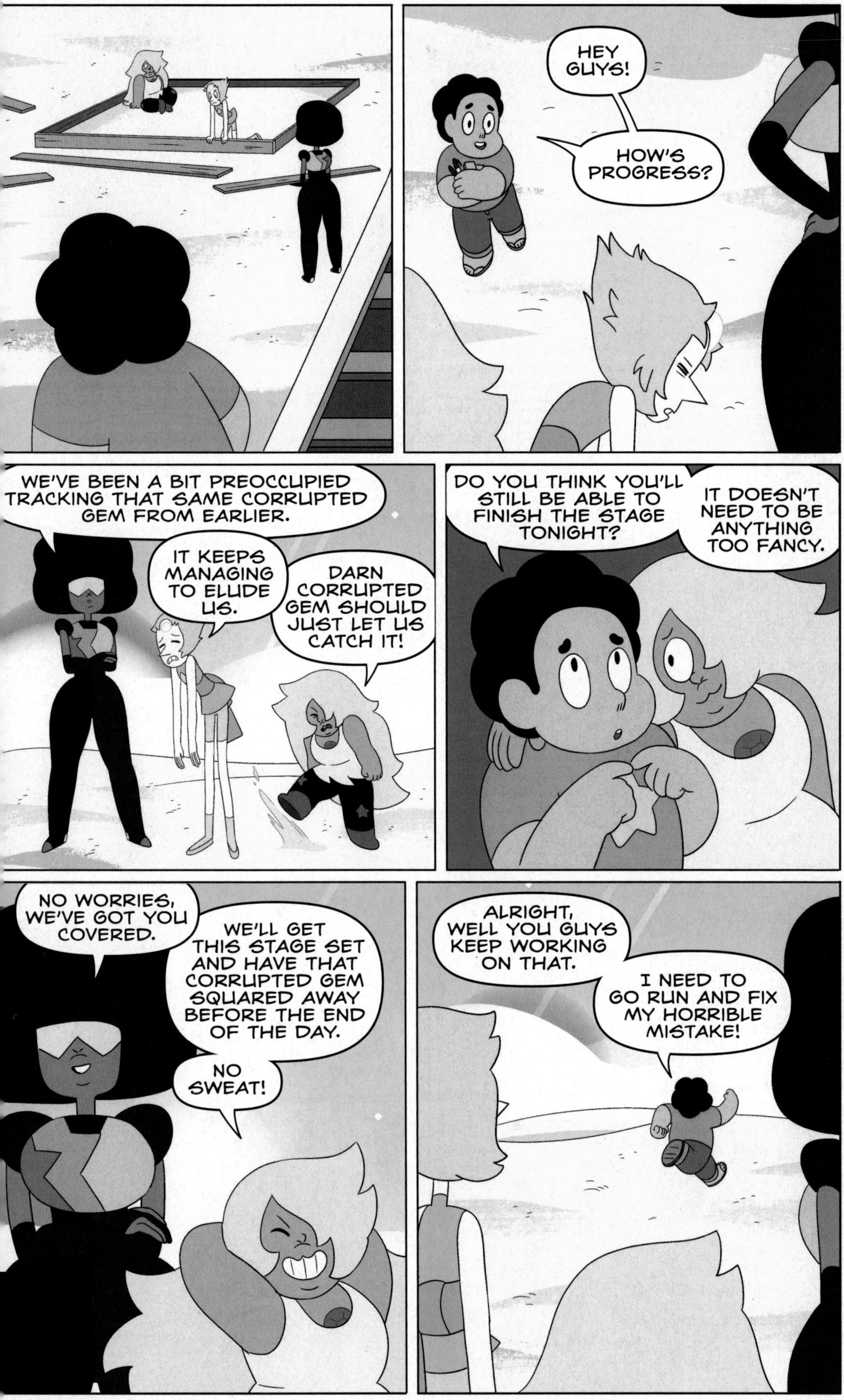
HEY GUYS!
HOW'S PROGRESS?
WE'VE BEEN A BIT PREOCCUPIED TRACKING THAT SAME CORRUPTED GEM FROM EARLIER.
IT KEEPS MANAGING TO ELUDE US.
DARN CORRUPTED GEM SHOULD JUST LET US CATCH IT!
DO YOU THINK YOU'LL STILL BE ABLE TO FINISH THE STAGE TONIGHT?
IT DOESN'T NEED TO BE ANYTHING TOO FANCY.
NO WORRIES, WE'VE GOT YOU COVERED.
WE'LL GET THIS STAGE SET AND HAVE THAT CORRUPTED GEM SQUARED AWAY BEFORE THE END OF THE DAY.
NO SWEAT!
ALRIGHT, WELL YOU GUYS KEEP WORKING ON THAT.
I NEED TO GO RUN AND FIX MY HORRIBLE MISTAKE!

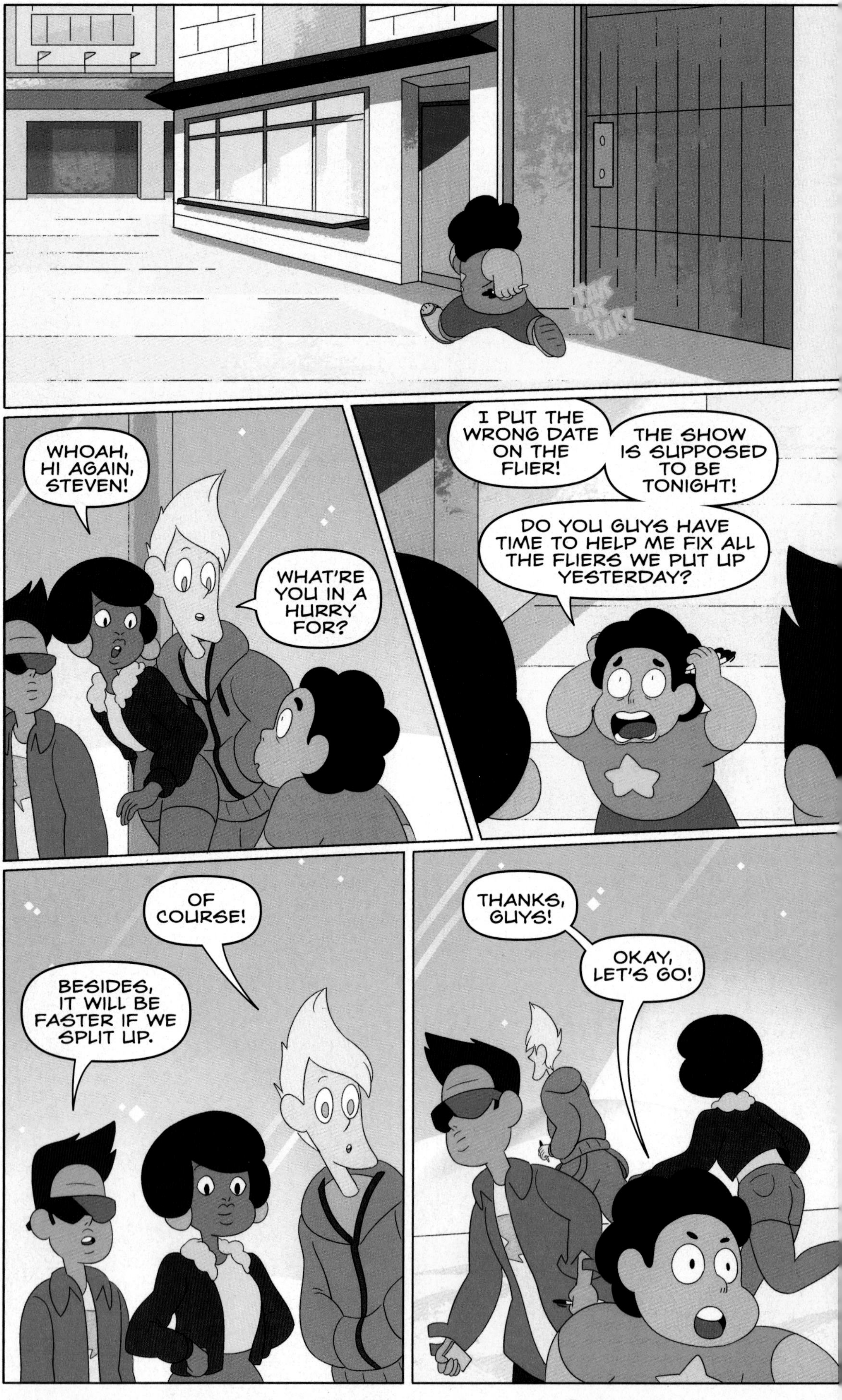
TAK TAK TAK!
WHOAH, HI AGAIN, STEVEN!
WHAT'RE YOU IN A HURRY FOR?
I PUT THE WRONG DATE ON THE FLIER!
THE SHOW IS SUPPOSED TO BE TONIGHT!
DO YOU GUYS HAVE TIME TO HELP ME FIX ALL THE FLIERS WE PUT UP YESTERDAY?
OF COURSE!
BESIDES, IT WILL BE FASTER IF WE SPLIT UP.
THANKS, GUYS!
OKAY, LET'S GO!

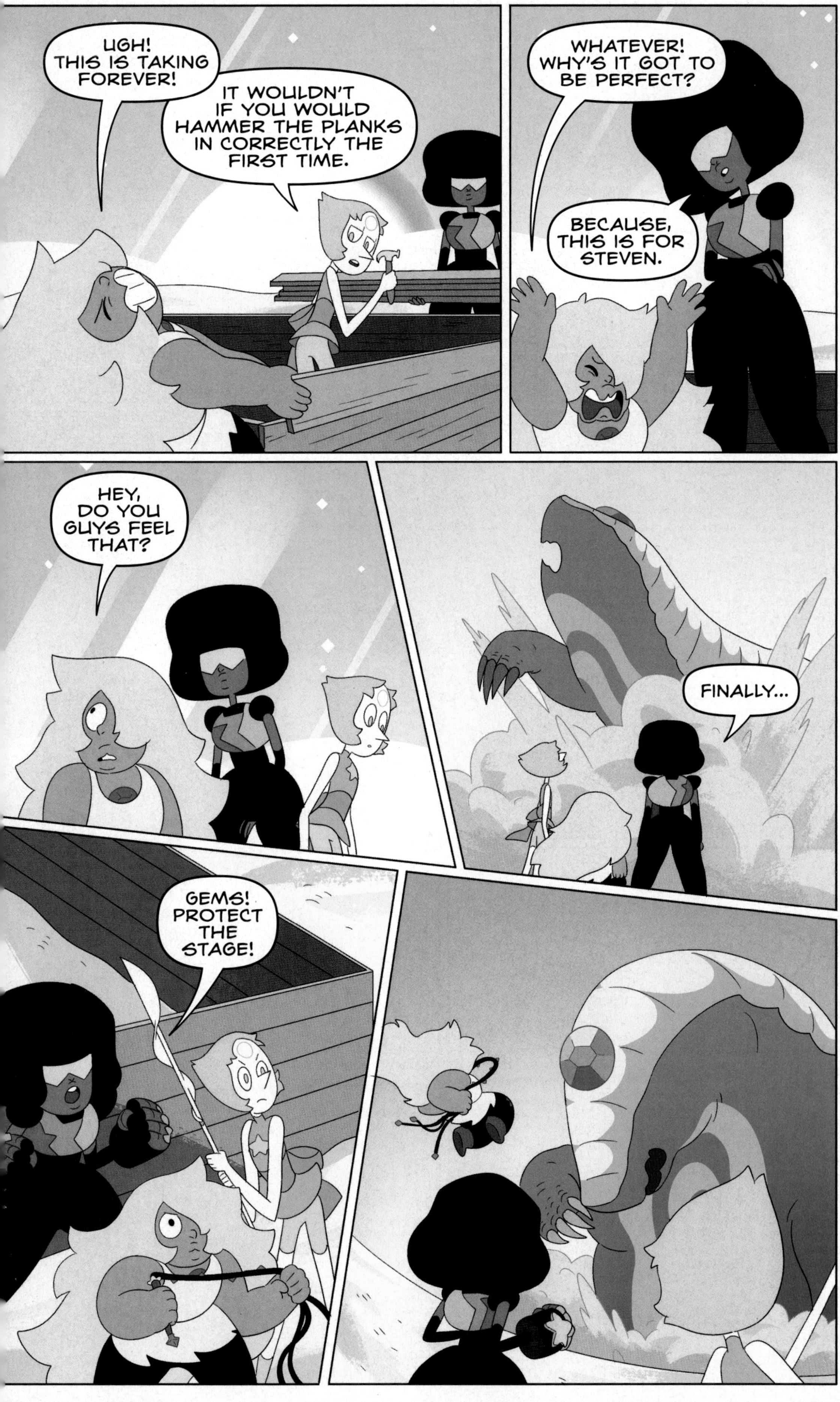
UGH! THIS IS TAKING FOREVER!
IT WOULDN'T IF YOU WOULD HAMMER THE PLANKS IN CORRECTLY THE FIRST TIME.
WHATEVER! WHY'S IT GOT TO BE PERFECT?
BECAUSE, THIS IS FOR STEVEN.
HEY, DO YOU GUYS FEEL THAT?
FINALLY...
GEMS! PROTECT THE STAGE!

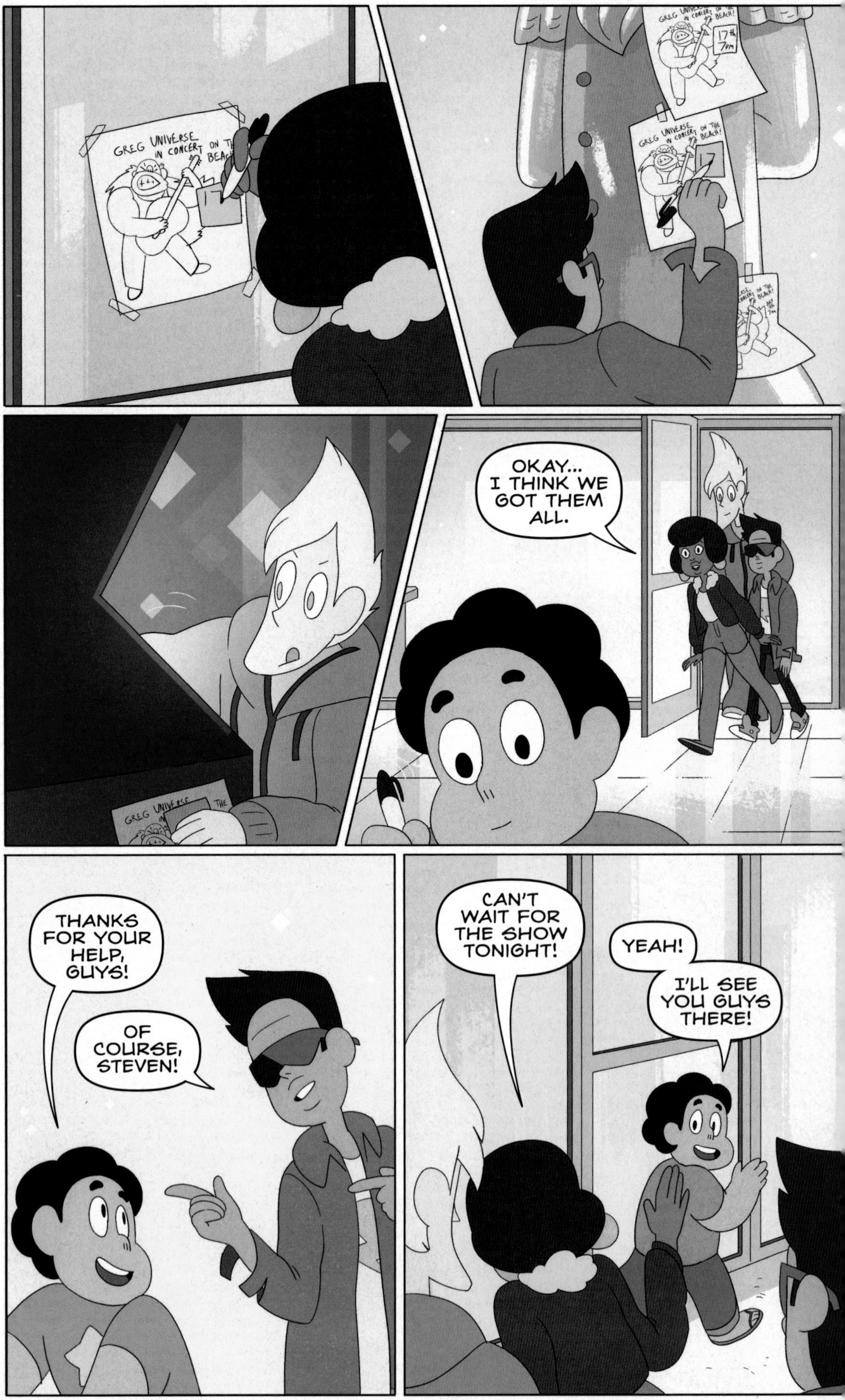
GREG UNIVERSE IN CONCERT ON THE BEACH
GREG UNIVERSE IN CONCERT ON THE BEACH!
17th 7PM
OKAY... I THINK WE GOT THEM ALL.
THANKS FOR YOUR HELP, GUYS!
OF COURSE, STEVEN!
CAN'T WAIT FOR THE SHOW TONIGHT!
YEAH!
I'LL SEE YOU GUYS THERE!

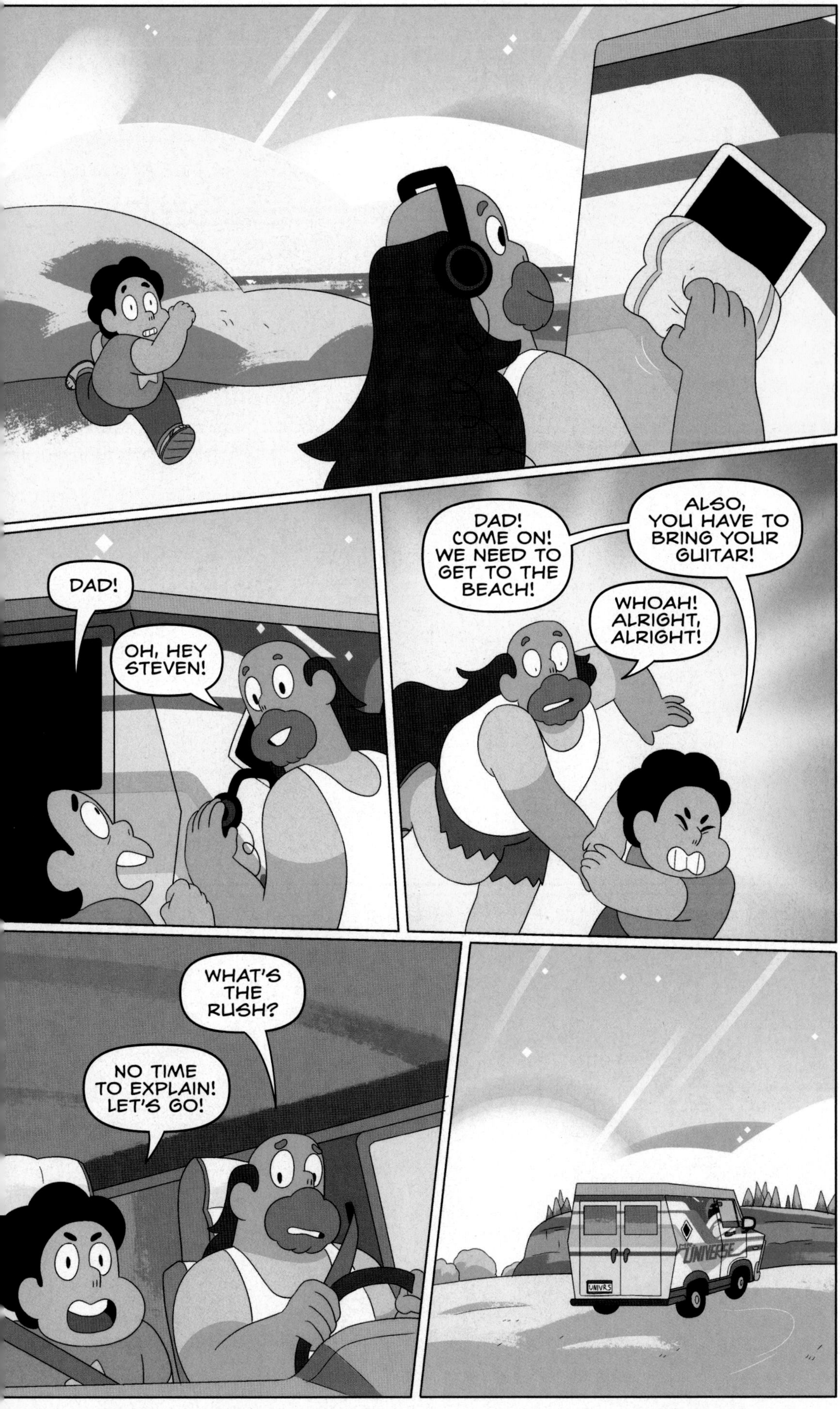
DAD!
OH, HEY STEVEN!
DAD! COME ON! WE NEED TO GET TO THE BEACH!
ALSO, YOU HAVE TO BRING YOUR GUITAR!
WHOAH! ALRIGHT, ALRIGHT!
WHAT'S THE RUSH?
NO TIME TO EXPLAIN! LET'S GO!
UNIVERSE
UNIVRS

WHOAH, SLOW DOWN! WHERE'S THE FIRE, KIDDO?

BWOOO

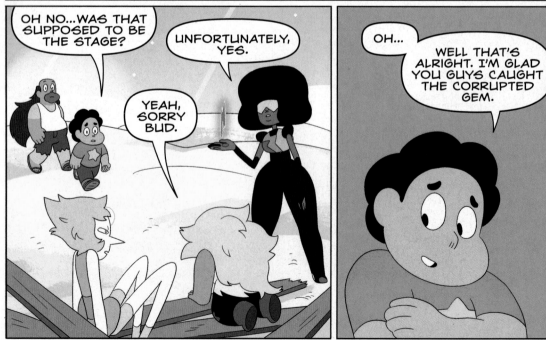

OH NO...WAS THAT SUPPOSED TO BE THE STAGE?

UNFORTUNATELY, YES.

YEAH, SORRY BUD.

OH...

WELL THAT'S ALRIGHT. I'M GLAD YOU GUYS CAUGHT THE CORRUPTED GEM.

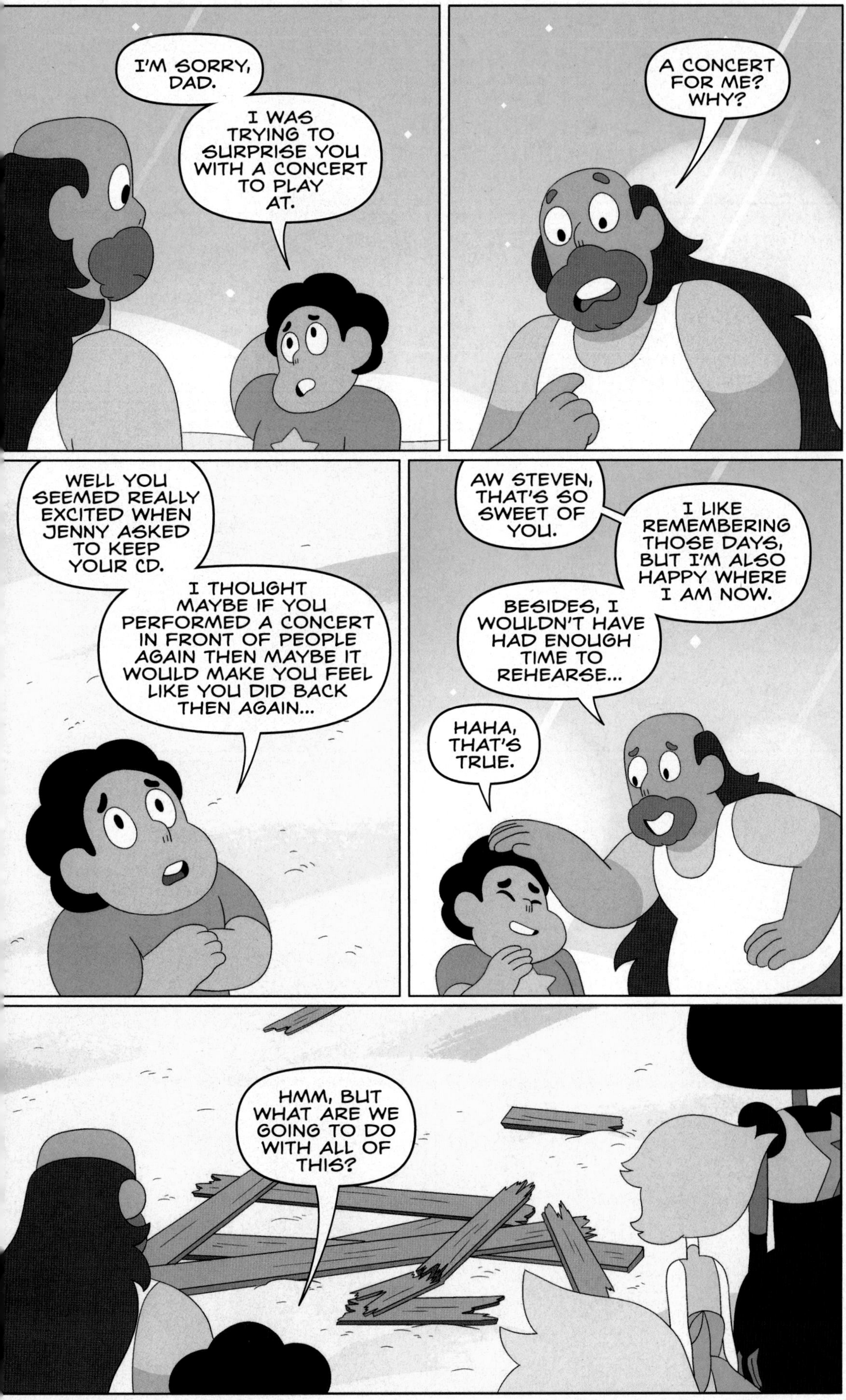
I'M SORRY, DAD.
I WAS TRYING TO SURPRISE YOU WITH A CONCERT TO PLAY AT.
A CONCERT FOR ME? WHY?
WELL YOU SEEMED REALLY EXCITED WHEN JENNY ASKED TO KEEP YOUR CD.
I THOUGHT MAYBE IF YOU PERFORMED A CONCERT IN FRONT OF PEOPLE AGAIN THEN MAYBE IT WOULD MAKE YOU FEEL LIKE YOU DID BACK THEN AGAIN...
AW STEVEN, THAT'S SO SWEET OF YOU.
I LIKE REMEMBERING THOSE DAYS, BUT I'M ALSO HAPPY WHERE I AM NOW.
BESIDES, I WOULDN'T HAVE HAD ENOUGH TIME TO REHEARSE...
HAHA, THAT'S TRUE.
HMM, BUT WHAT ARE WE GOING TO DO WITH ALL OF THIS?

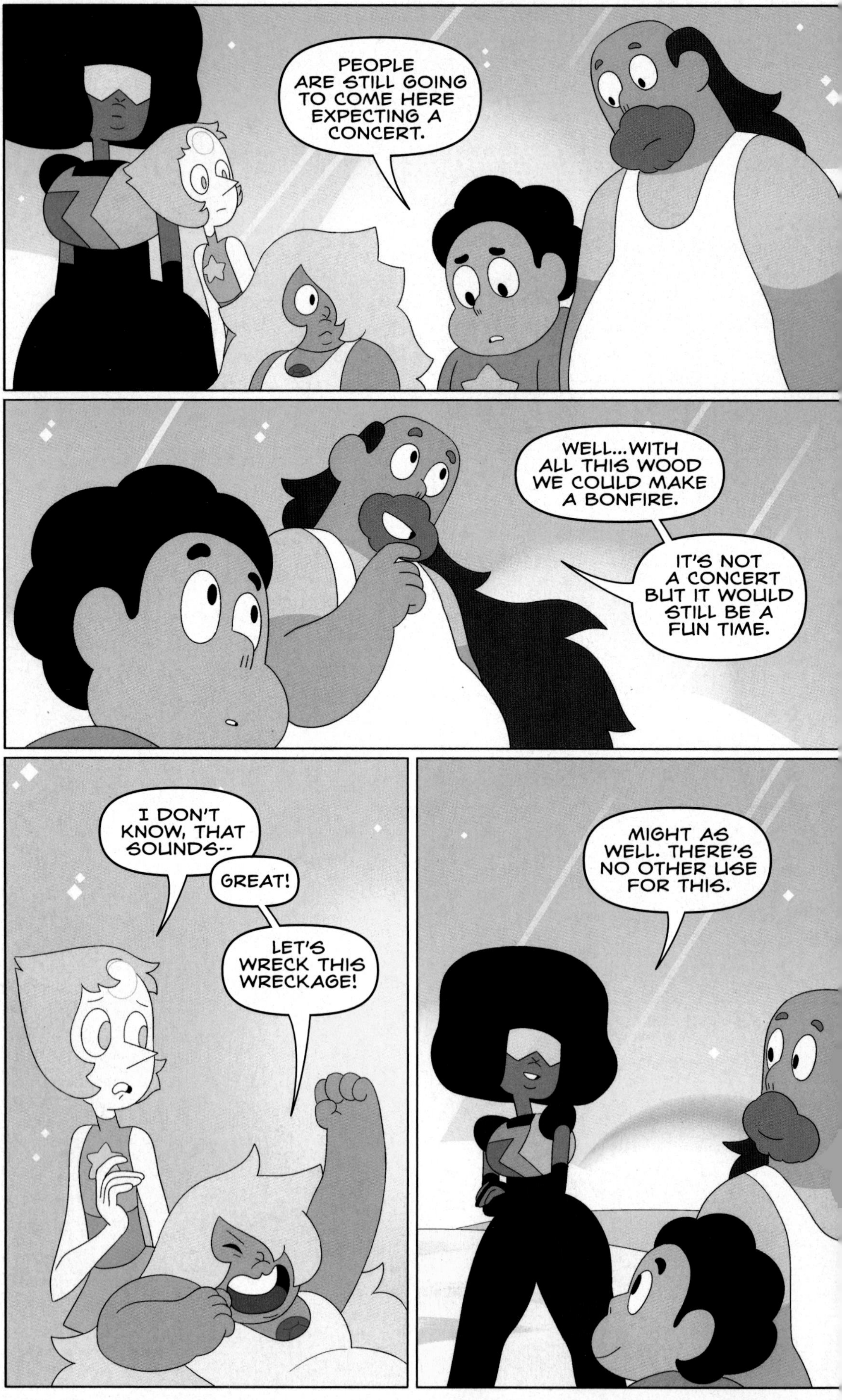
PEOPLE ARE STILL GOING TO COME HERE EXPECTING A CONCERT.
WELL...WITH ALL THIS WOOD WE COULD MAKE A BONFIRE.
IT'S NOT A CONCERT BUT IT WOULD STILL BE A FUN TIME.
I DON'T KNOW, THAT SOUNDS--
GREAT!
LET'S WRECK THIS WRECKAGE!
MIGHT AS WELL. THERE'S NO OTHER USE FOR THIS.

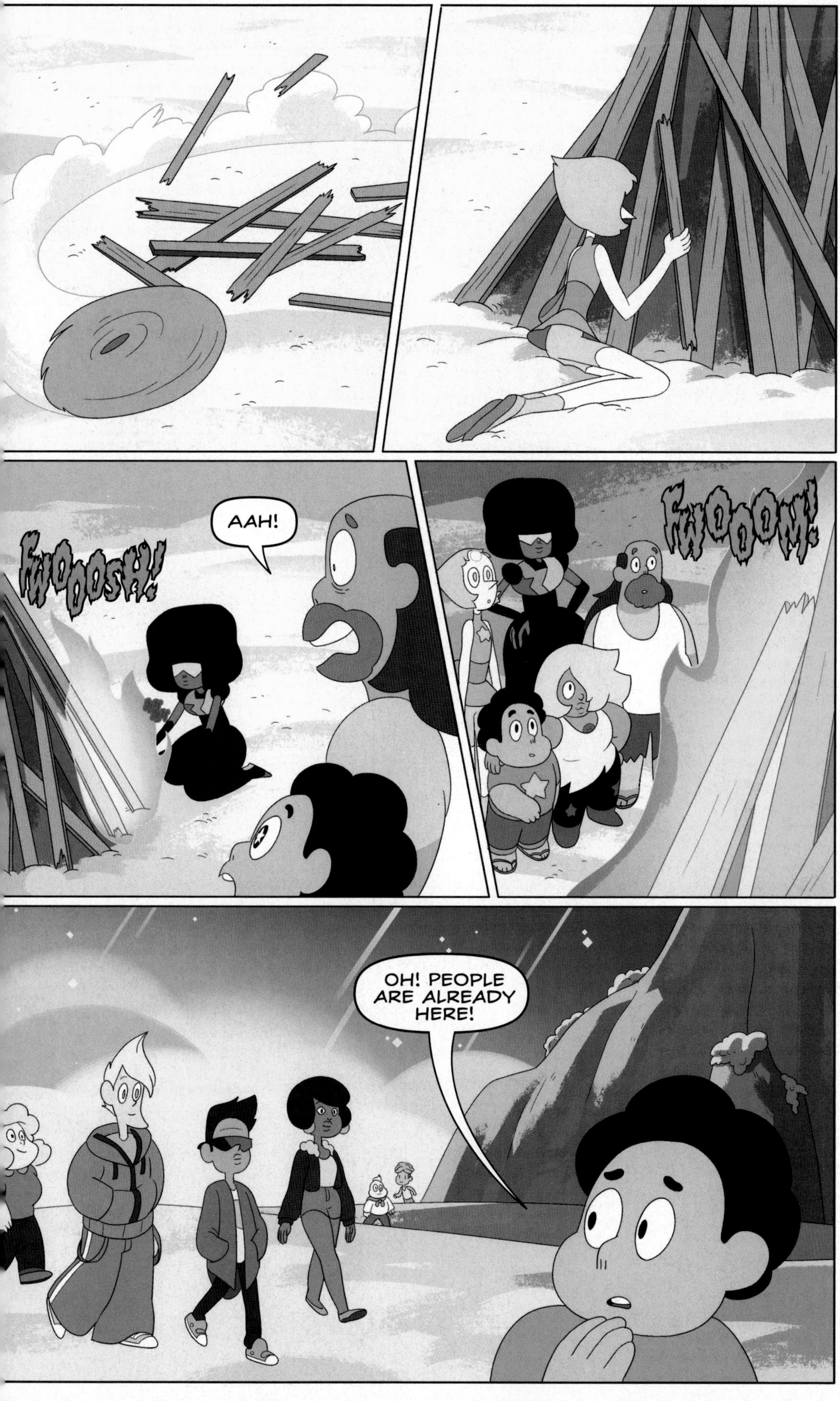
FWOOOSH!
AAH!
FWOOOOM!
OH! PEOPLE ARE ALREADY HERE!

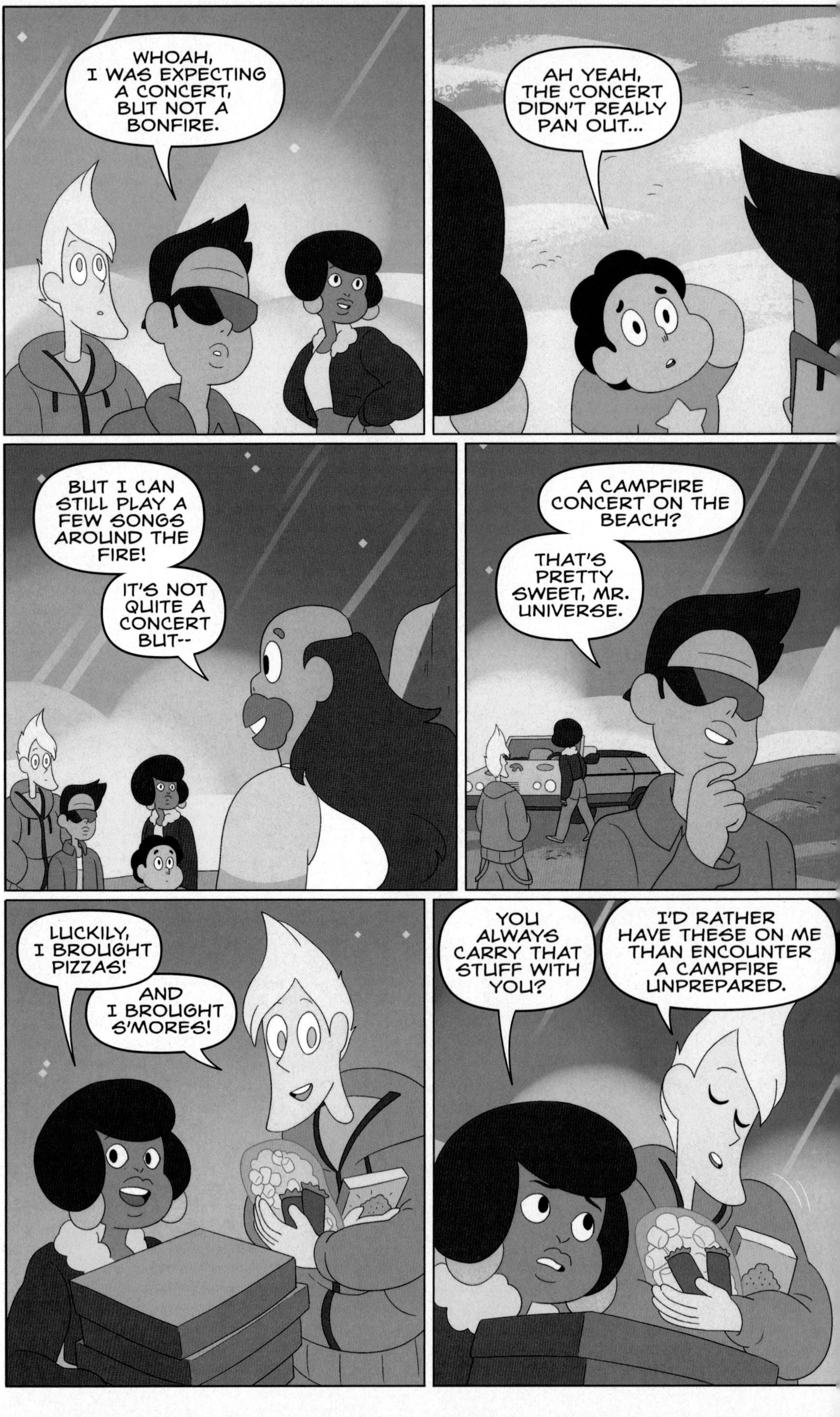
WHOAH, I WAS EXPECTING A CONCERT, BUT NOT A BONFIRE.
AH YEAH, THE CONCERT DIDN'T REALLY PAN OUT...
BUT I CAN STILL PLAY A FEW SONGS AROUND THE FIRE!
IT'S NOT QUITE A CONCERT BUT--
A CAMPFIRE CONCERT ON THE BEACH?
THAT'S PRETTY SWEET, MR. UNIVERSE.
LUCKILY, I BROUGHT PIZZAS!
AND I BROUGHT S'MORES!
YOU ALWAYS CARRY THAT STUFF WITH YOU?
I'D RATHER HAVE THESE ON ME THAN ENCOUNTER A CAMPFIRE UNPREPARED.

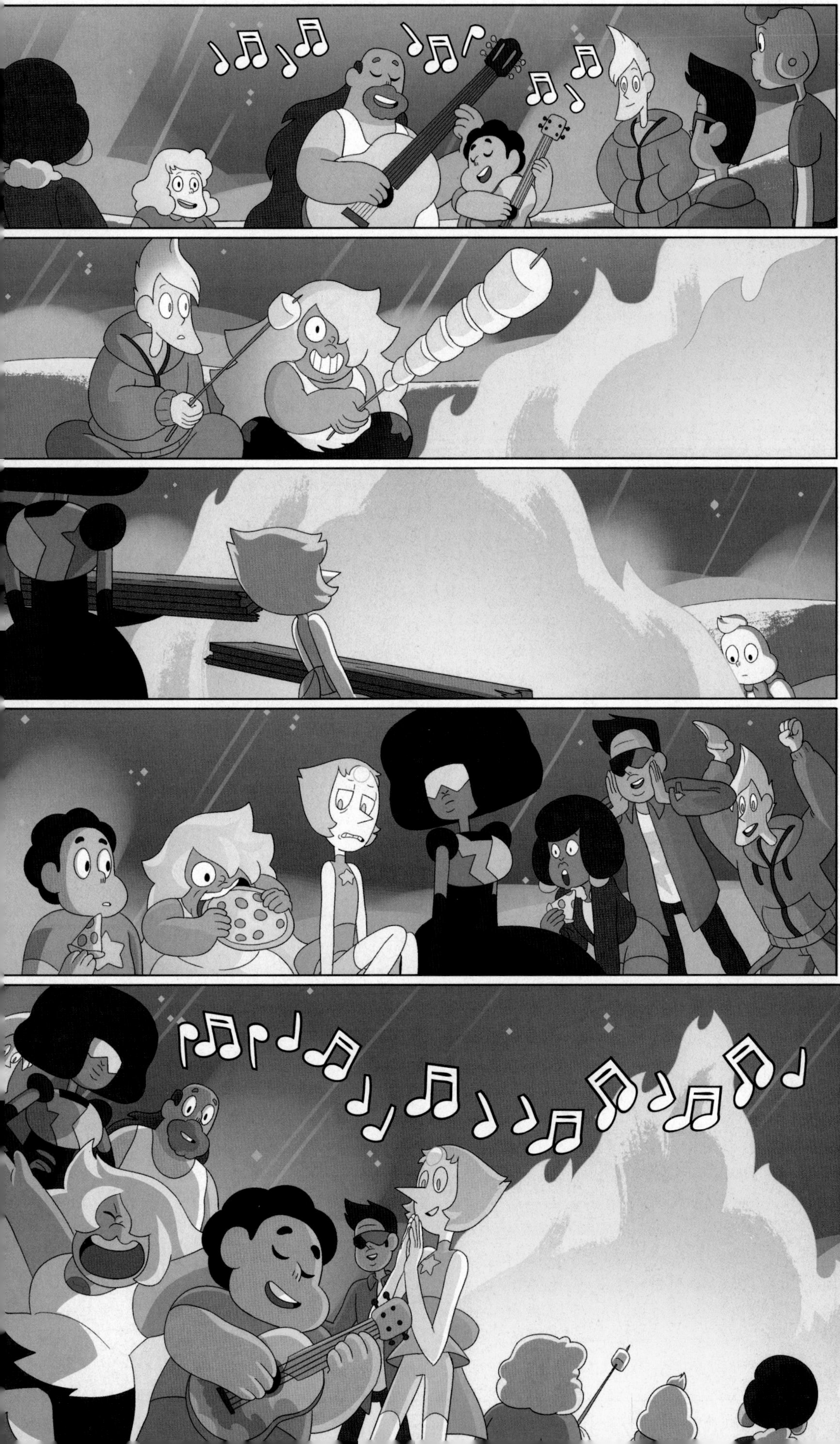

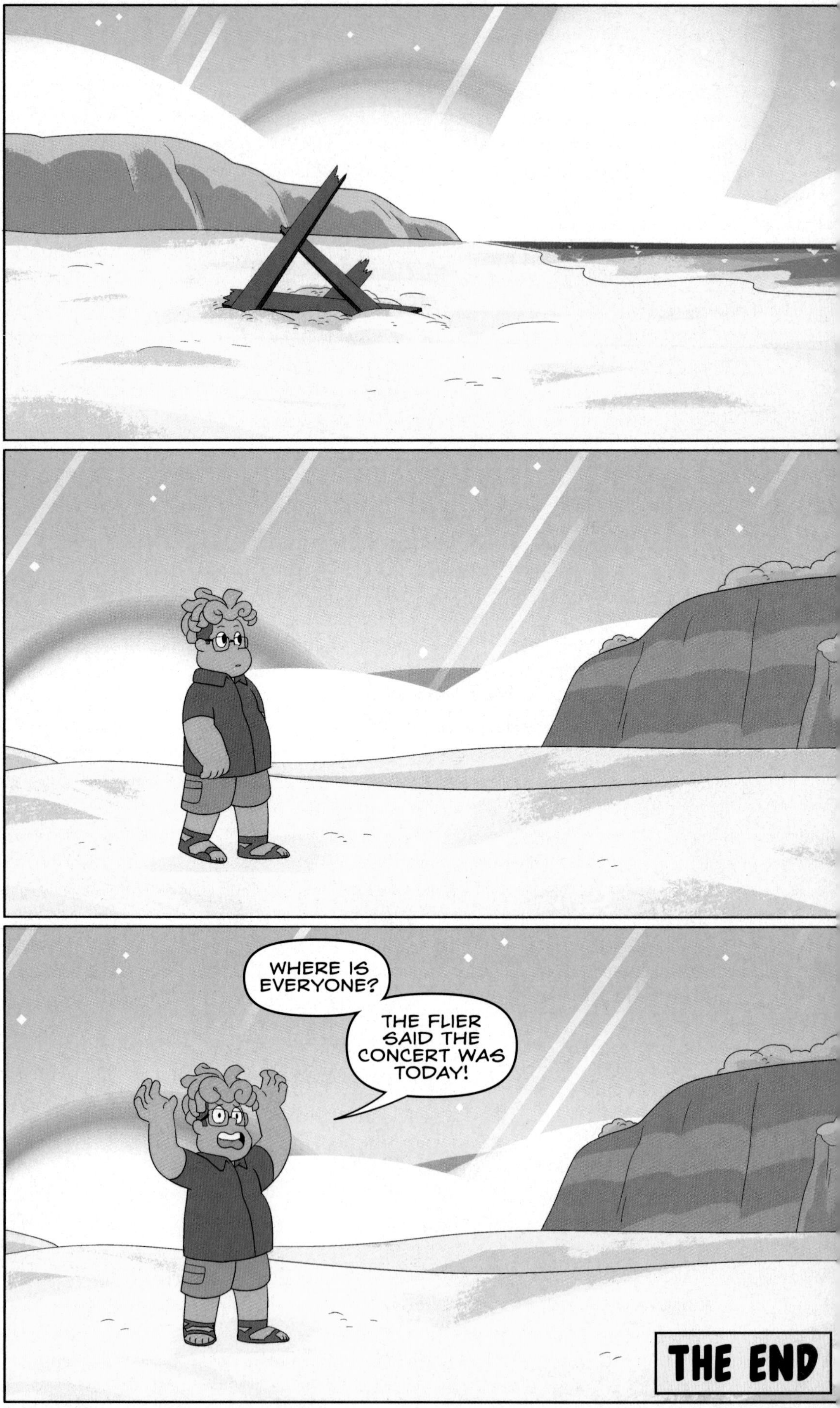
WHERE IS EVERYONE?
THE FLIER SAID THE CONCERT WAS TODAY!
THE END

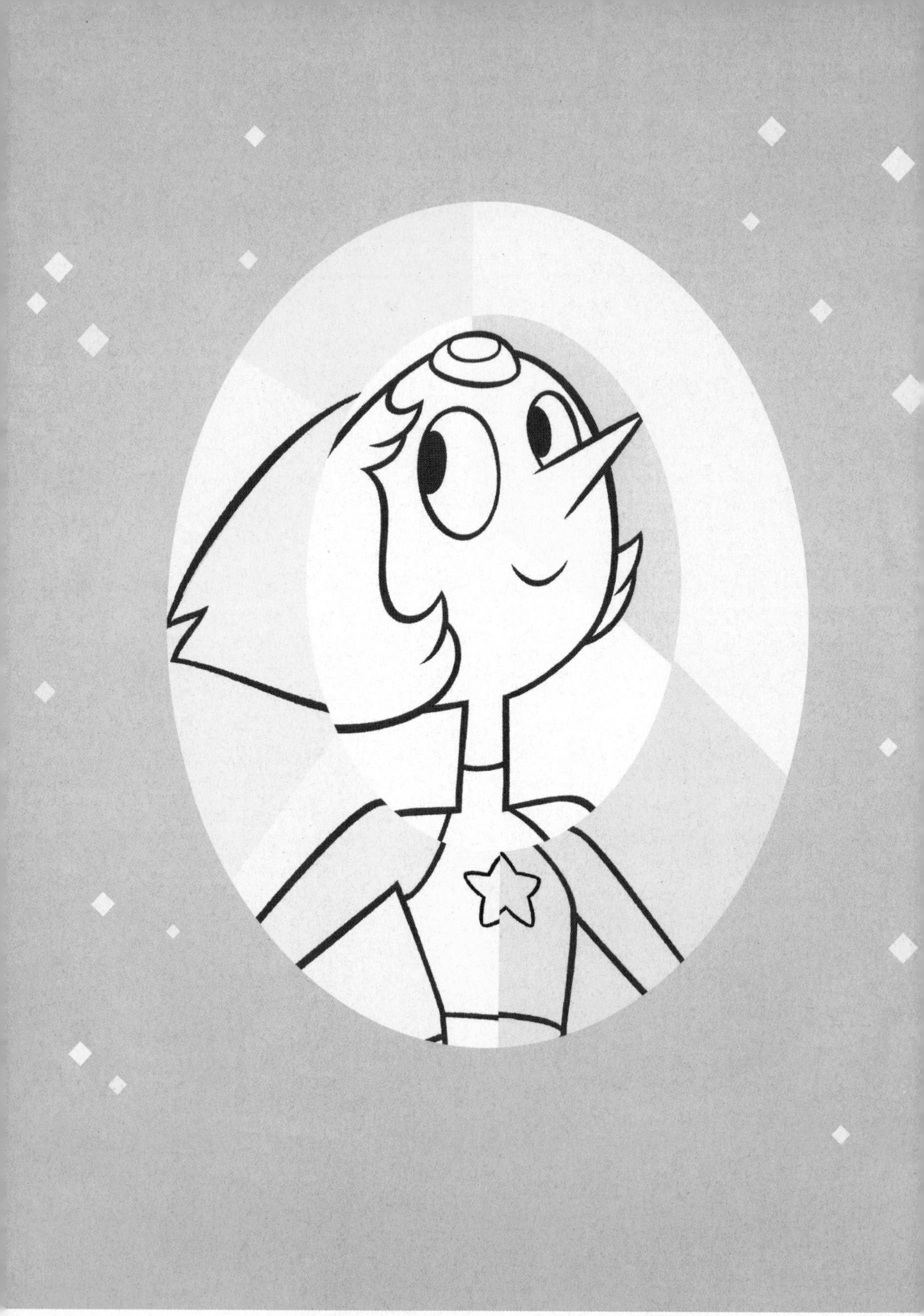

CHAPTER FIFTEEN

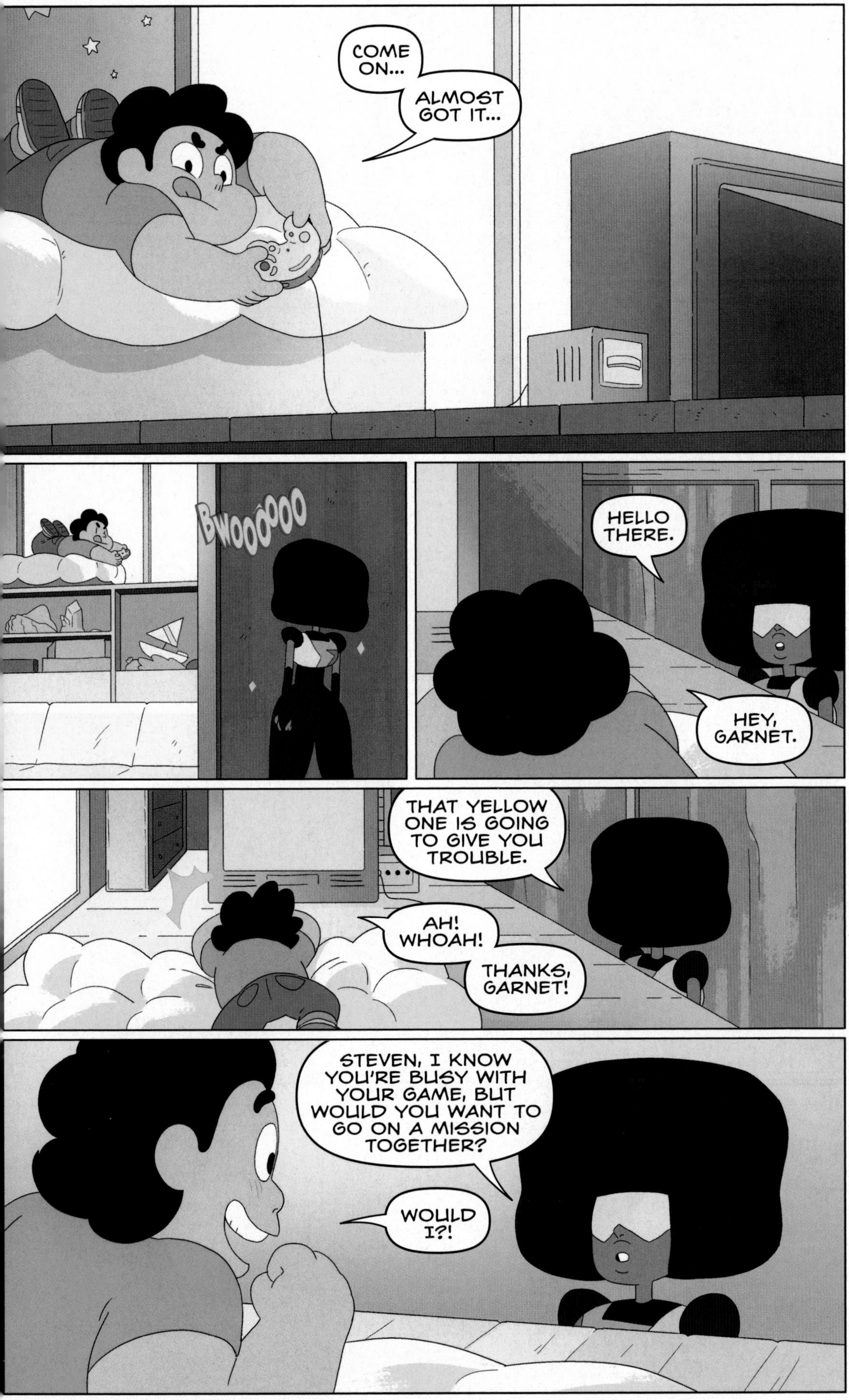
COME ON...
ALMOST GOT IT...
BWOOÔOOO
HELLO THERE.
HEY, GARNET.
THAT YELLOW ONE IS GOING TO GIVE YOU TROUBLE.
AH! WHOAH!
THANKS, GARNET!
STEVEN, I KNOW YOU'RE BUSY WITH YOUR GAME, BUT WOULD YOU WANT TO GO ON A MISSION TOGETHER?
WOULD I?!

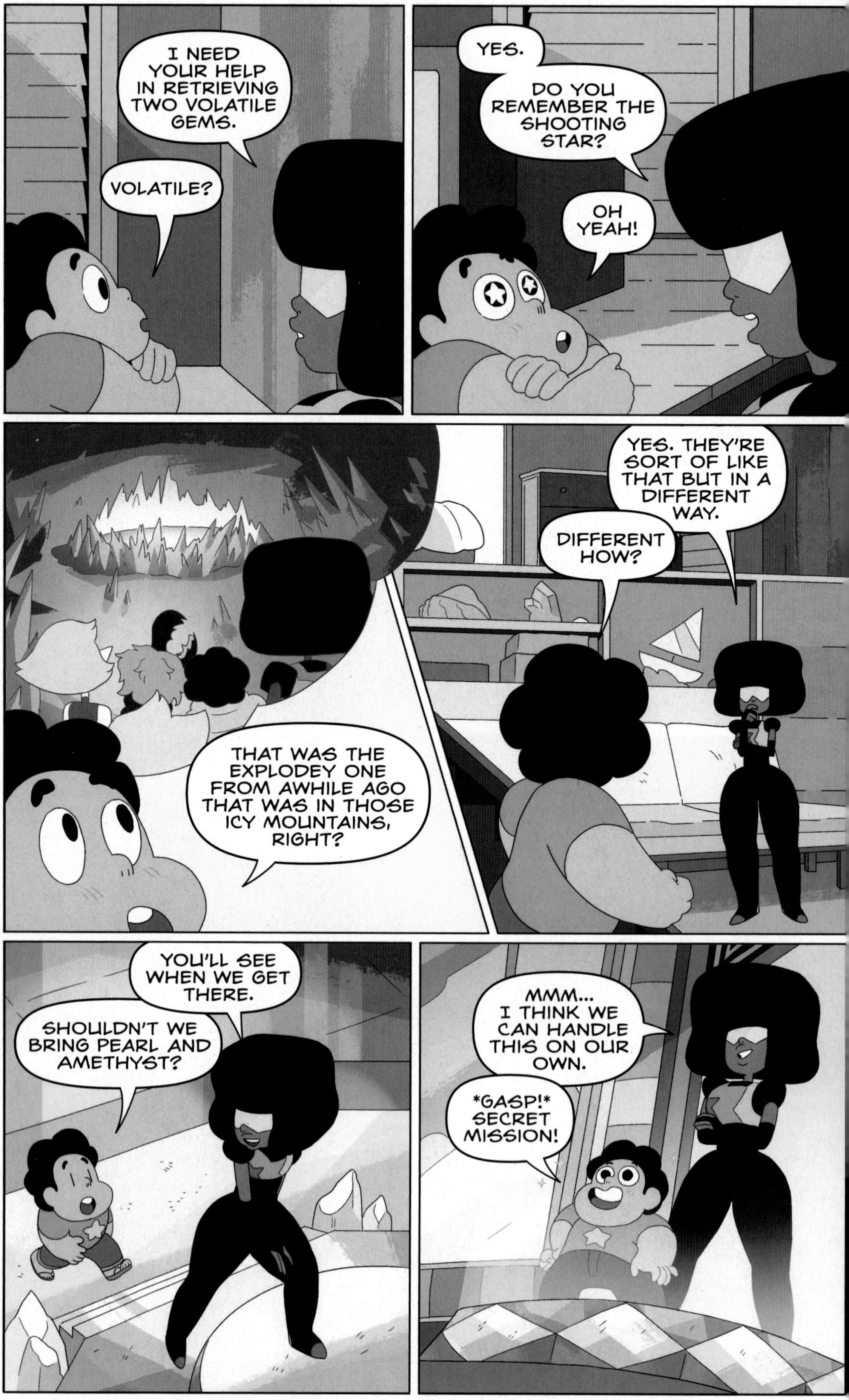
I NEED YOUR HELP IN RETRIEVING TWO VOLATILE GEMS.
VOLATILE?
YES.
DO YOU REMEMBER THE SHOOTING STAR?
OH YEAH!
THAT WAS THE EXPLODEY ONE FROM AWHILE AGO THAT WAS IN THOSE ICY MOUNTAINS, RIGHT?
YES. THEY'RE SORT OF LIKE THAT BUT IN A DIFFERENT WAY.
DIFFERENT HOW?
SHOULDN'T WE BRING PEARL AND AMETHYST?
YOU'LL SEE WHEN WE GET THERE.
MMM... I THINK WE CAN HANDLE THIS ON OUR OWN.
GASP! SECRET MISSION!

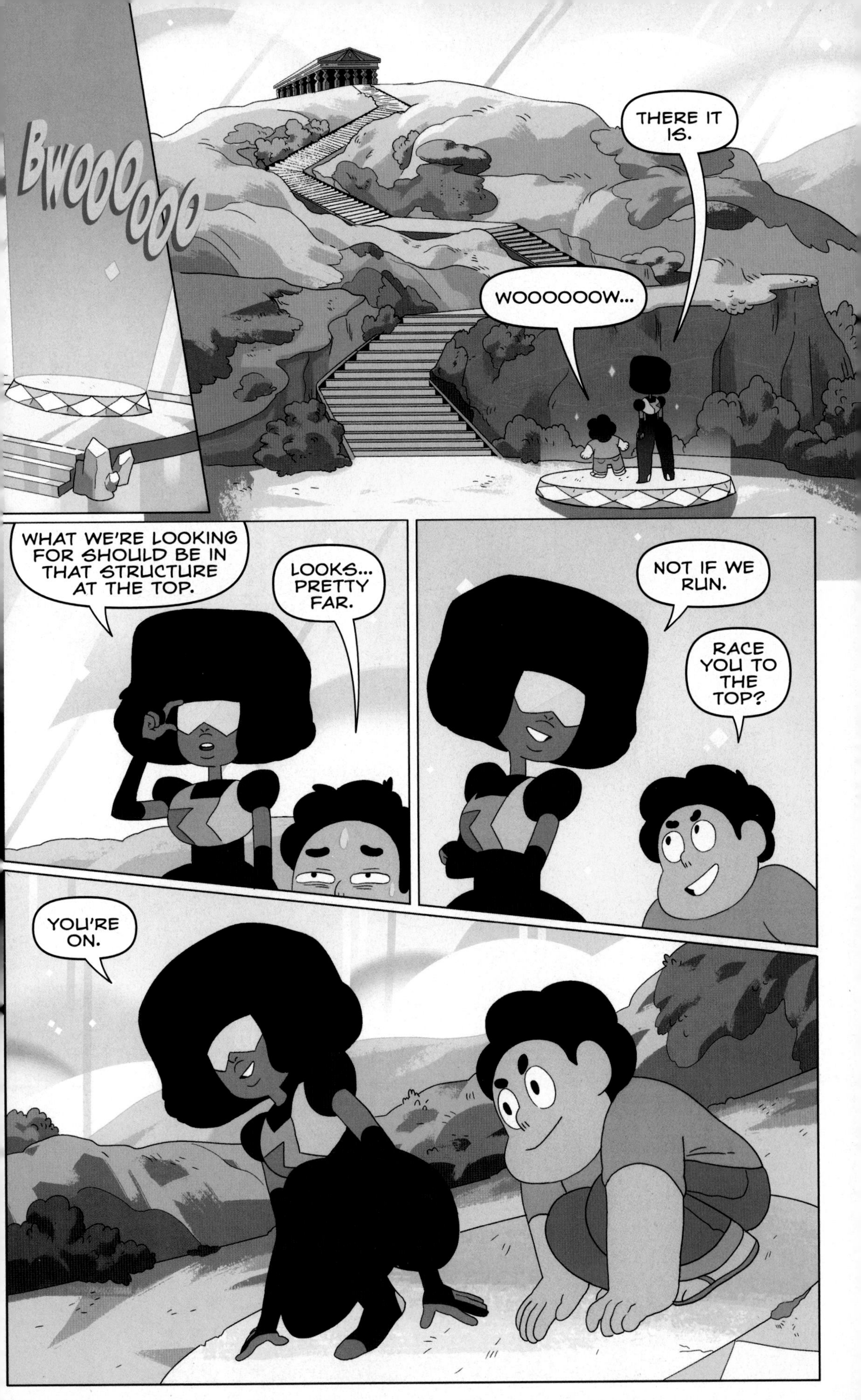
BWOOOOOO
THERE IT IS.
WOOOOOOW...
WHAT WE'RE LOOKING FOR SHOULD BE IN THAT STRUCTURE AT THE TOP.
LOOKS... PRETTY FAR.
NOT IF WE RUN.
RACE YOU TO THE TOP?
YOU'RE ON.

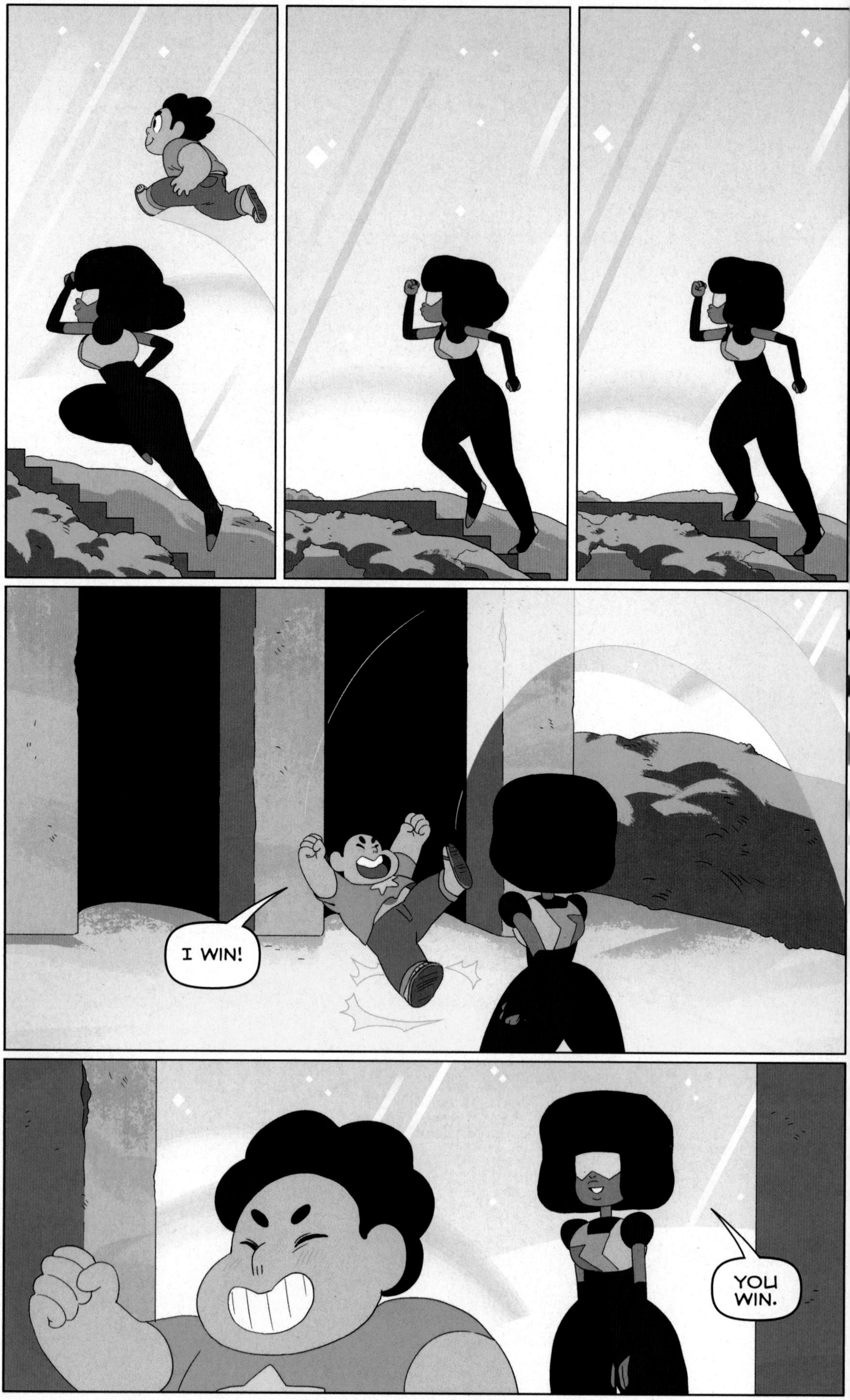
I WIN!
YOU WIN.

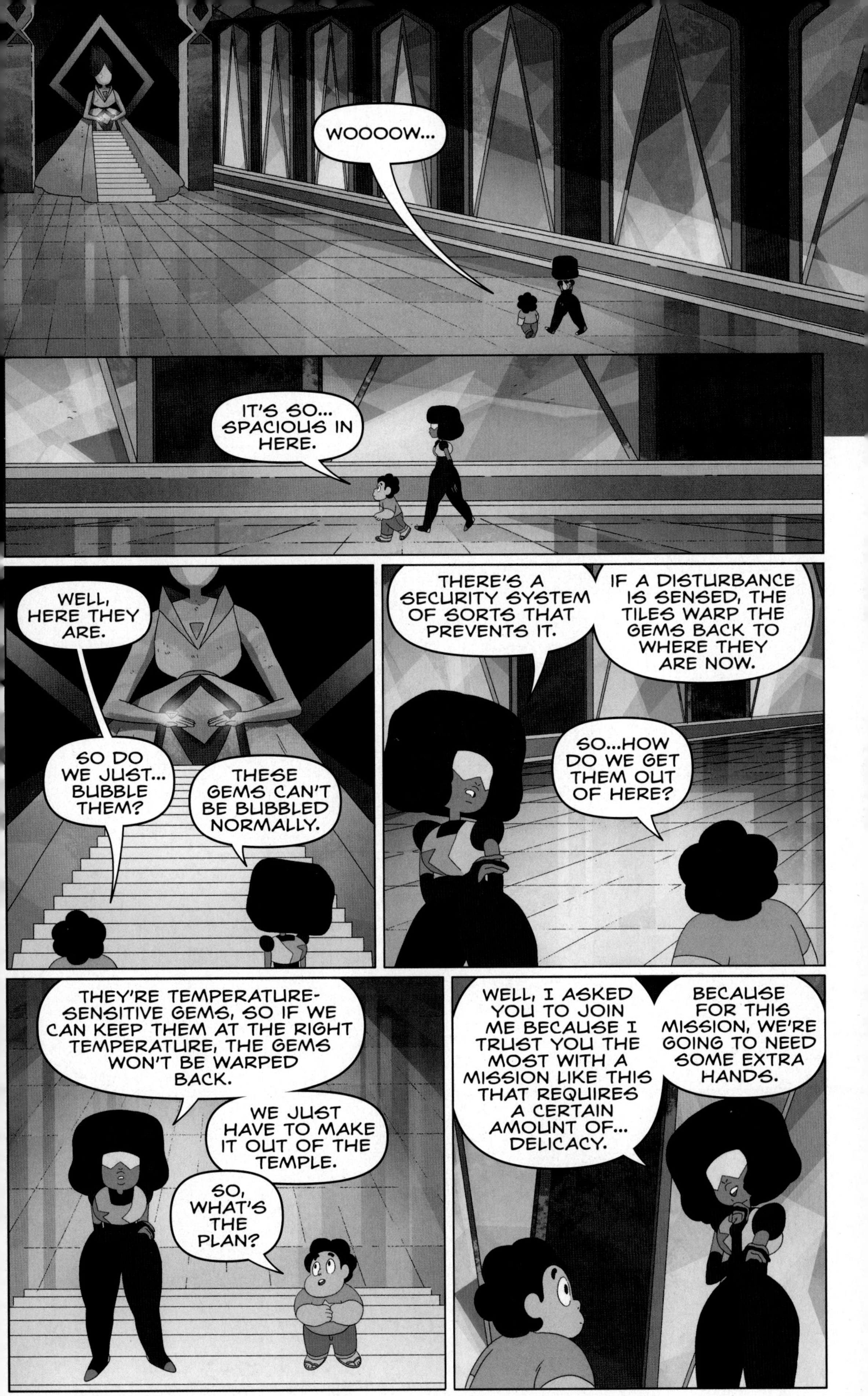
WOOOOW...
IT'S SO... SPACIOUS IN HERE.
WELL, HERE THEY ARE.
SO DO WE JUST... BUBBLE THEM?
THESE GEMS CAN'T BE BUBBLED NORMALLY.
THERE'S A SECURITY SYSTEM OF SORTS THAT PREVENTS IT.
IF A DISTURBANCE IS SENSED, THE TILES WARP THE GEMS BACK TO WHERE THEY ARE NOW.
SO...HOW DO WE GET THEM OUT OF HERE?
THEY'RE TEMPERATURE-SENSITIVE GEMS, SO IF WE CAN KEEP THEM AT THE RIGHT TEMPERATURE, THE GEMS WON'T BE WARPED BACK.
WE JUST HAVE TO MAKE IT OUT OF THE TEMPLE.
SO, WHAT'S THE PLAN?
WELL, I ASKED YOU TO JOIN ME BECAUSE I TRUST YOU THE MOST WITH A MISSION LIKE THIS THAT REQUIRES A CERTAIN AMOUNT OF... DELICACY.
BECAUSE FOR THIS MISSION, WE'RE GOING TO NEED SOME EXTRA HANDS.

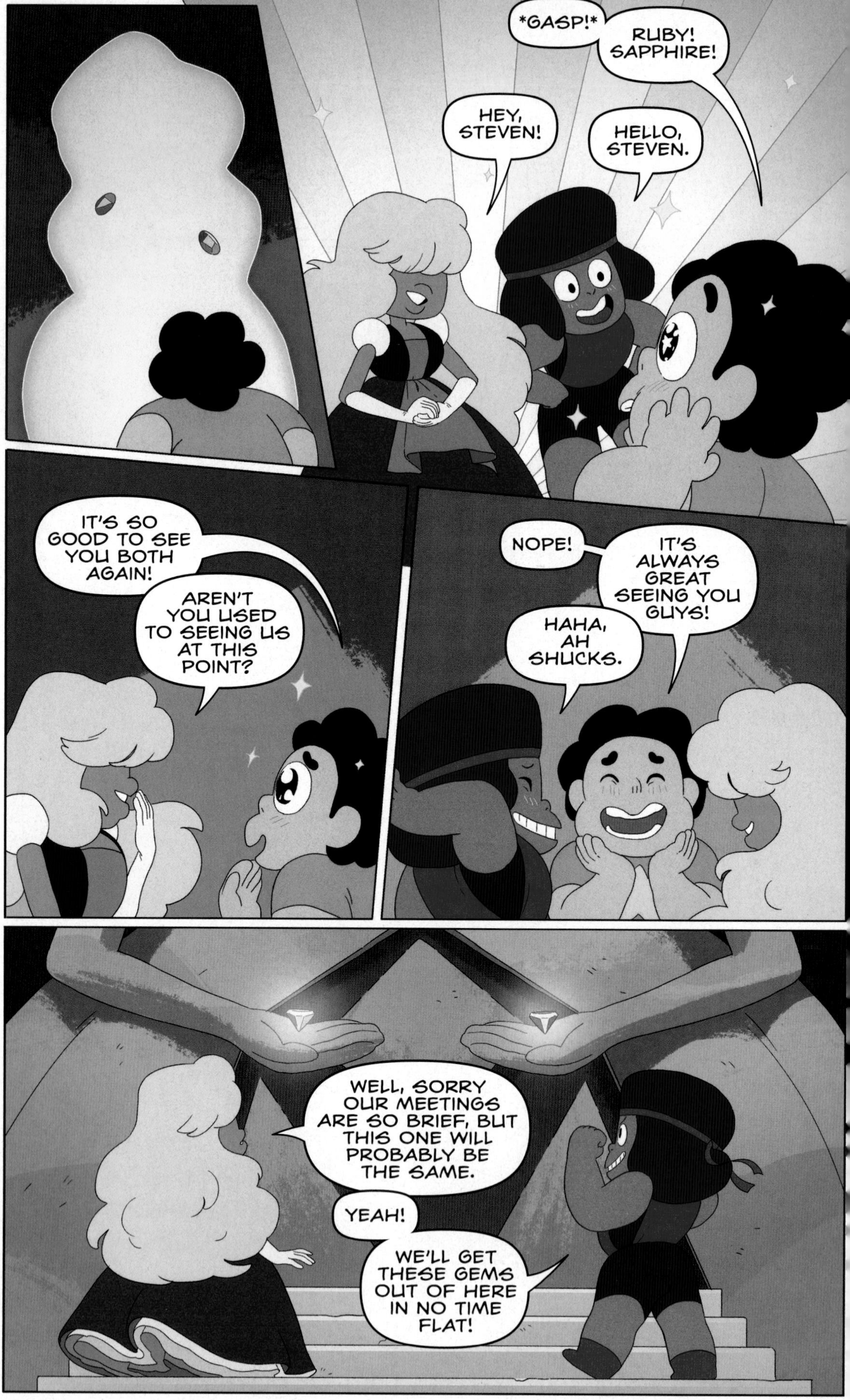
GASP!
RUBY! SAPPHIRE!
HEY, STEVEN!
HELLO, STEVEN.
IT'S SO GOOD TO SEE YOU BOTH AGAIN!
AREN'T YOU USED TO SEEING US AT THIS POINT?
NOPE!
IT'S ALWAYS GREAT SEEING YOU GUYS!
HAHA, AH SHUCKS.
WELL, SORRY OUR MEETINGS ARE SO BRIEF, BUT THIS ONE WILL PROBABLY BE THE SAME.
YEAH!
WE'LL GET THESE GEMS OUT OF HERE IN NO TIME FLAT!

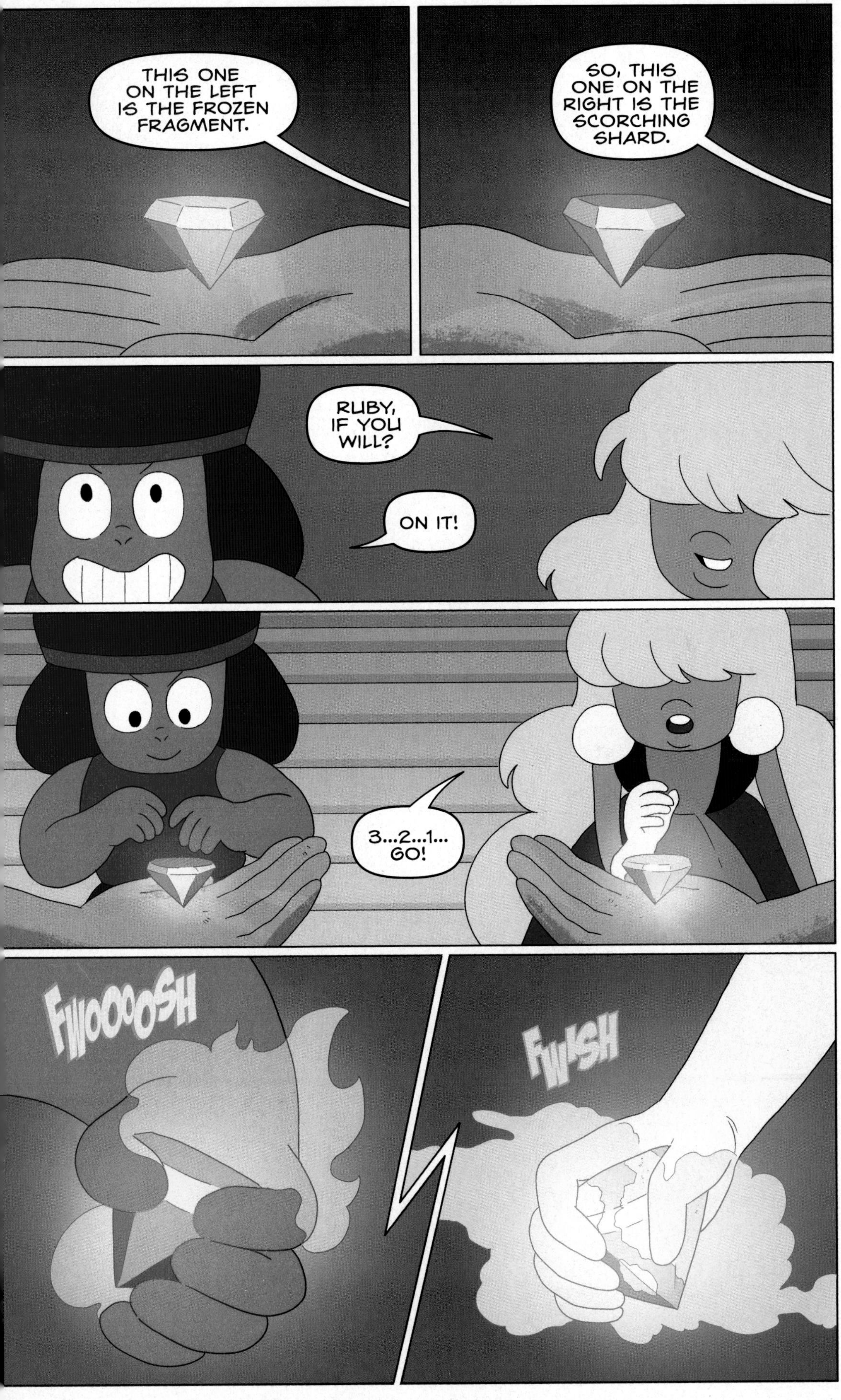
THIS ONE ON THE LEFT IS THE FROZEN FRAGMENT.
SO, THIS ONE ON THE RIGHT IS THE SCORCHING SHARD.
RUBY, IF YOU WILL?
ON IT!
3...2...1... GO!
FWOOOOSH
FWISH

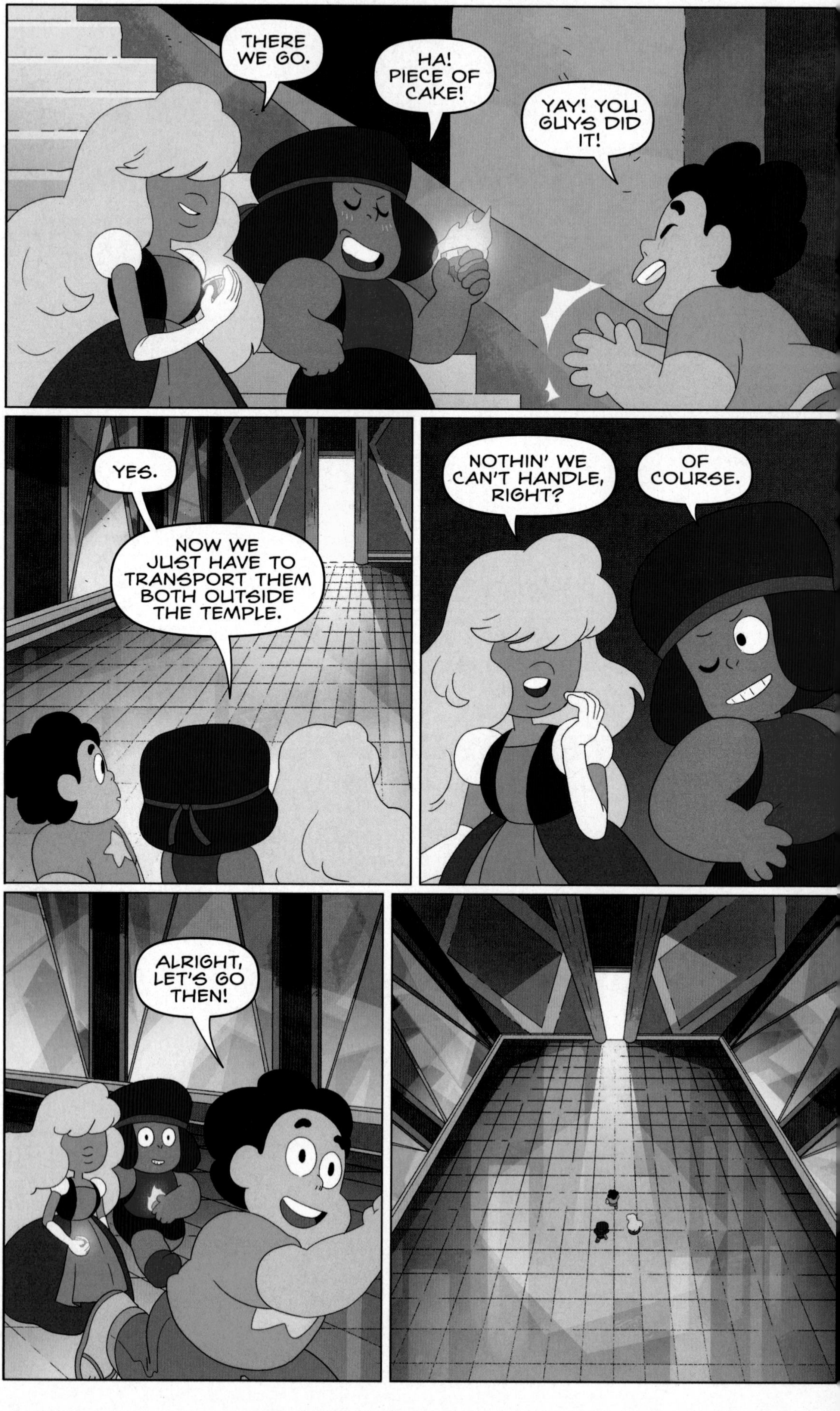
THERE WE GO.
HA! PIECE OF CAKE!
YAY! YOU GUYS DID IT!
YES.
NOW WE JUST HAVE TO TRANSPORT THEM BOTH OUTSIDE THE TEMPLE.
NOTHIN' WE CAN'T HANDLE, RIGHT?
OF COURSE.
ALRIGHT, LET'S GO THEN!

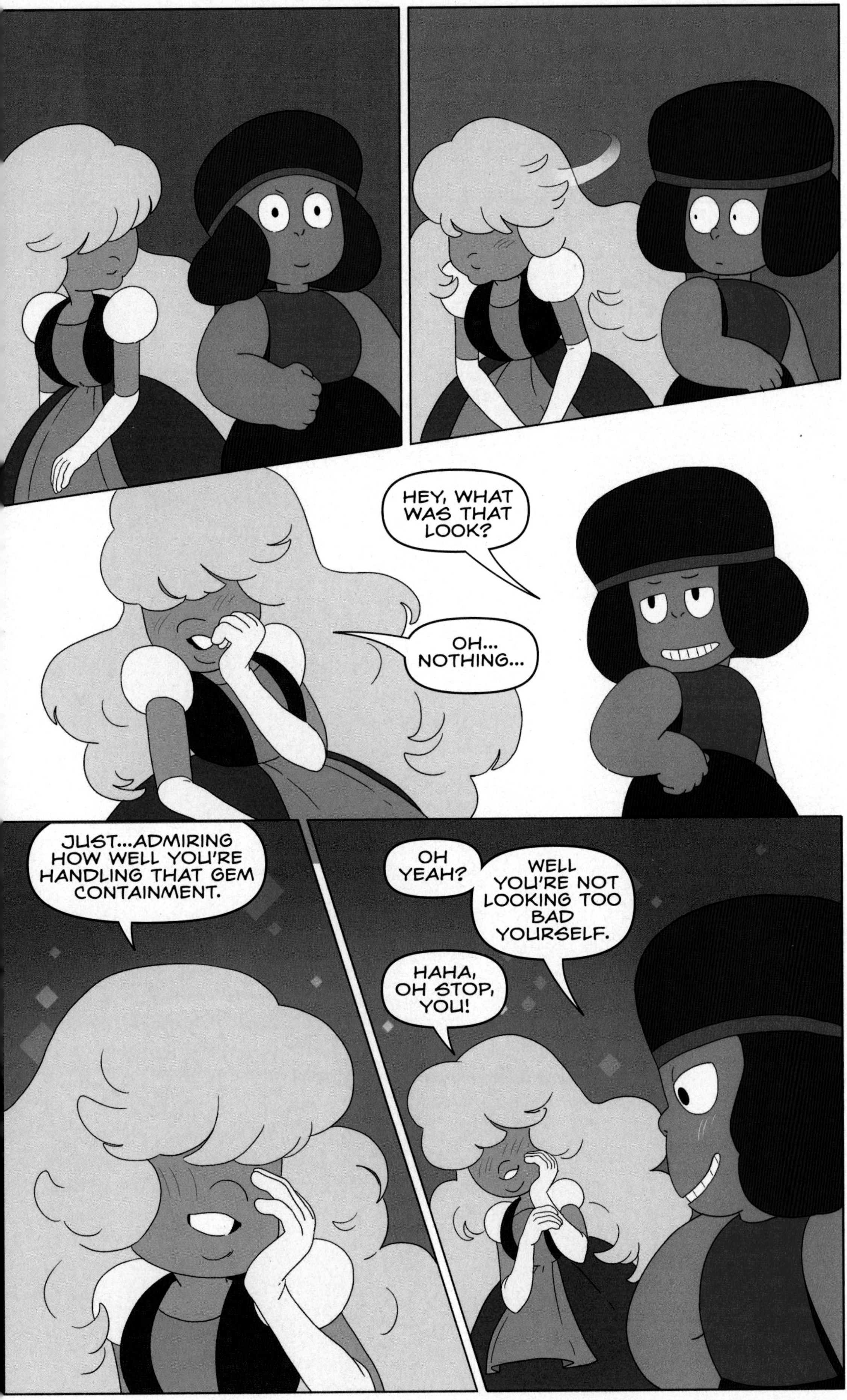
HEY, WHAT WAS THAT LOOK?
OH... NOTHING...
JUST...ADMIRING HOW WELL YOU'RE HANDLING THAT GEM CONTAINMENT.
OH YEAH?
WELL YOU'RE NOT LOOKING TOO BAD YOURSELF.
HAHA, OH STOP, YOU!

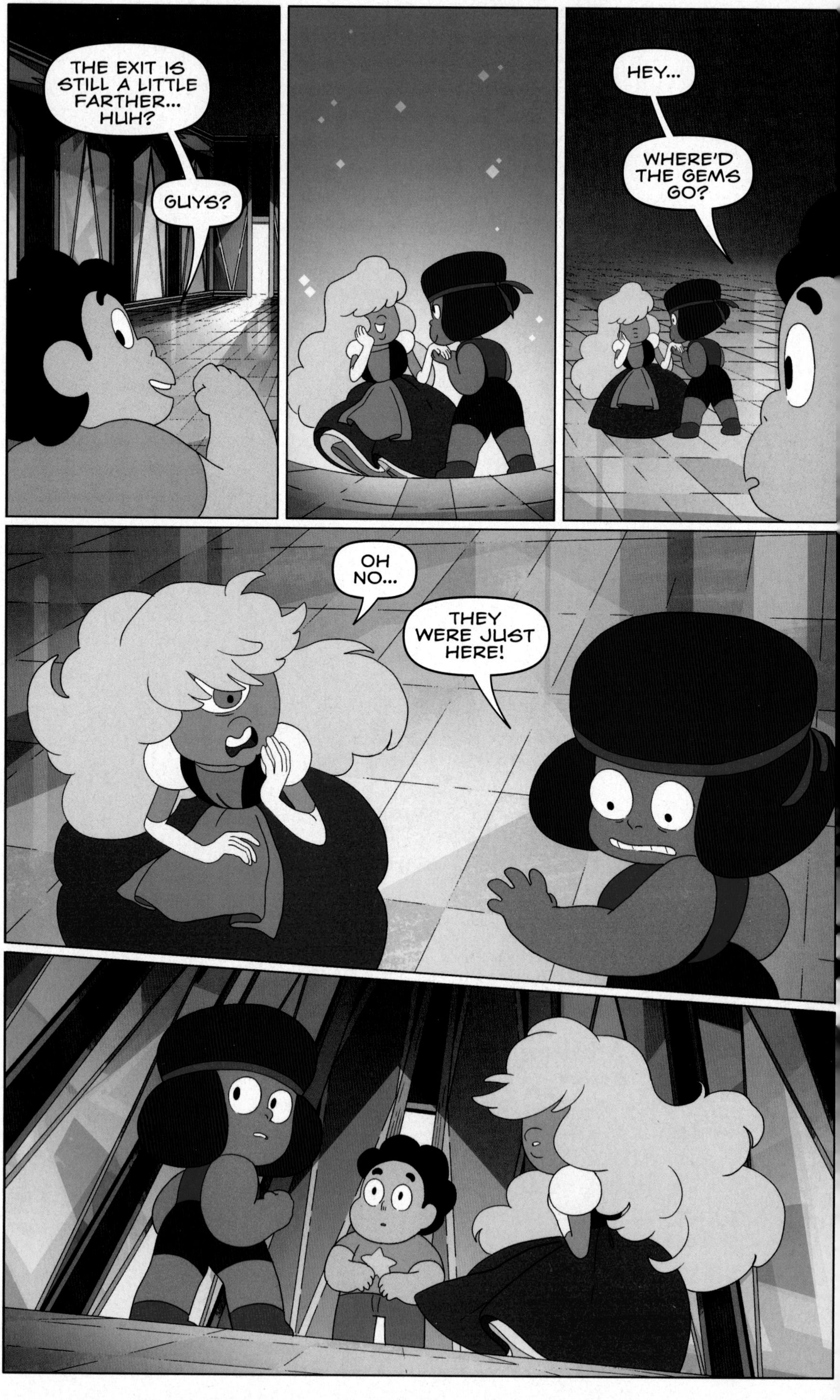
THE EXIT IS STILL A LITTLE FARTHER... HUH?
GUYS?
HEY...
WHERE'D THE GEMS GO?
OH NO...
THEY WERE JUST HERE!

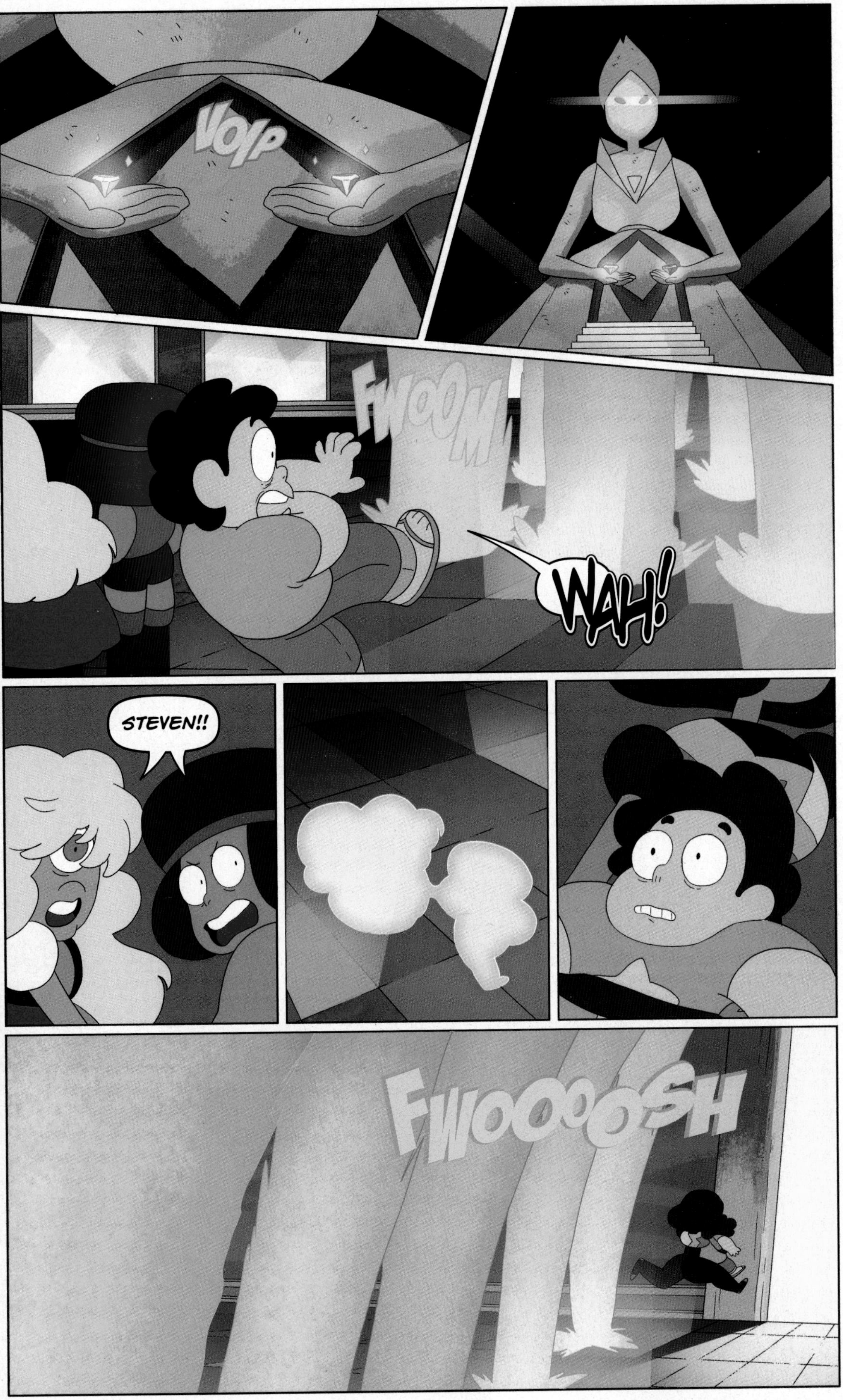
VOIP
FWOOM
WAH!
STEVEN!!
FWOOOOSH

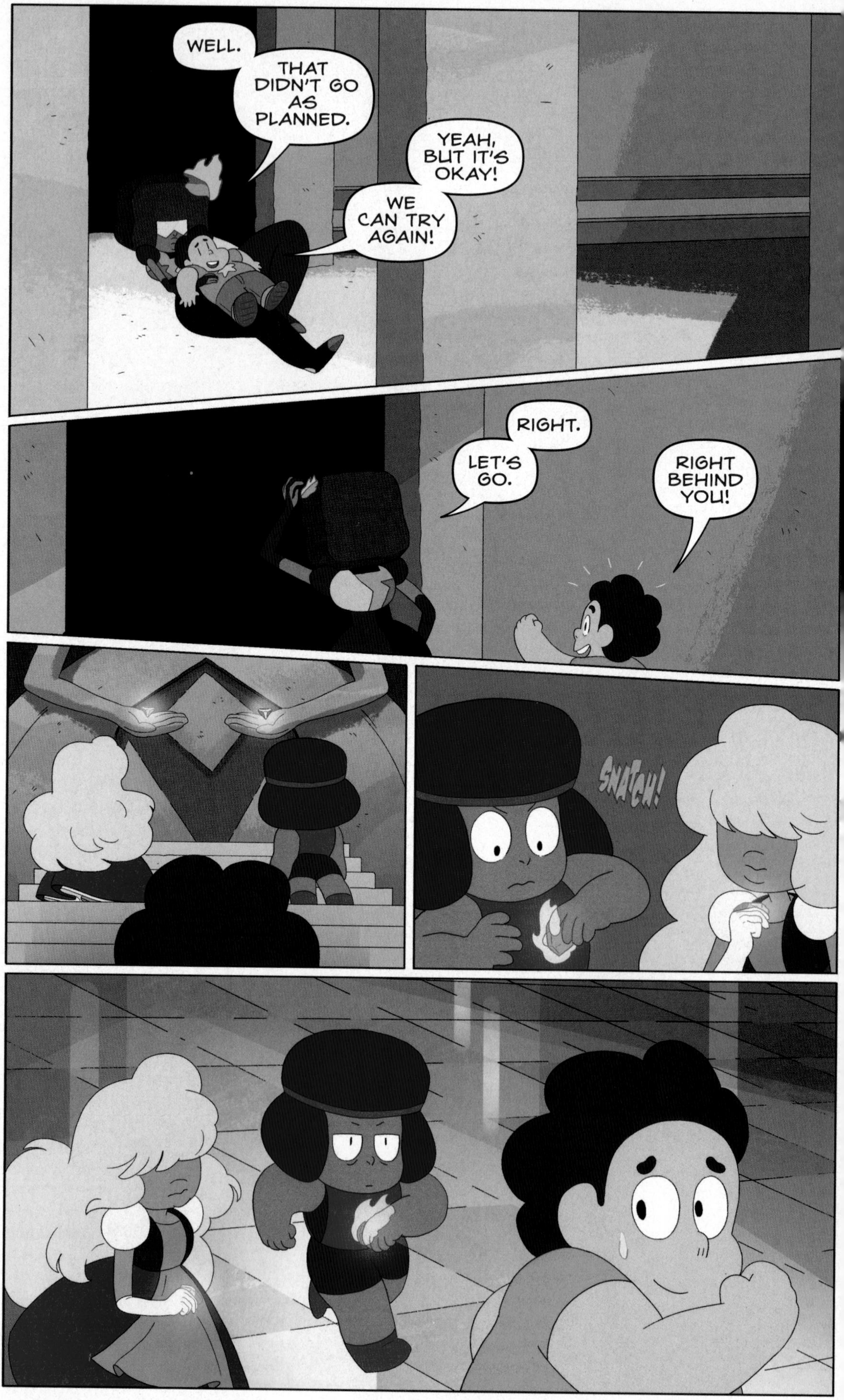
WELL.
THAT DIDN'T GO AS PLANNED.
YEAH, BUT IT'S OKAY!
WE CAN TRY AGAIN!
RIGHT.
LET'S GO.
RIGHT BEHIND YOU!
SNATCH!

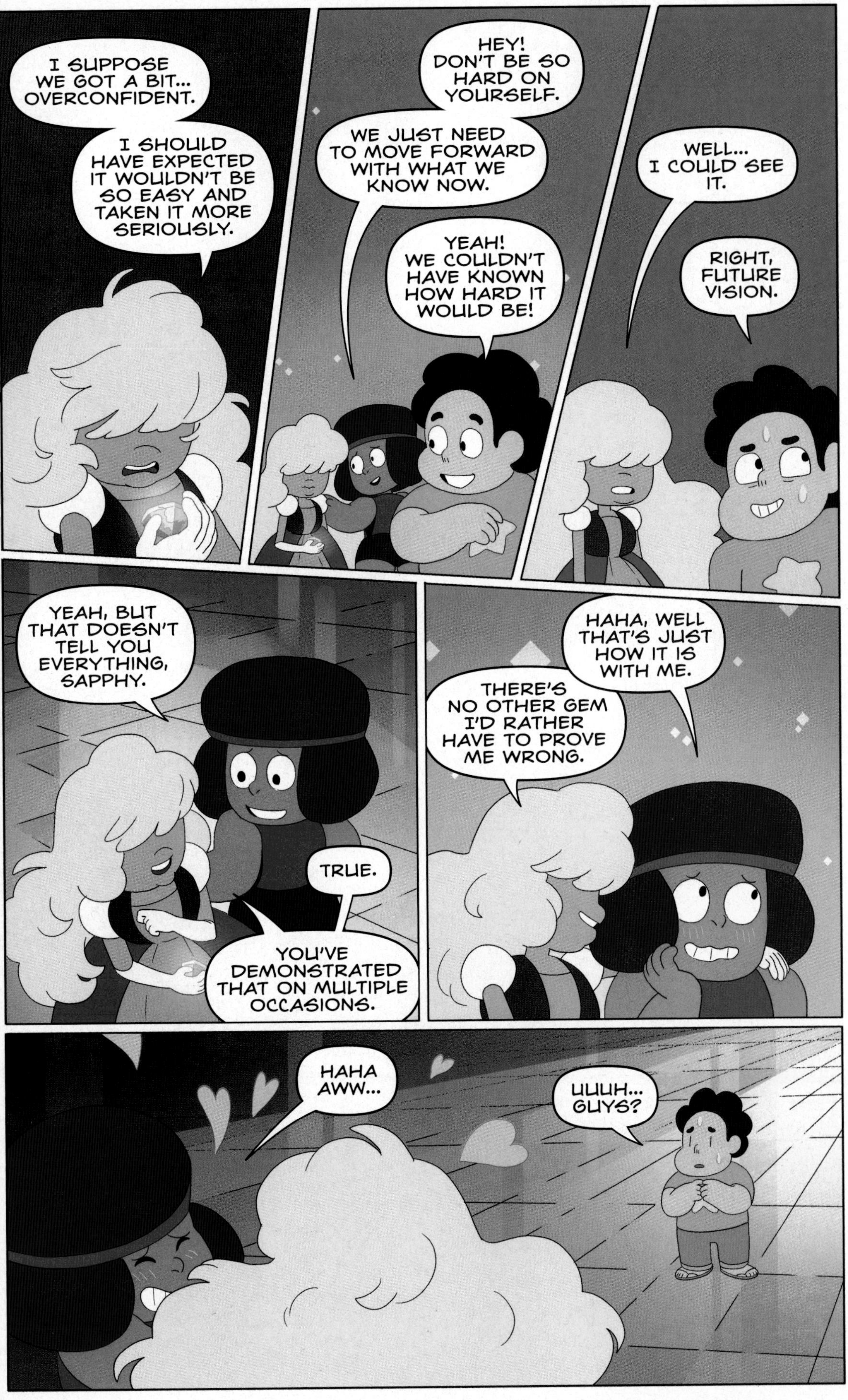
I SUPPOSE WE GOT A BIT... OVERCONFIDENT.
I SHOULD HAVE EXPECTED IT WOULDN'T BE SO EASY AND TAKEN IT MORE SERIOUSLY.
HEY! DON'T BE SO HARD ON YOURSELF.
WE JUST NEED TO MOVE FORWARD WITH WHAT WE KNOW NOW.
YEAH! WE COULDN'T HAVE KNOWN HOW HARD IT WOULD BE!
WELL... I COULD SEE IT.
RIGHT, FUTURE VISION.
YEAH, BUT THAT DOESN'T TELL YOU EVERYTHING, SAPPHY.
TRUE.
YOU'VE DEMONSTRATED THAT ON MULTIPLE OCCASIONS.
HAHA, WELL THAT'S JUST HOW IT IS WITH ME.
THERE'S NO OTHER GEM I'D RATHER HAVE TO PROVE ME WRONG.
HAHA AWW...
UUUH... GUYS?

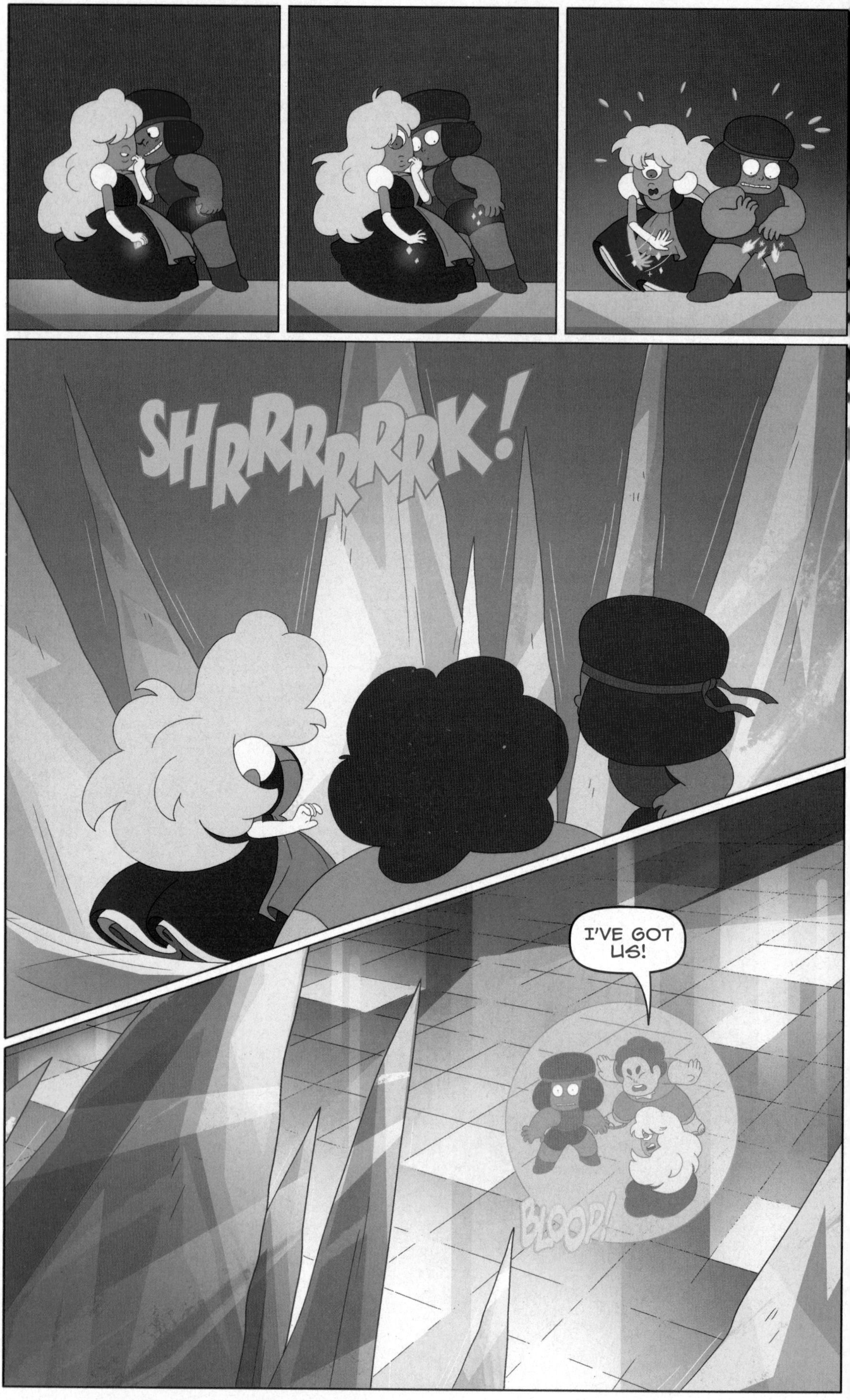
SHRRRRRRK!
I'VE GOT US!
BLOOP!

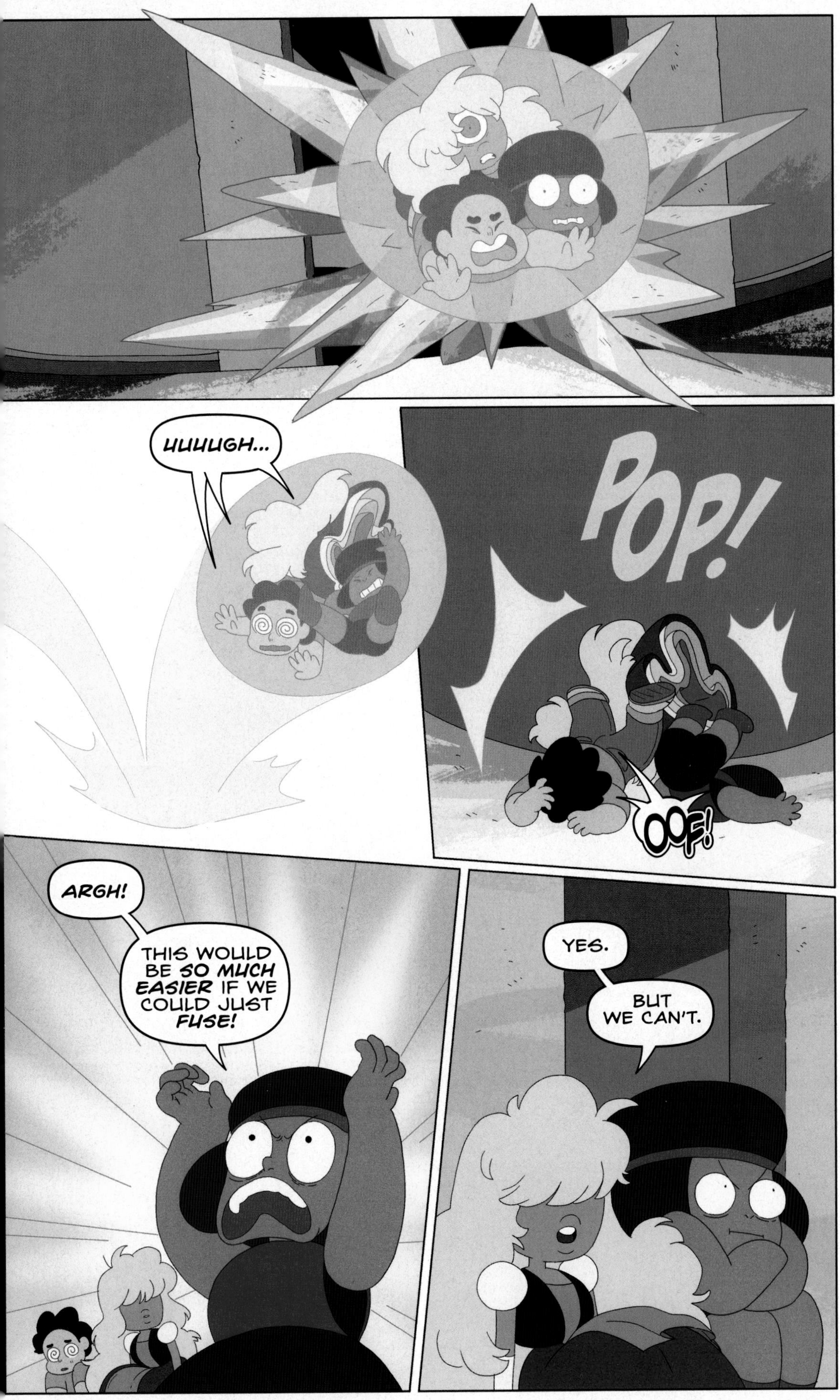
UUUUGH...
POP!
OOF!
ARGH!
THIS WOULD BE SO MUCH EASIER IF WE COULD JUST FUSE!
YES.
BUT WE CAN'T.

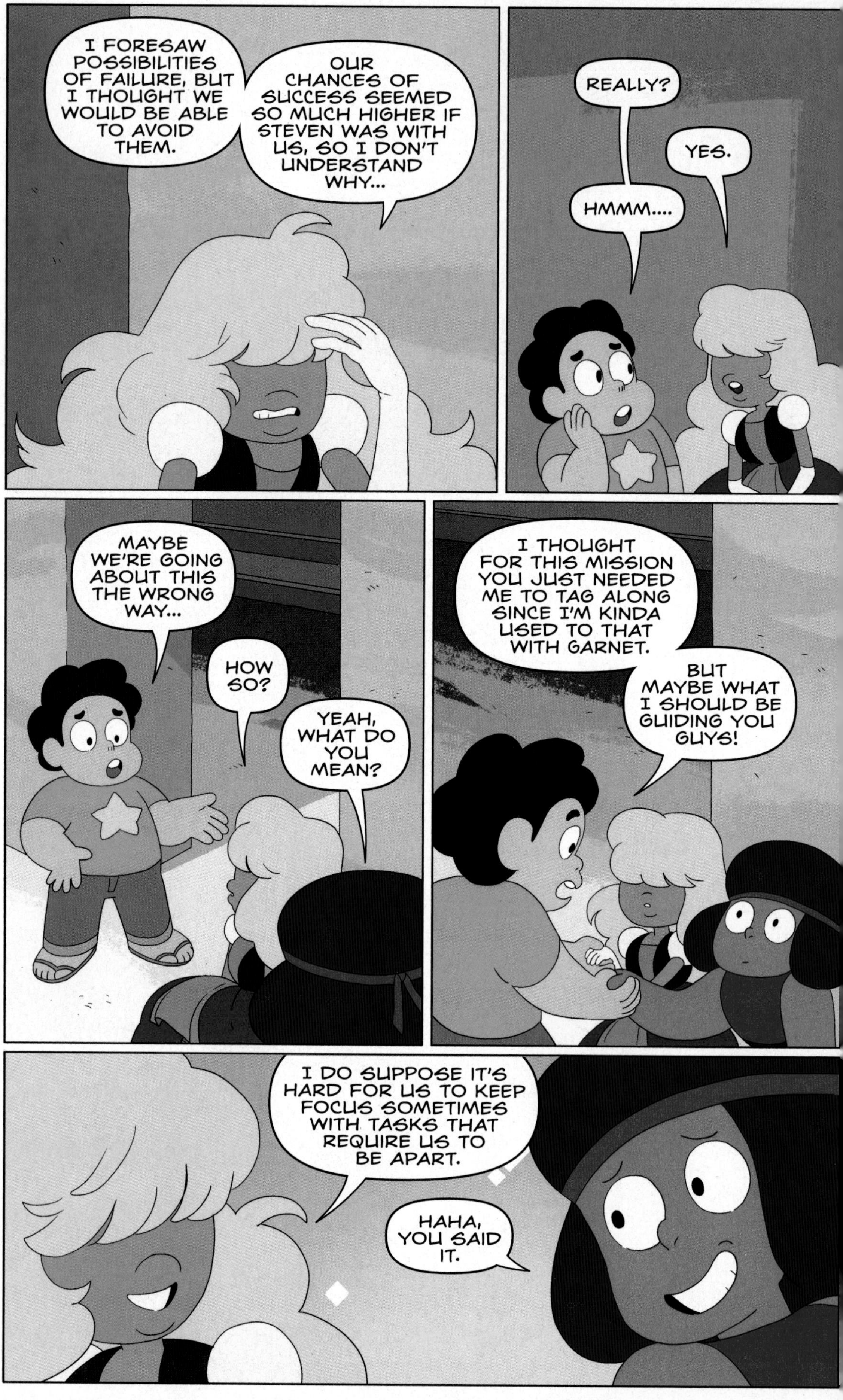
I FORESAW POSSIBILITIES OF FAILURE, BUT I THOUGHT WE WOULD BE ABLE TO AVOID THEM.
OUR CHANCES OF SUCCESS SEEMED SO MUCH HIGHER IF STEVEN WAS WITH US, SO I DON'T UNDERSTAND WHY...
REALLY?
YES.
HMMM....
MAYBE WE'RE GOING ABOUT THIS THE WRONG WAY...
HOW SO?
YEAH, WHAT DO YOU MEAN?
I THOUGHT FOR THIS MISSION YOU JUST NEEDED ME TO TAG ALONG SINCE I'M KINDA USED TO THAT WITH GARNET.
BUT MAYBE WHAT I SHOULD BE GUIDING YOU GUYS!
I DO SUPPOSE IT'S HARD FOR US TO KEEP FOCUS SOMETIMES WITH TASKS THAT REQUIRE US TO BE APART.
HAHA, YOU SAID IT.

WE COULD USE A LITTLE HELP TO KEEP OUR ATTENTION.

IT'S SETTLED THEN!

ONWARD, TEAM!

LEAD THE WAY FEARLESS LEADER, HAHA!

RIGHT BEHIND YOU, STEVEN.

ALRIGHT, LET'S DO THIS THE SAME AS BEFORE.

OKAY, ON MY MARK, GRAB THE GEMS.

1...2...

3!!

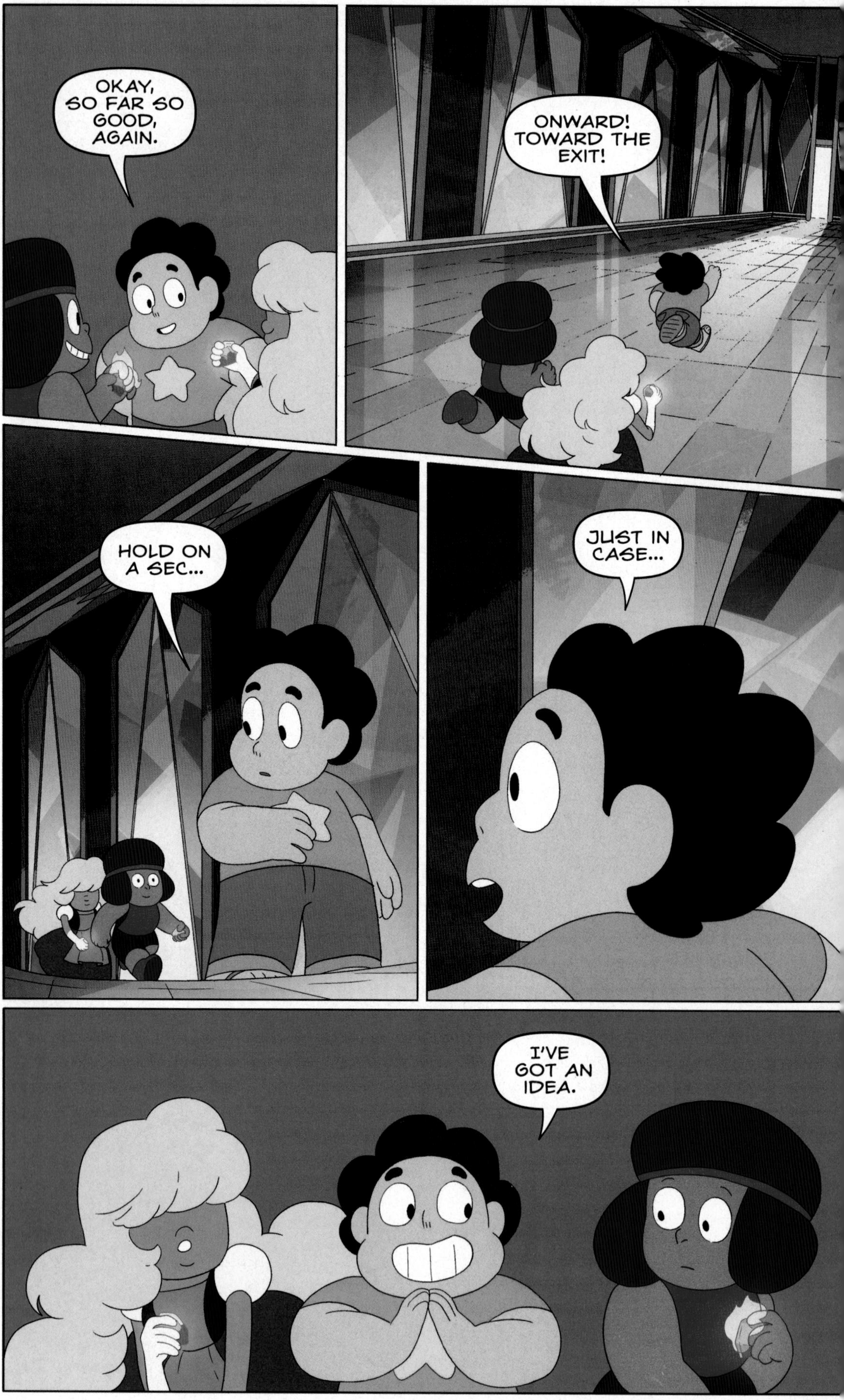
OKAY, SO FAR SO GOOD, AGAIN.
ONWARD! TOWARD THE EXIT!
HOLD ON A SEC...
JUST IN CASE...
I'VE GOT AN IDEA.

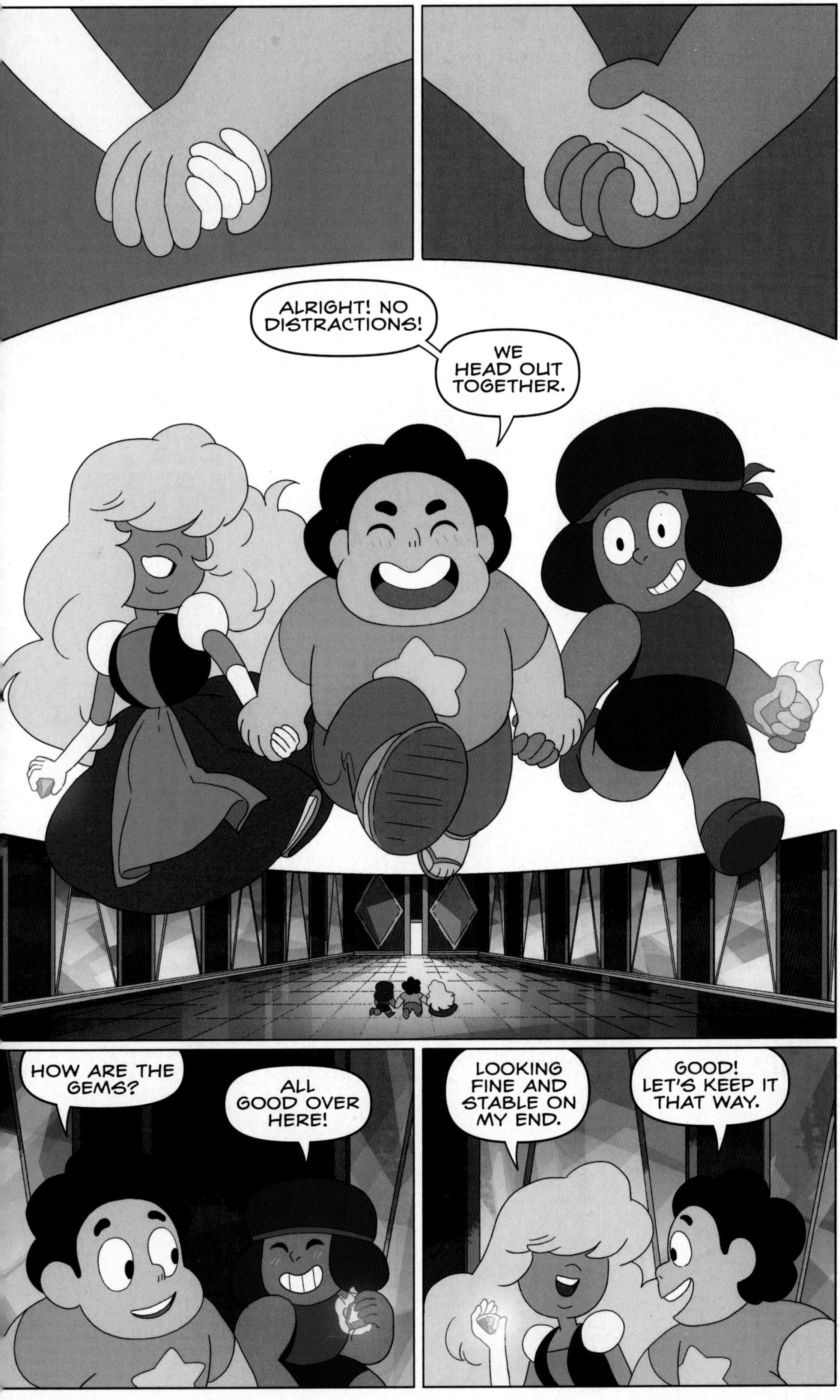
ALRIGHT! NO DISTRACTIONS!
WE HEAD OUT TOGETHER.
HOW ARE THE GEMS?
ALL GOOD OVER HERE!
LOOKING FINE AND STABLE ON MY END.
GOOD! LET'S KEEP IT THAT WAY.

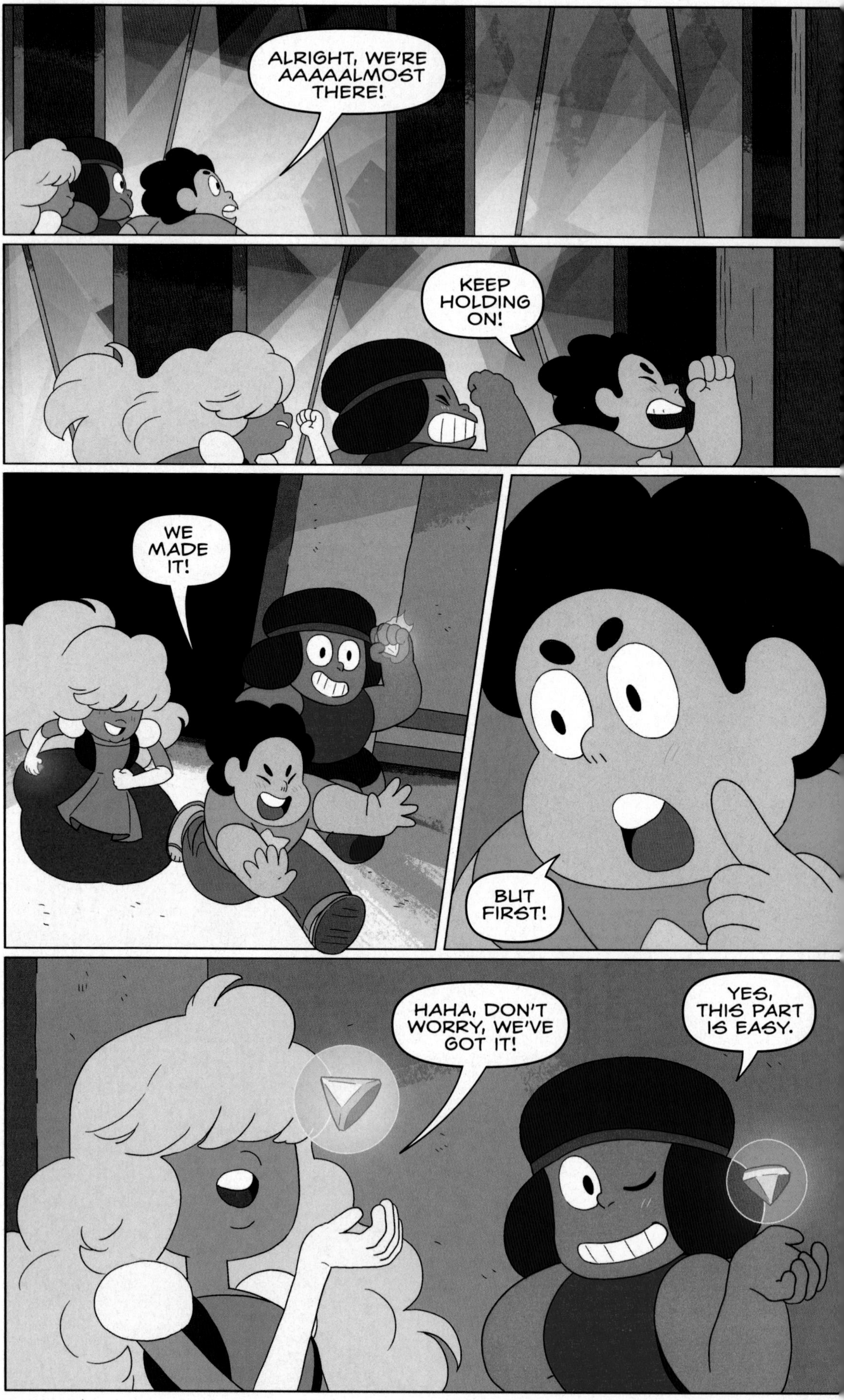
ALRIGHT, WE'RE AAAAALMOST THERE!
KEEP HOLDING ON!
WE MADE IT!
BUT FIRST!
HAHA, DON'T WORRY, WE'VE GOT IT!
YES, THIS PART IS EASY.

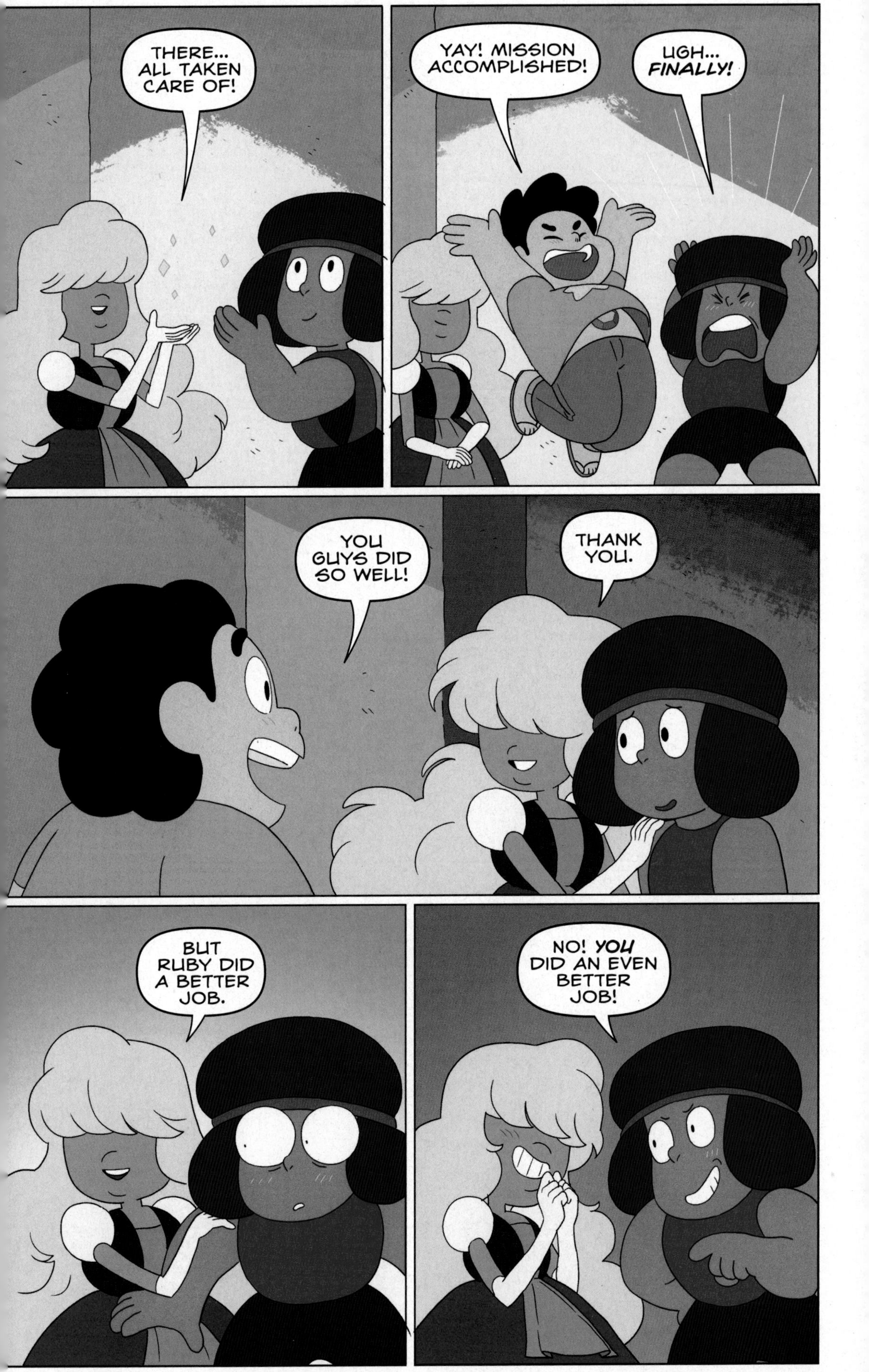
THERE... ALL TAKEN CARE OF!
YAY! MISSION ACCOMPLISHED!
UGH... *FINALLY!*
YOU GUYS DID SO WELL!
THANK YOU.
BUT RUBY DID A BETTER JOB.
NO! *YOU* DID AN EVEN BETTER JOB!

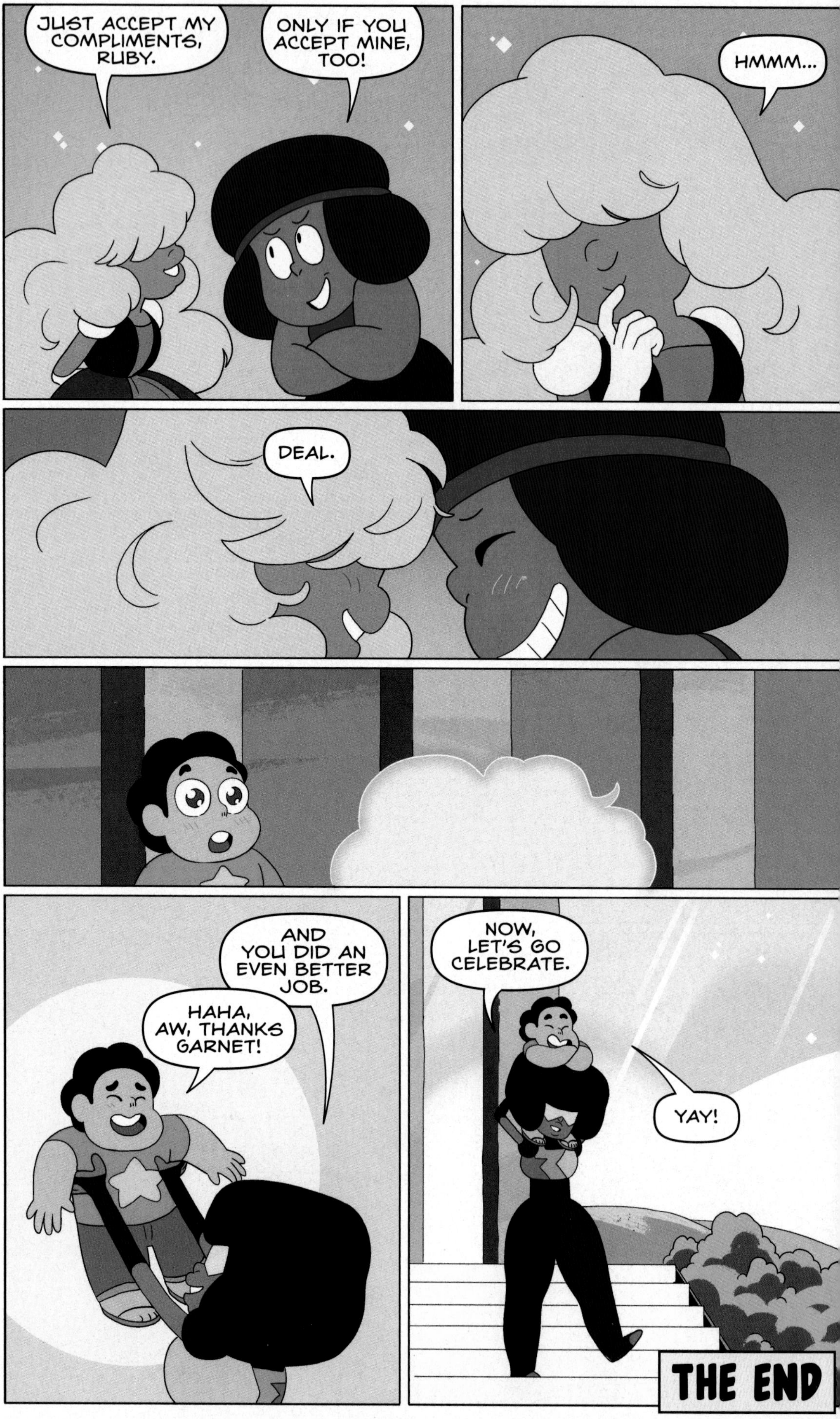
JUST ACCEPT MY COMPLIMENTS, RUBY.
ONLY IF YOU ACCEPT MINE, TOO!
HMMM...
DEAL.
AND YOU DID AN EVEN BETTER JOB.
HAHA, AW, THANKS GARNET!
NOW, LET'S GO CELEBRATE.
YAY!
THE END

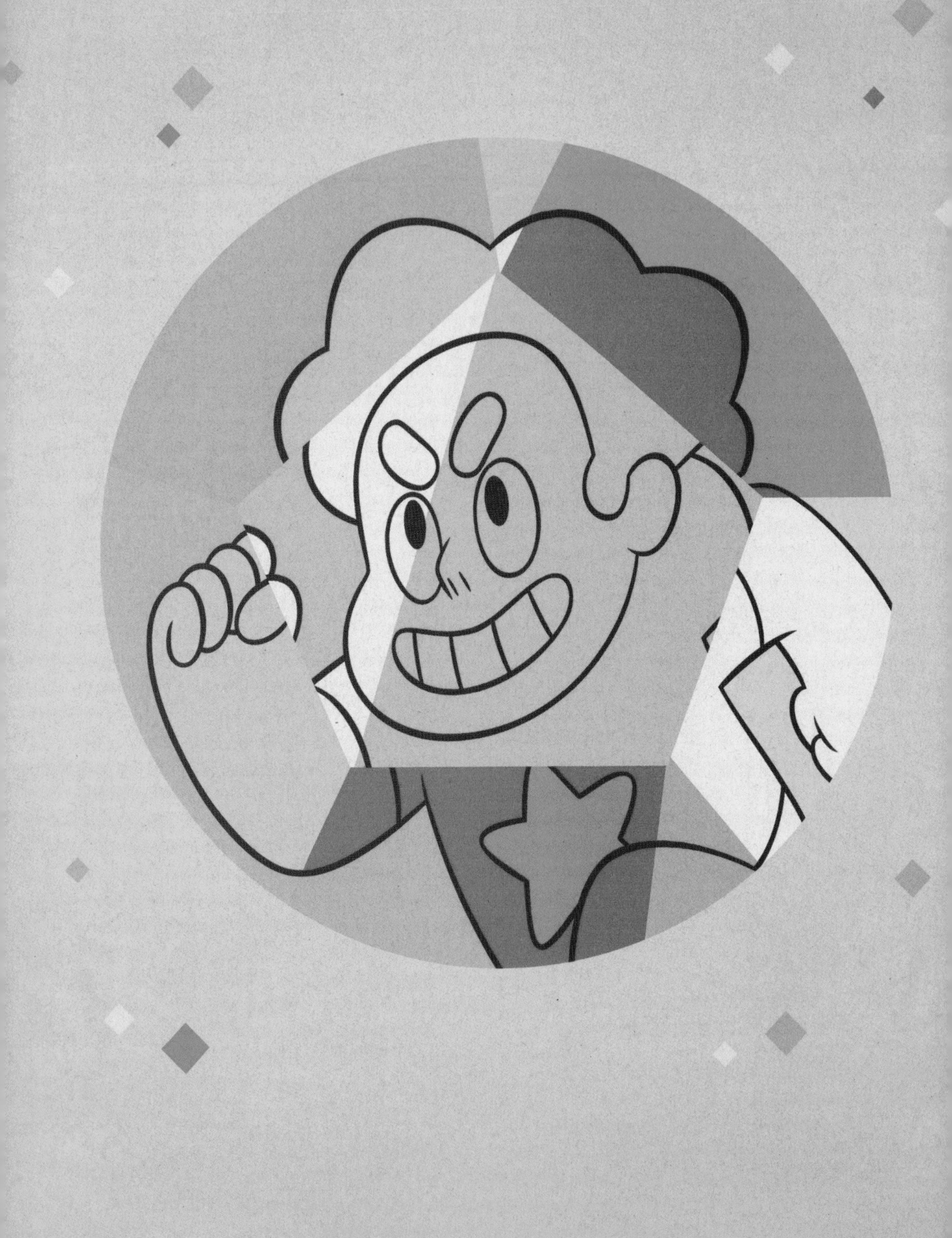

CHAPTER SIXTEEN

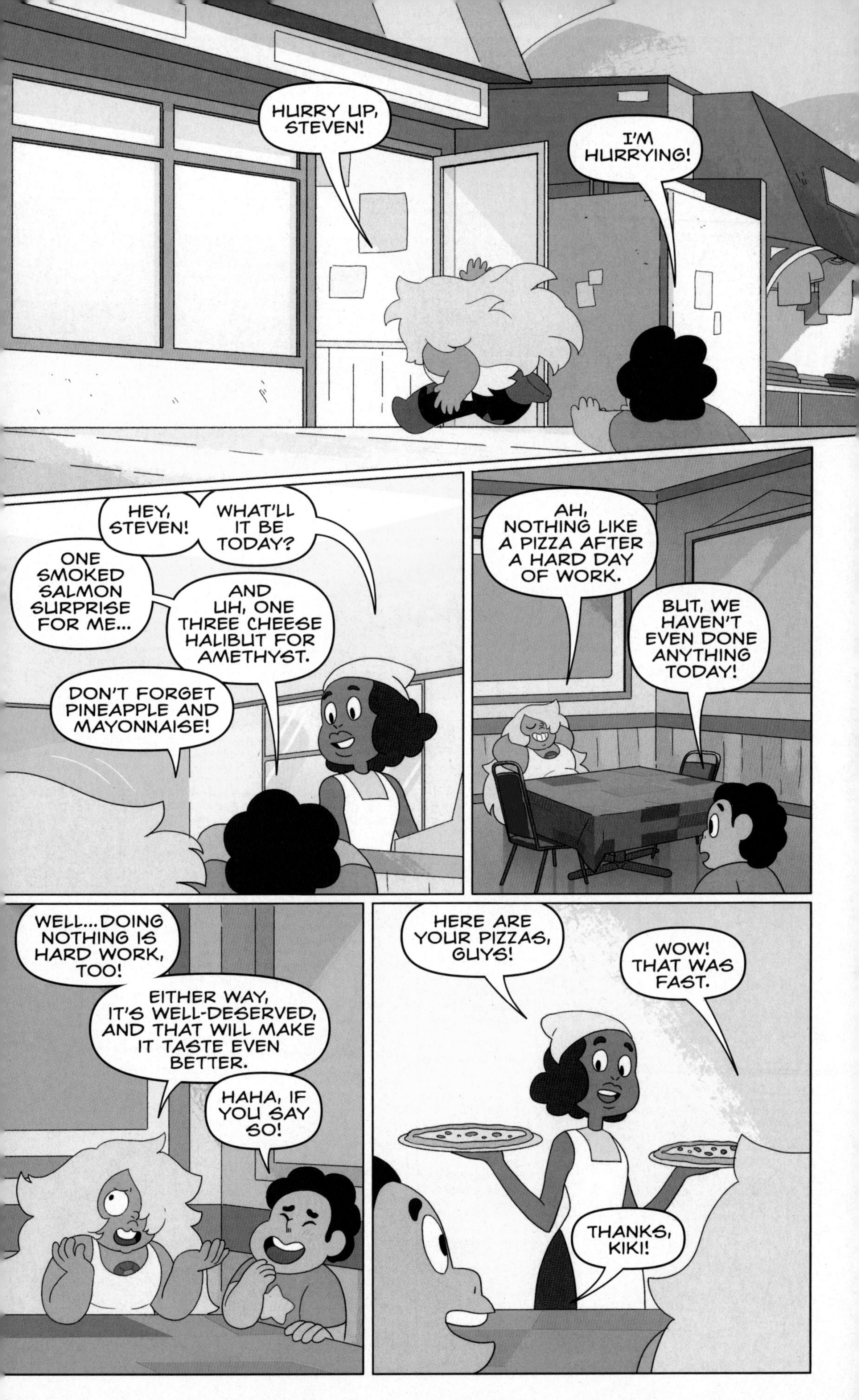
HURRY UP, STEVEN!
I'M HURRYING!
HEY, STEVEN!
WHAT'LL IT BE TODAY?
ONE SMOKED SALMON SURPRISE FOR ME...
AND UH, ONE THREE CHEESE HALIBUT FOR AMETHYST.
DON'T FORGET PINEAPPLE AND MAYONNAISE!
AH, NOTHING LIKE A PIZZA AFTER A HARD DAY OF WORK.
BUT, WE HAVEN'T EVEN DONE ANYTHING TODAY!
WELL...DOING NOTHING IS HARD WORK, TOO!
EITHER WAY, IT'S WELL-DESERVED, AND THAT WILL MAKE IT TASTE EVEN BETTER.
HAHA, IF YOU SAY SO!
HERE ARE YOUR PIZZAS, GUYS!
WOW! THAT WAS FAST.
THANKS, KIKI!

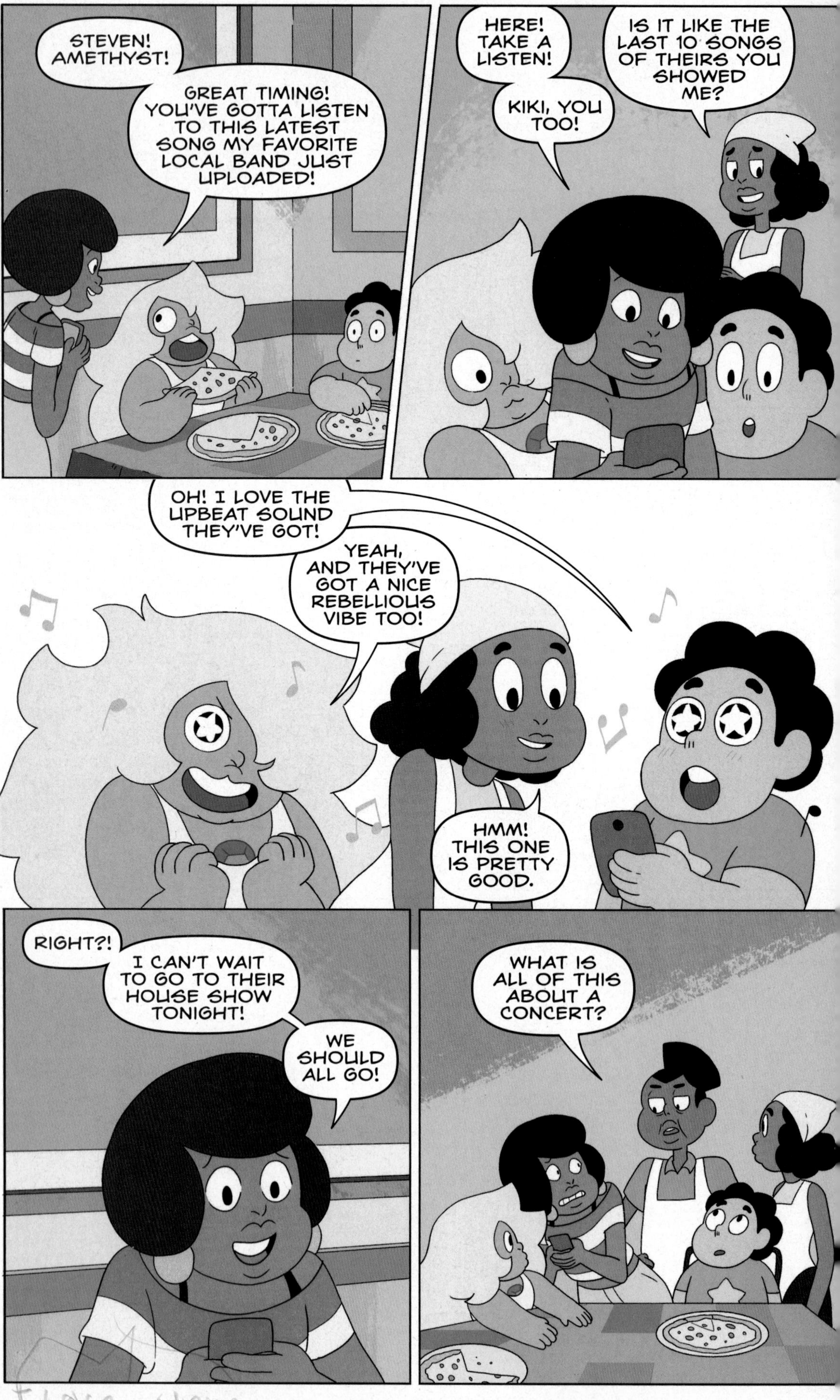
STEVEN! AMETHYST!
GREAT TIMING! YOU'VE GOTTA LISTEN TO THIS LATEST SONG MY FAVORITE LOCAL BAND JUST UPLOADED!
HERE! TAKE A LISTEN!
KIKI, YOU TOO!
IS IT LIKE THE LAST 10 SONGS OF THEIRS YOU SHOWED ME?
OH! I LOVE THE UPBEAT SOUND THEY'VE GOT!
YEAH, AND THEY'VE GOT A NICE REBELLIOUS VIBE TOO!
HMM! THIS ONE IS PRETTY GOOD.
RIGHT?!
I CAN'T WAIT TO GO TO THEIR HOUSE SHOW TONIGHT!
WE SHOULD ALL GO!
WHAT IS ALL OF THIS ABOUT A CONCERT?

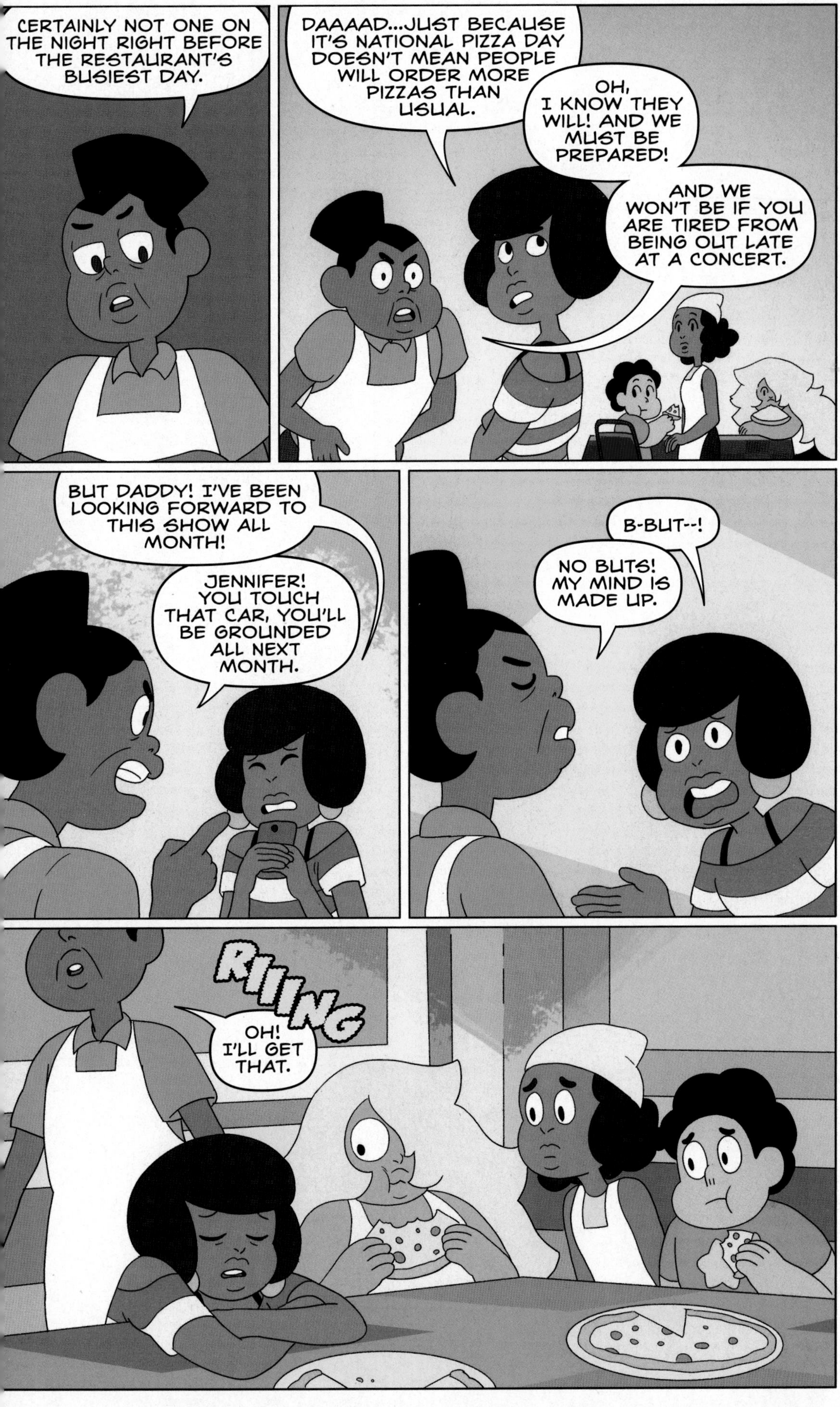

CERTAINLY NOT ONE ON THE NIGHT RIGHT BEFORE THE RESTAURANT'S BUSIEST DAY.
DAAAAD...JUST BECAUSE IT'S NATIONAL PIZZA DAY DOESN'T MEAN PEOPLE WILL ORDER MORE PIZZAS THAN USUAL.
OH, I KNOW THEY WILL! AND WE MUST BE PREPARED!
AND WE WON'T BE IF YOU ARE TIRED FROM BEING OUT LATE AT A CONCERT.
BUT DADDY! I'VE BEEN LOOKING FORWARD TO THIS SHOW ALL MONTH!
JENNIFER! YOU TOUCH THAT CAR, YOU'LL BE GROUNDED ALL NEXT MONTH.
B-BUT--!
NO BUTS! MY MIND IS MADE UP.
RIIING
OH! I'LL GET THAT.

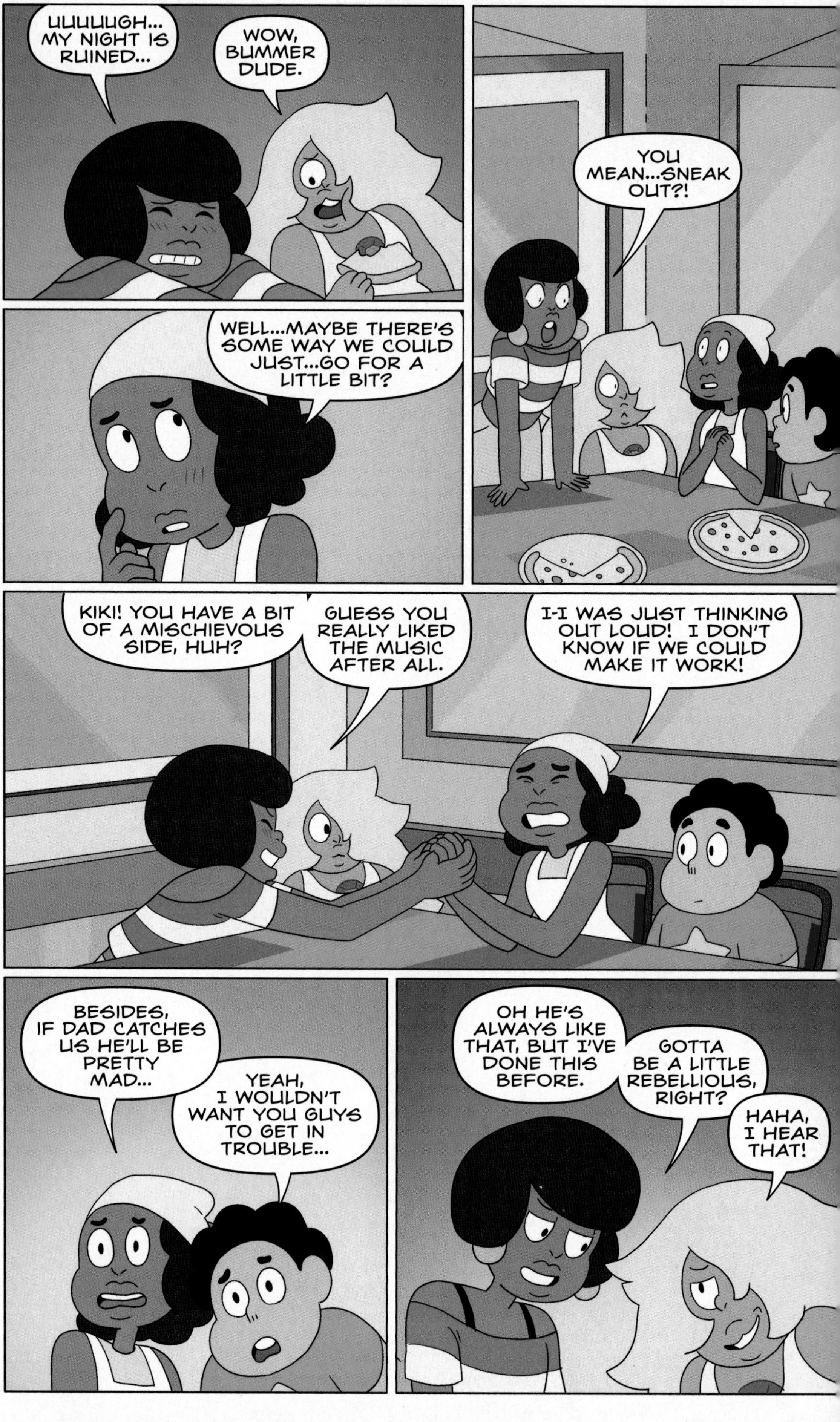
UUUUUGH... MY NIGHT IS RUINED...
WOW, BUMMER DUDE.
WELL...MAYBE THERE'S SOME WAY WE COULD JUST...GO FOR A LITTLE BIT?
YOU MEAN...SNEAK OUT?!
KIKI! YOU HAVE A BIT OF A MISCHIEVOUS SIDE, HUH?
GUESS YOU REALLY LIKED THE MUSIC AFTER ALL.
I-I WAS JUST THINKING OUT LOUD! I DON'T KNOW IF WE COULD MAKE IT WORK!
BESIDES, IF DAD CATCHES US HE'LL BE PRETTY MAD...
YEAH, I WOULDN'T WANT YOU GUYS TO GET IN TROUBLE...
OH HE'S ALWAYS LIKE THAT, BUT I'VE DONE THIS BEFORE.
GOTTA BE A LITTLE REBELLIOUS, RIGHT?
HAHA, I HEAR THAT!

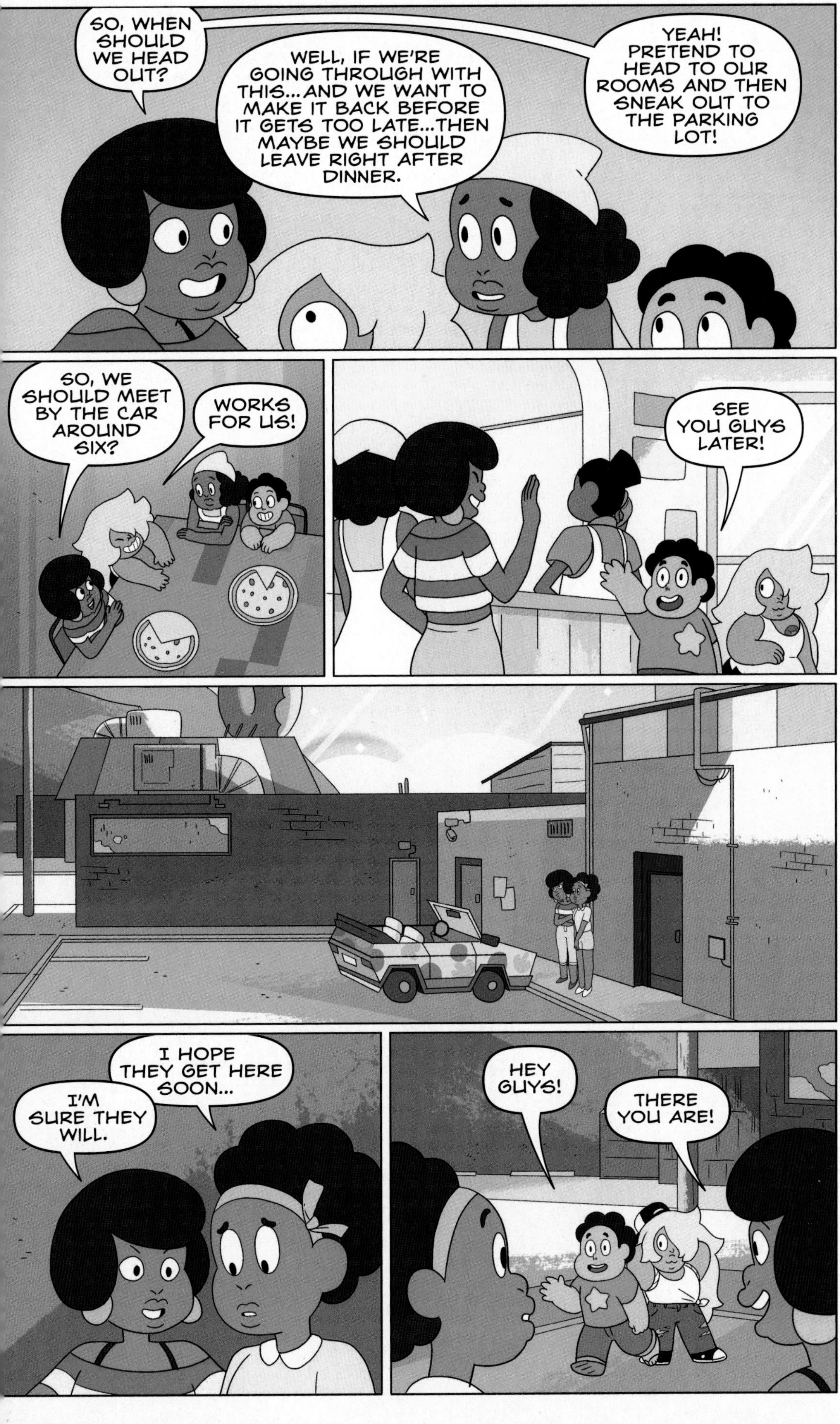
SO, WHEN SHOULD WE HEAD OUT?
WELL, IF WE'RE GOING THROUGH WITH THIS...AND WE WANT TO MAKE IT BACK BEFORE IT GETS TOO LATE...THEN MAYBE WE SHOULD LEAVE RIGHT AFTER DINNER.
YEAH! PRETEND TO HEAD TO OUR ROOMS AND THEN SNEAK OUT TO THE PARKING LOT!
SO, WE SHOULD MEET BY THE CAR AROUND SIX?
WORKS FOR US!
SEE YOU GUYS LATER!
I HOPE THEY GET HERE SOON...
I'M SURE THEY WILL.
HEY GUYS!
THERE YOU ARE!

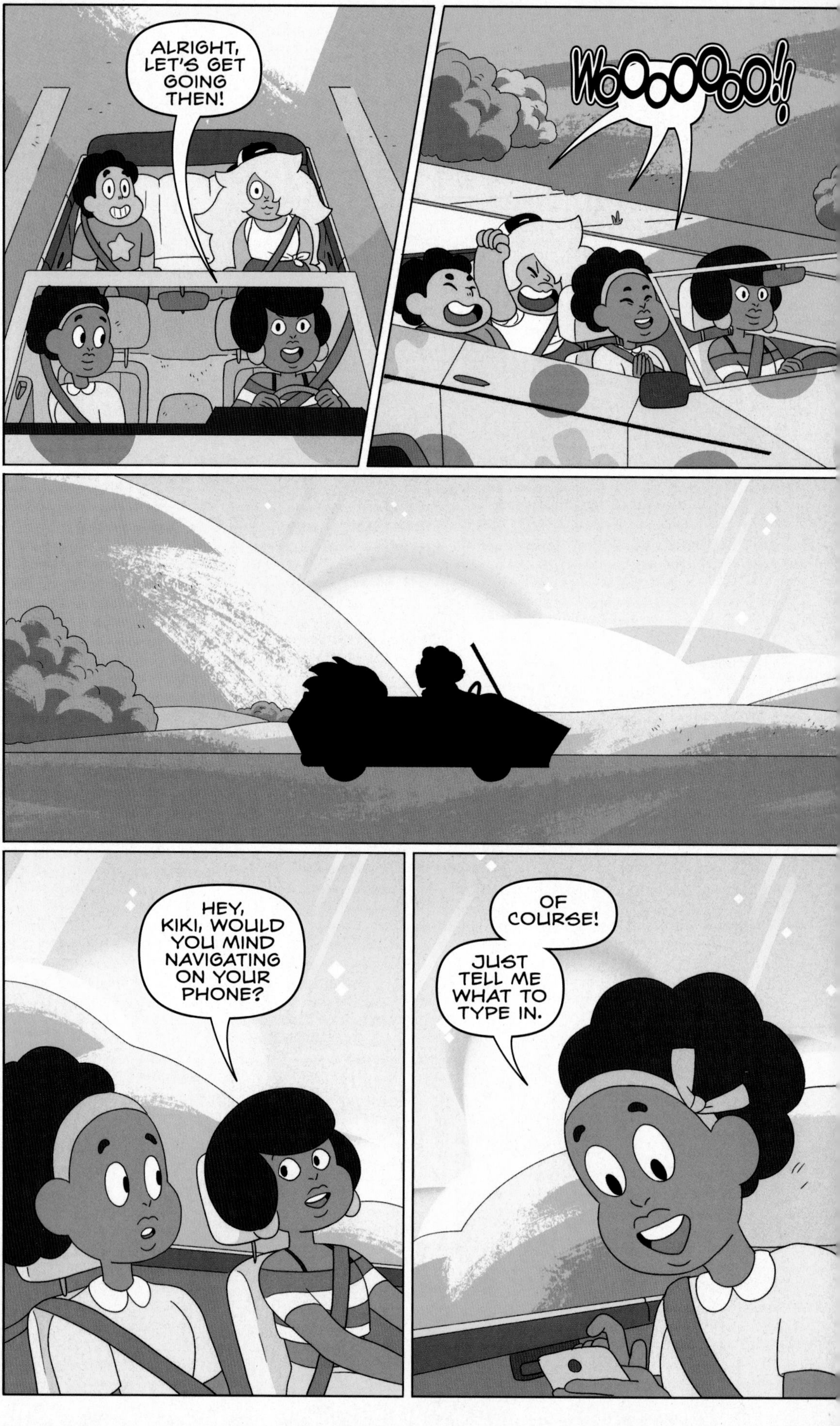
ALRIGHT, LET'S GET GOING THEN!
WOOOOOOOO!!
HEY, KIKI, WOULD YOU MIND NAVIGATING ON YOUR PHONE?
OF COURSE!
JUST TELL ME WHAT TO TYPE IN.

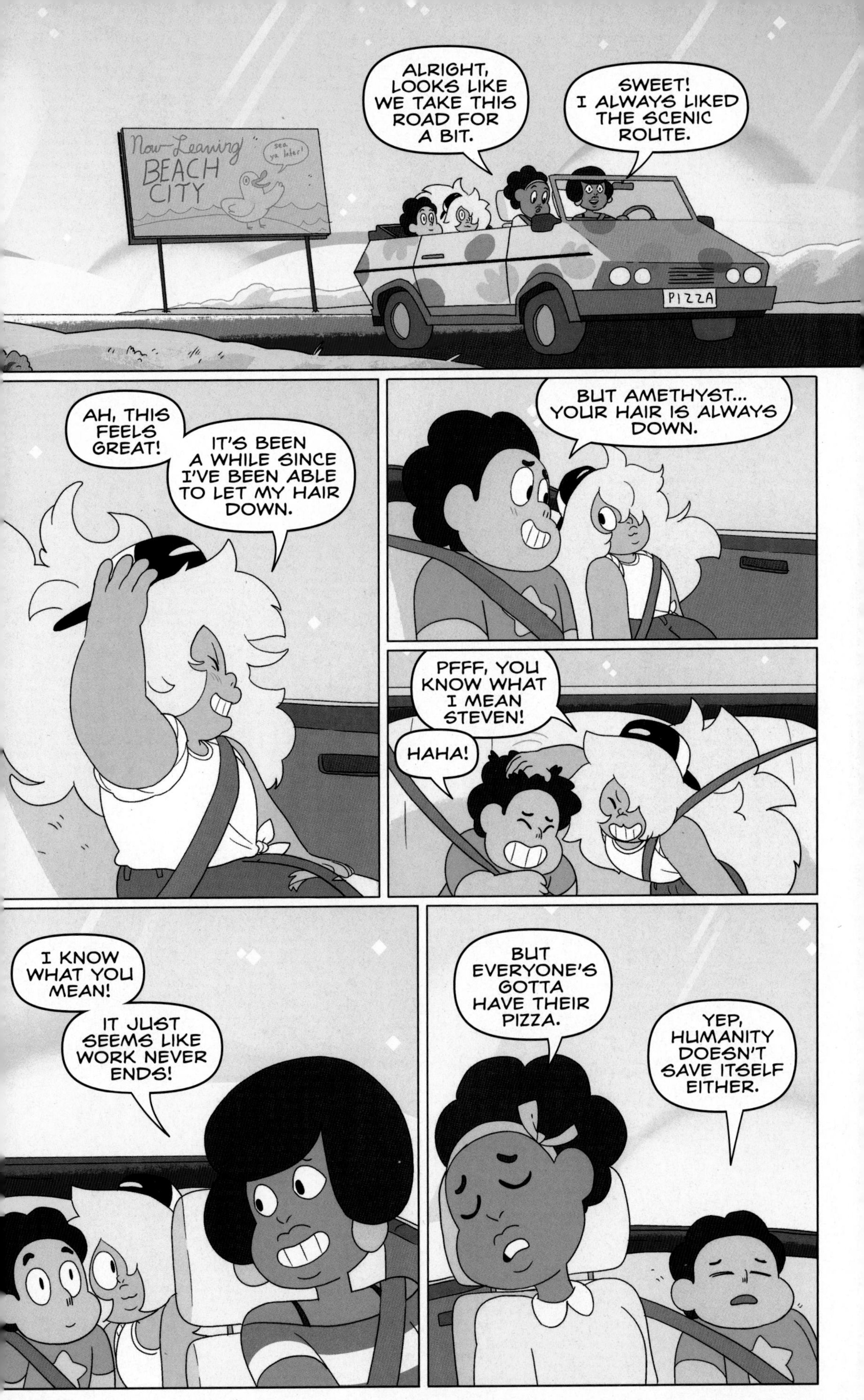
Now-Leaning BEACH CITY
sea ya later!
ALRIGHT, LOOKS LIKE WE TAKE THIS ROAD FOR A BIT.
SWEET! I ALWAYS LIKED THE SCENIC ROUTE.
PIZZA
AH, THIS FEELS GREAT!
IT'S BEEN A WHILE SINCE I'VE BEEN ABLE TO LET MY HAIR DOWN.
BUT AMETHYST... YOUR HAIR IS ALWAYS DOWN.
PFFF, YOU KNOW WHAT I MEAN STEVEN!
HAHA!
I KNOW WHAT YOU MEAN!
IT JUST SEEMS LIKE WORK NEVER ENDS!
BUT EVERYONE'S GOTTA HAVE THEIR PIZZA.
YEP, HUMANITY DOESN'T SAVE ITSELF EITHER.

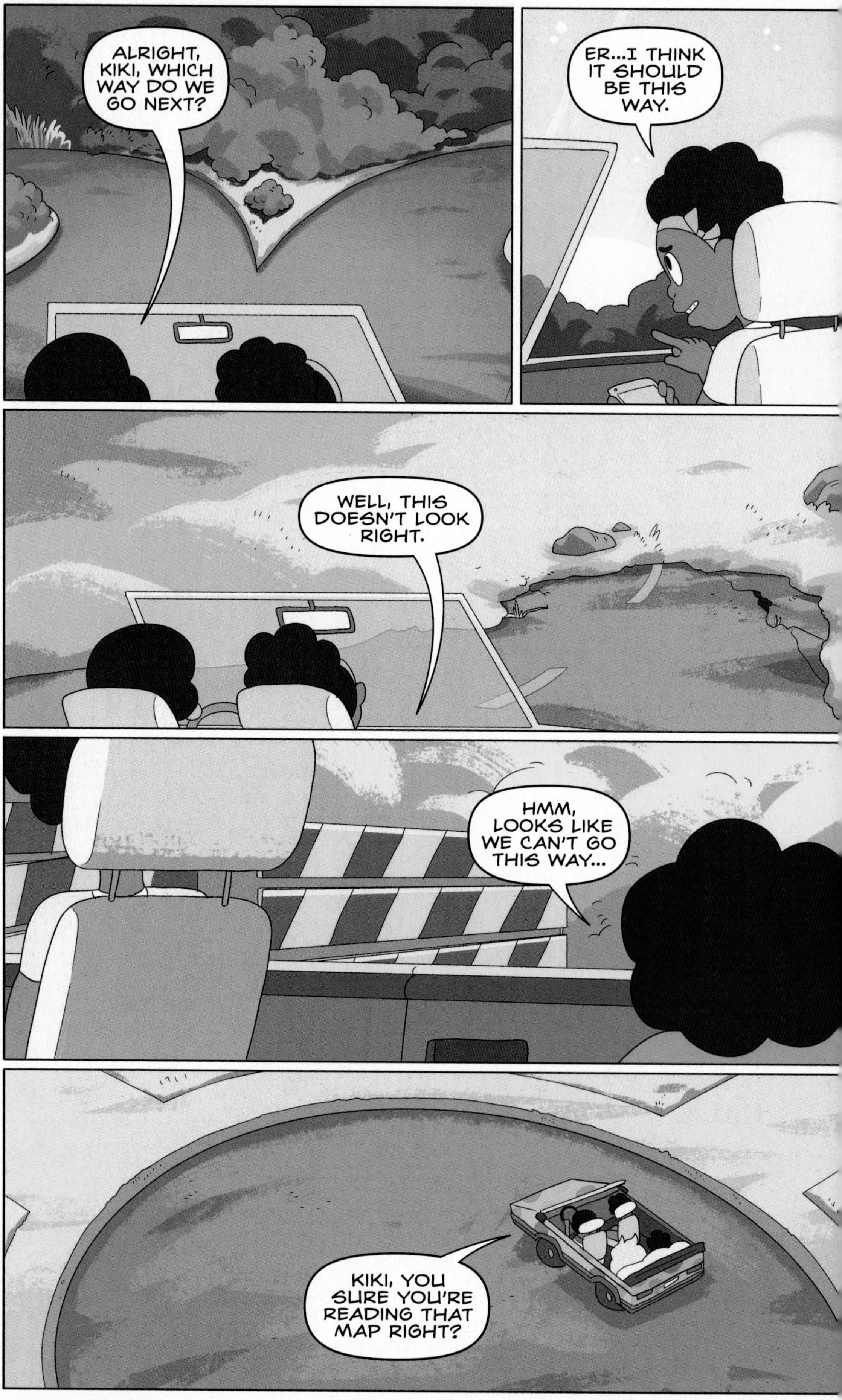
ALRIGHT, KIKI, WHICH WAY DO WE GO NEXT?
ER...I THINK IT SHOULD BE THIS WAY.
WELL, THIS DOESN'T LOOK RIGHT.
HMM, LOOKS LIKE WE CAN'T GO THIS WAY...
KIKI, YOU SURE YOU'RE READING THAT MAP RIGHT?

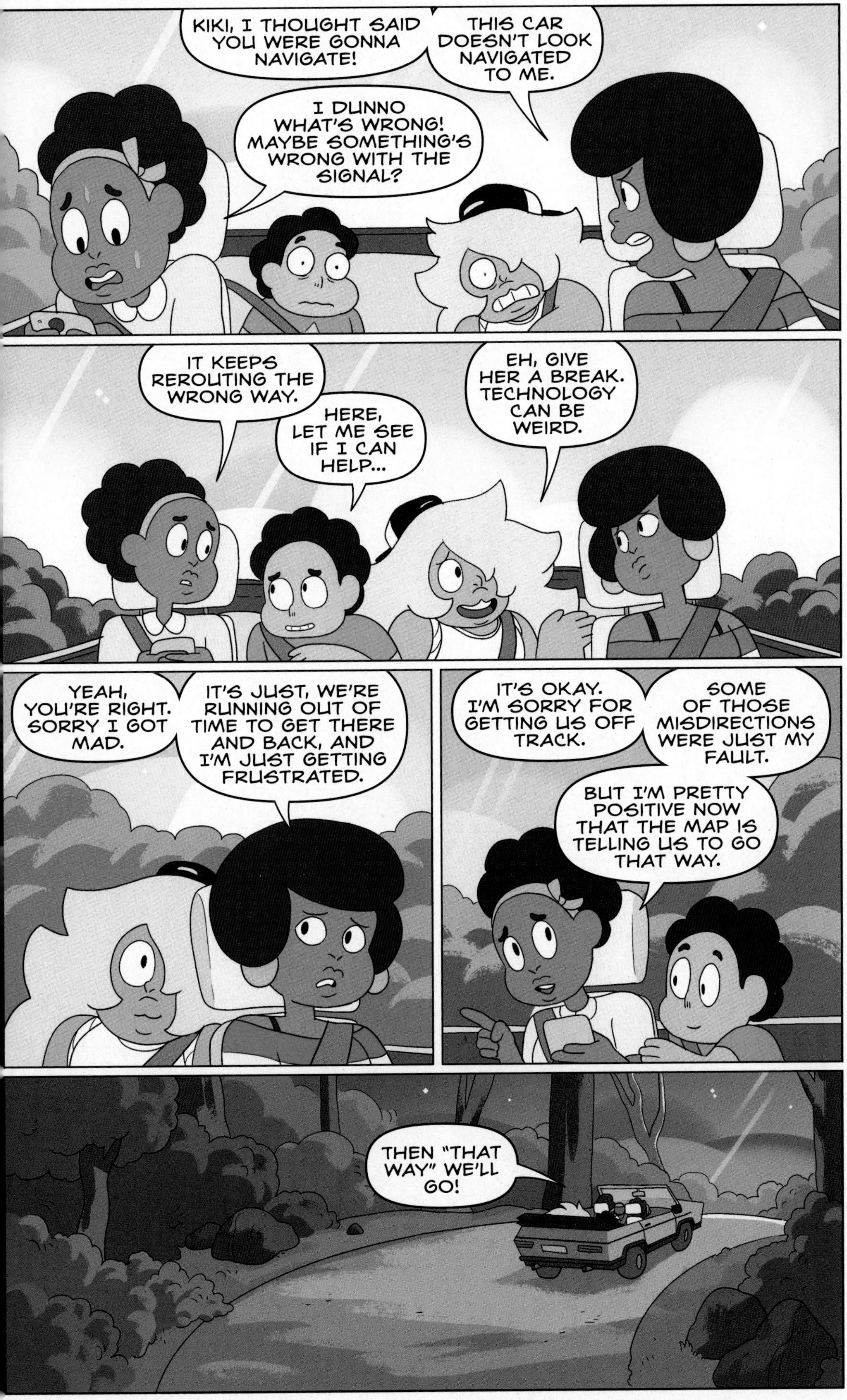
KIKI, I THOUGHT SAID YOU WERE GONNA NAVIGATE!
THIS CAR DOESN'T LOOK NAVIGATED TO ME.
I DUNNO WHAT'S WRONG! MAYBE SOMETHING'S WRONG WITH THE SIGNAL?
IT KEEPS REROUTING THE WRONG WAY.
HERE, LET ME SEE IF I CAN HELP...
EH, GIVE HER A BREAK. TECHNOLOGY CAN BE WEIRD.
YEAH, YOU'RE RIGHT. SORRY I GOT MAD.
IT'S JUST, WE'RE RUNNING OUT OF TIME TO GET THERE AND BACK, AND I'M JUST GETTING FRUSTRATED.
IT'S OKAY. I'M SORRY FOR GETTING US OFF TRACK.
SOME OF THOSE MISDIRECTIONS WERE JUST MY FAULT.
BUT I'M PRETTY POSITIVE NOW THAT THE MAP IS TELLING US TO GO THAT WAY.
THEN "THAT WAY" WE'LL GO!

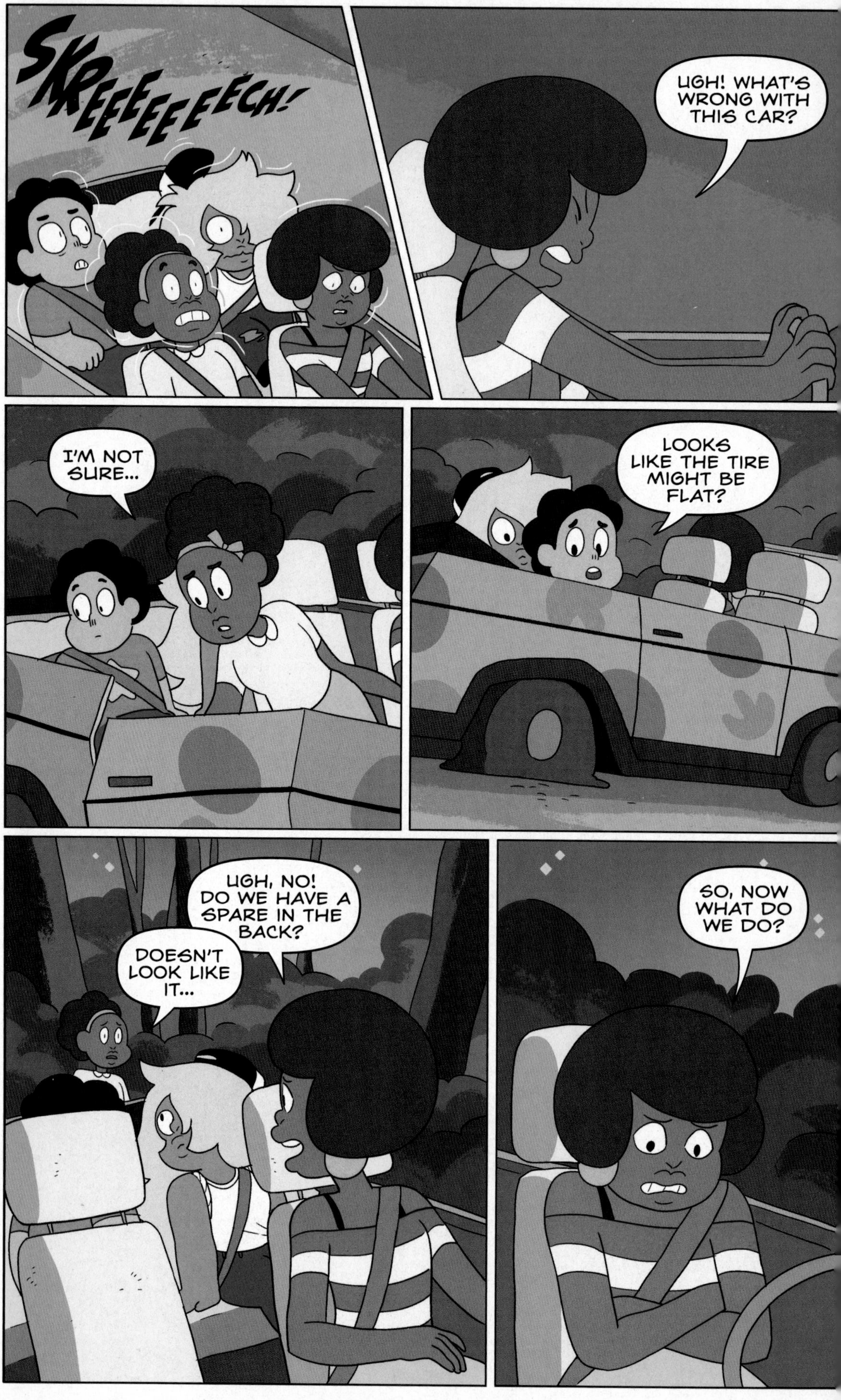
SKREEEEEEEECH!
UGH! WHAT'S WRONG WITH THIS CAR?
I'M NOT SURE...
LOOKS LIKE THE TIRE MIGHT BE FLAT?
UGH, NO! DO WE HAVE A SPARE IN THE BACK?
DOESN'T LOOK LIKE IT...
SO, NOW WHAT DO WE DO?

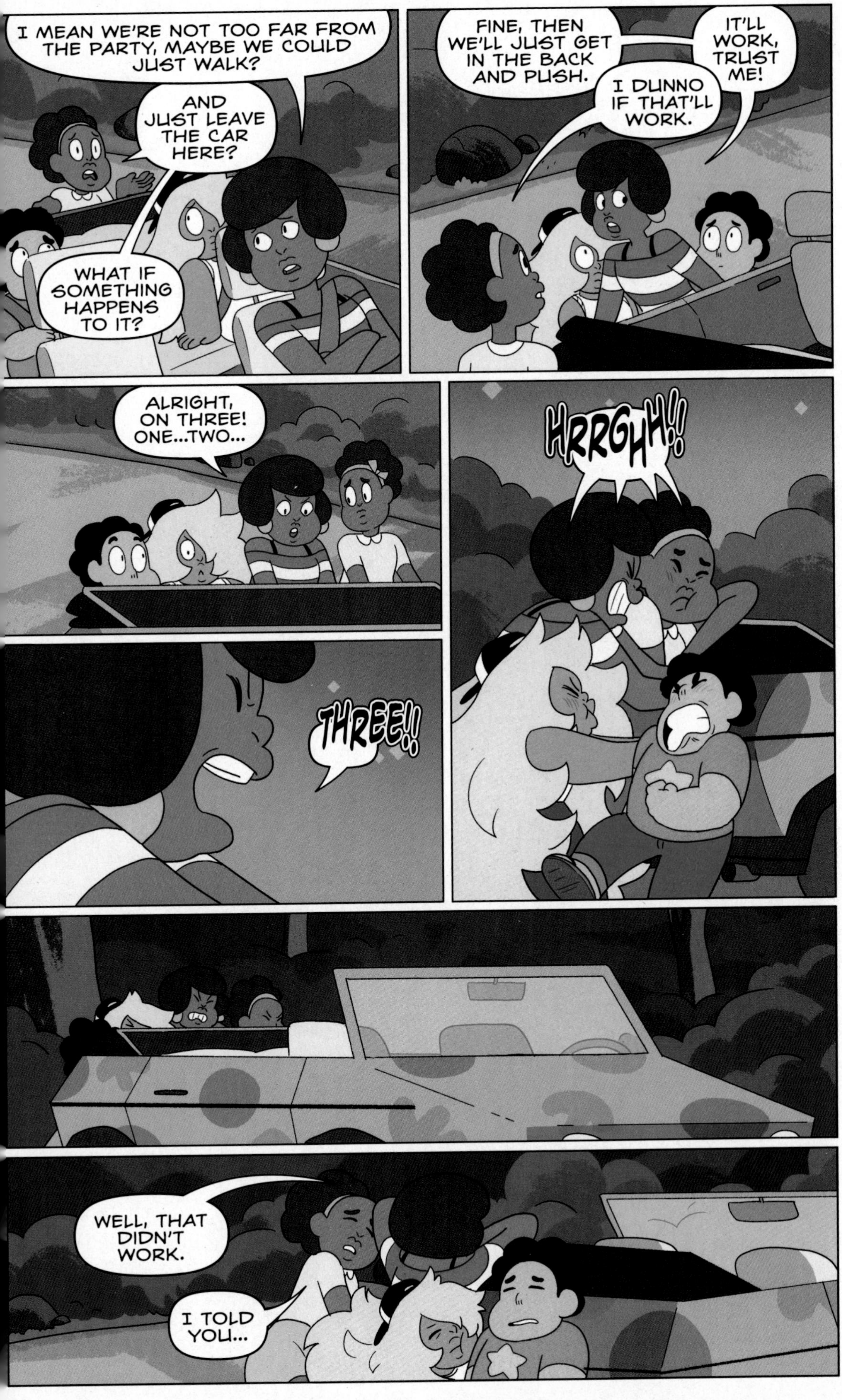
I MEAN WE'RE NOT TOO FAR FROM THE PARTY, MAYBE WE COULD JUST WALK?
AND JUST LEAVE THE CAR HERE?
WHAT IF SOMETHING HAPPENS TO IT?
FINE, THEN WE'LL JUST GET IN THE BACK AND PUSH.
IT'LL WORK, TRUST ME!
I DUNNO IF THAT'LL WORK.
ALRIGHT, ON THREE! ONE...TWO...
HRRGHH!!
THREE!!
WELL, THAT DIDN'T WORK.
I TOLD YOU...

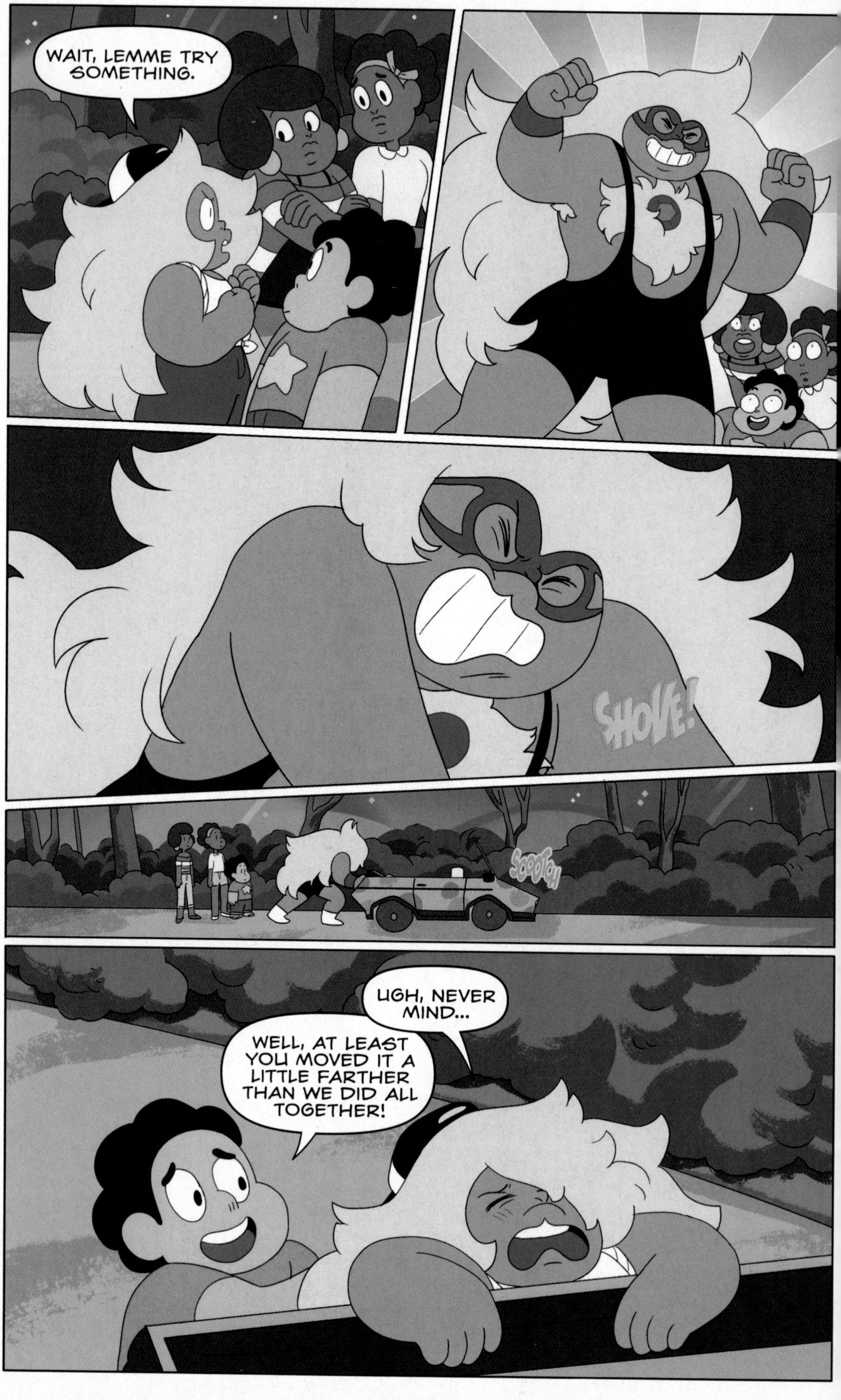
WAIT, LEMME TRY SOMETHING.
SHOVE!
SCOOTCH
UGH, NEVER MIND...
WELL, AT LEAST YOU MOVED IT A LITTLE FARTHER THAN WE DID ALL TOGETHER!

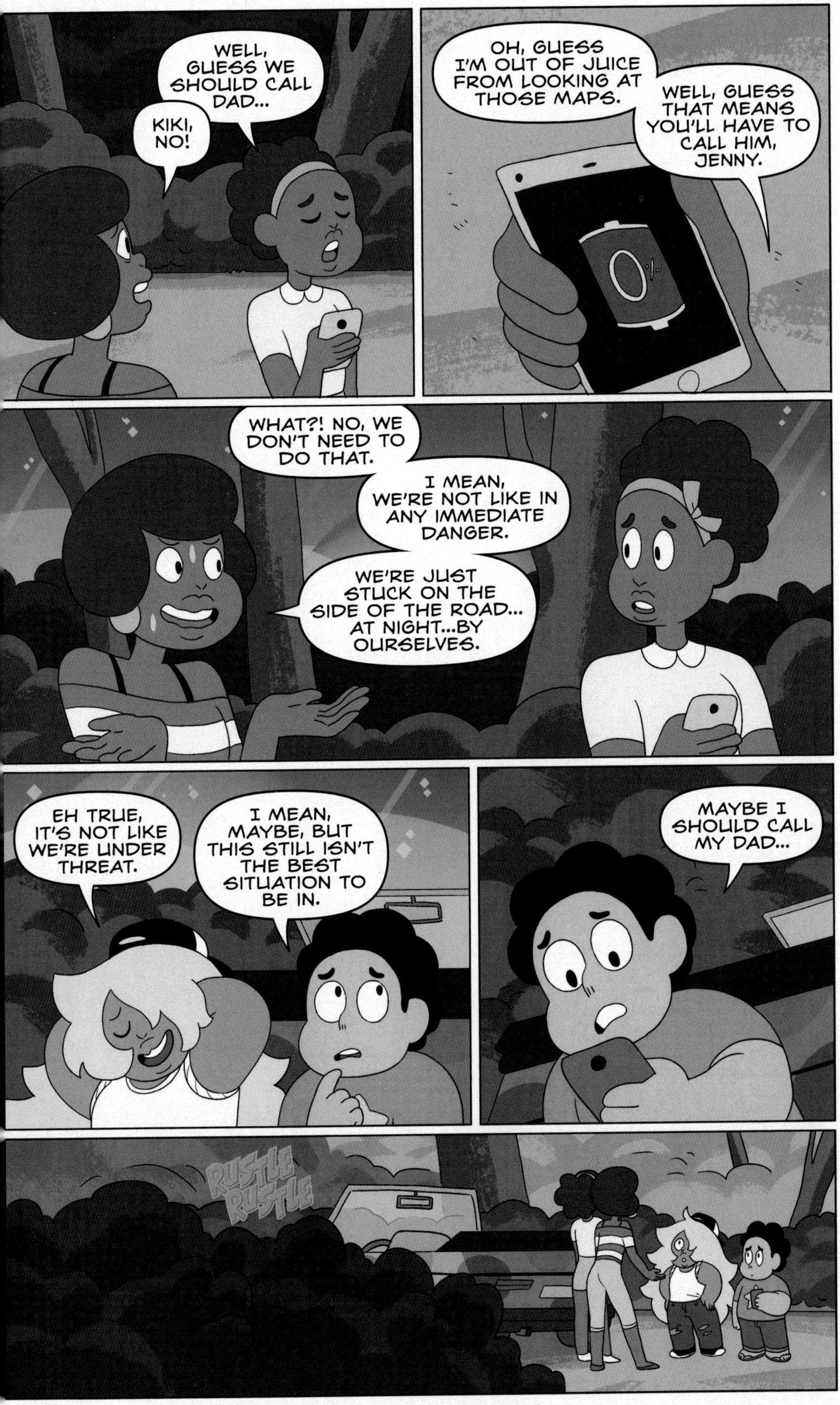

WELL, GUESS WE SHOULD CALL DAD...
KIKI, NO!
OH, GUESS I'M OUT OF JUICE FROM LOOKING AT THOSE MAPS.
WELL, GUESS THAT MEANS YOU'LL HAVE TO CALL HIM, JENNY.
0%
WHAT?! NO, WE DON'T NEED TO DO THAT.
I MEAN, WE'RE NOT LIKE IN ANY IMMEDIATE DANGER.
WE'RE JUST STUCK ON THE SIDE OF THE ROAD... AT NIGHT...BY OURSELVES.
EH TRUE, IT'S NOT LIKE WE'RE UNDER THREAT.
I MEAN, MAYBE, BUT THIS STILL ISN'T THE BEST SITUATION TO BE IN.
MAYBE I SHOULD CALL MY DAD...
RUSTLE RUSTLE

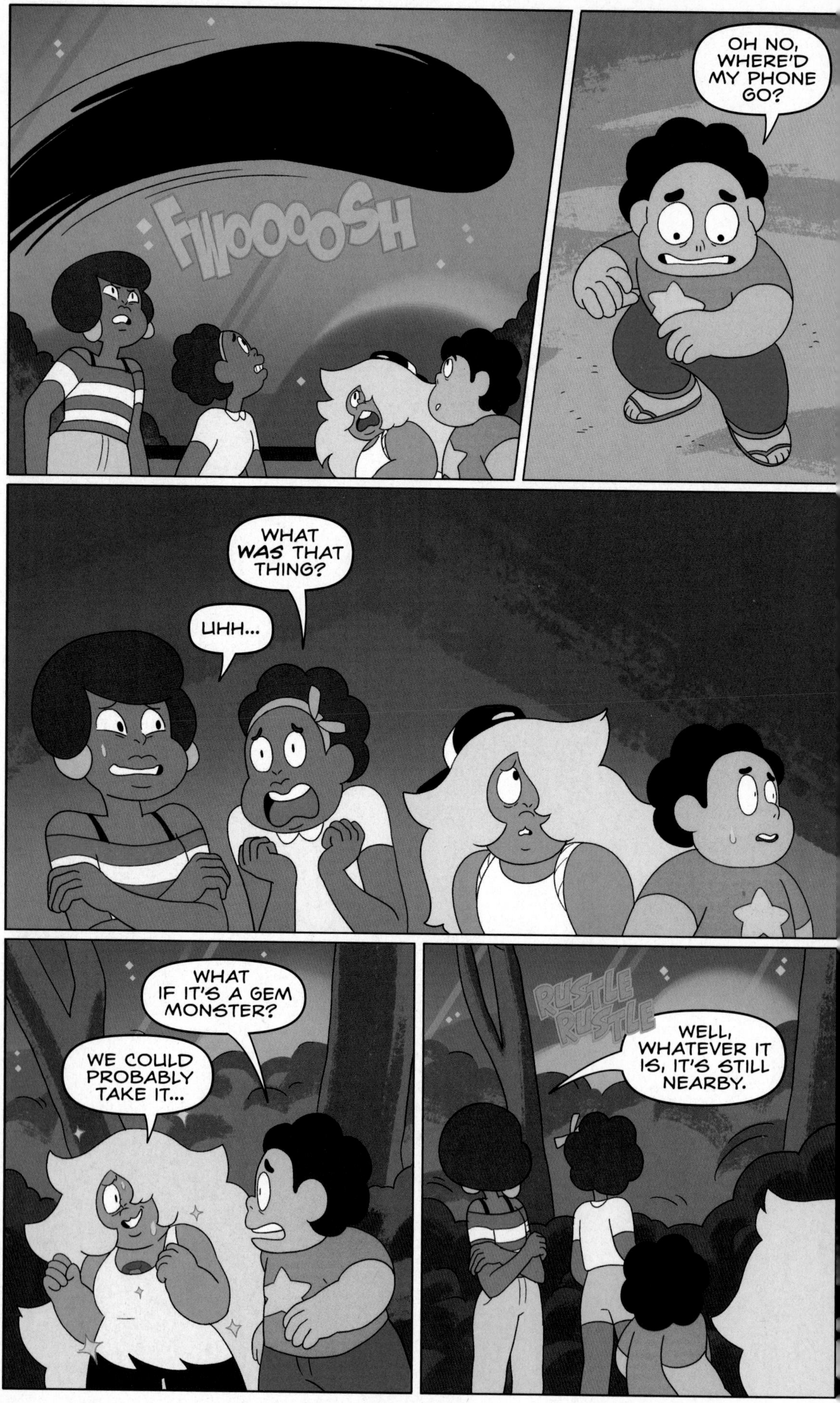
FWOOOOSH
OH NO, WHERE'D MY PHONE GO?
WHAT WAS THAT THING?
UHH...
WHAT IF IT'S A GEM MONSTER?
WE COULD PROBABLY TAKE IT...
RUSTLE RUSTLE
WELL, WHATEVER IT IS, IT'S STILL NEARBY.

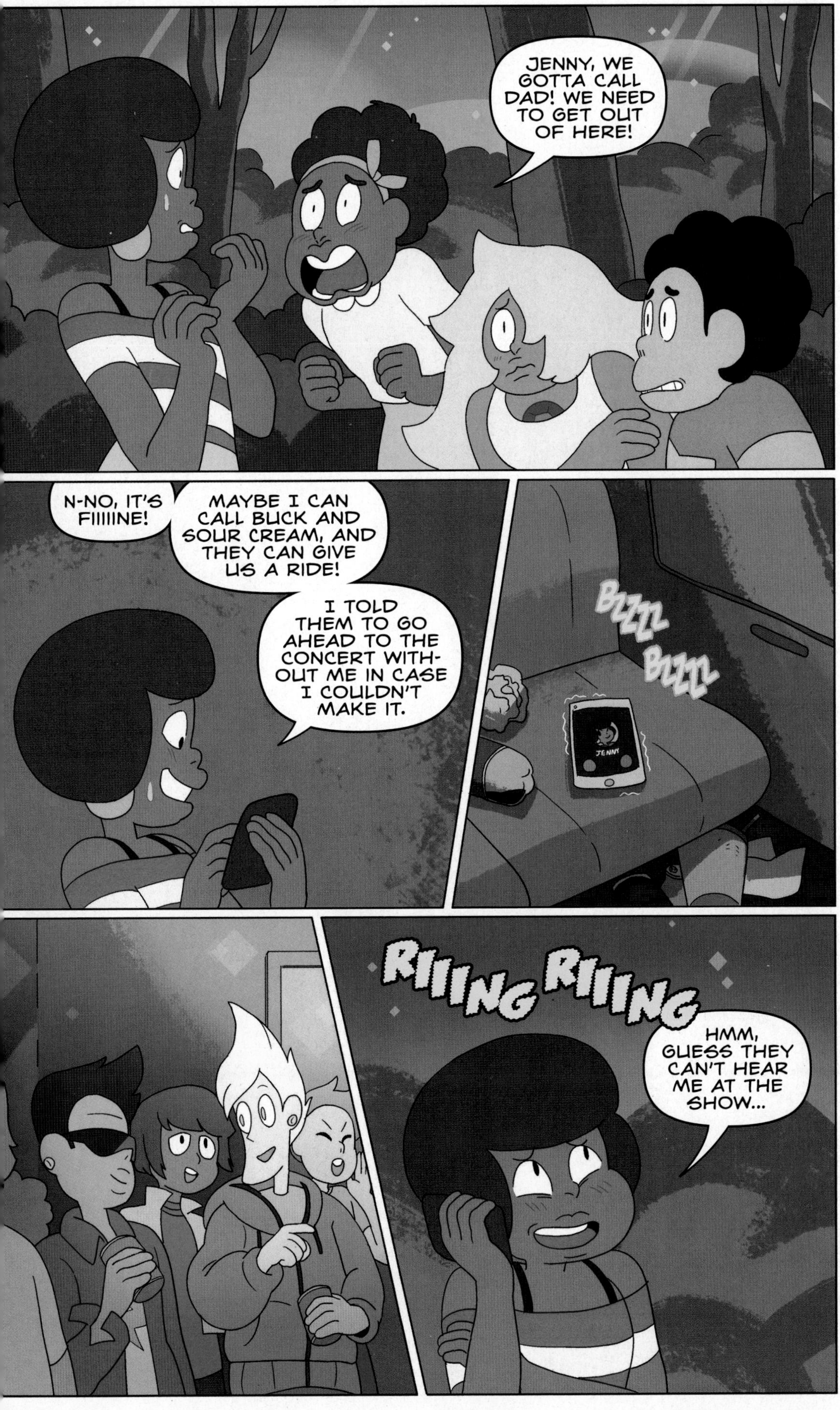
JENNY, WE GOTTA CALL DAD! WE NEED TO GET OUT OF HERE!
N-NO, IT'S FIIIINE!
MAYBE I CAN CALL BUCK AND SOUR CREAM, AND THEY CAN GIVE US A RIDE!
I TOLD THEM TO GO AHEAD TO THE CONCERT WITH-OUT ME IN CASE I COULDN'T MAKE IT.
BZZZZ
BZZZZ
JENNY
RIIING RIIING
HMM, GUESS THEY CAN'T HEAR ME AT THE SHOW...

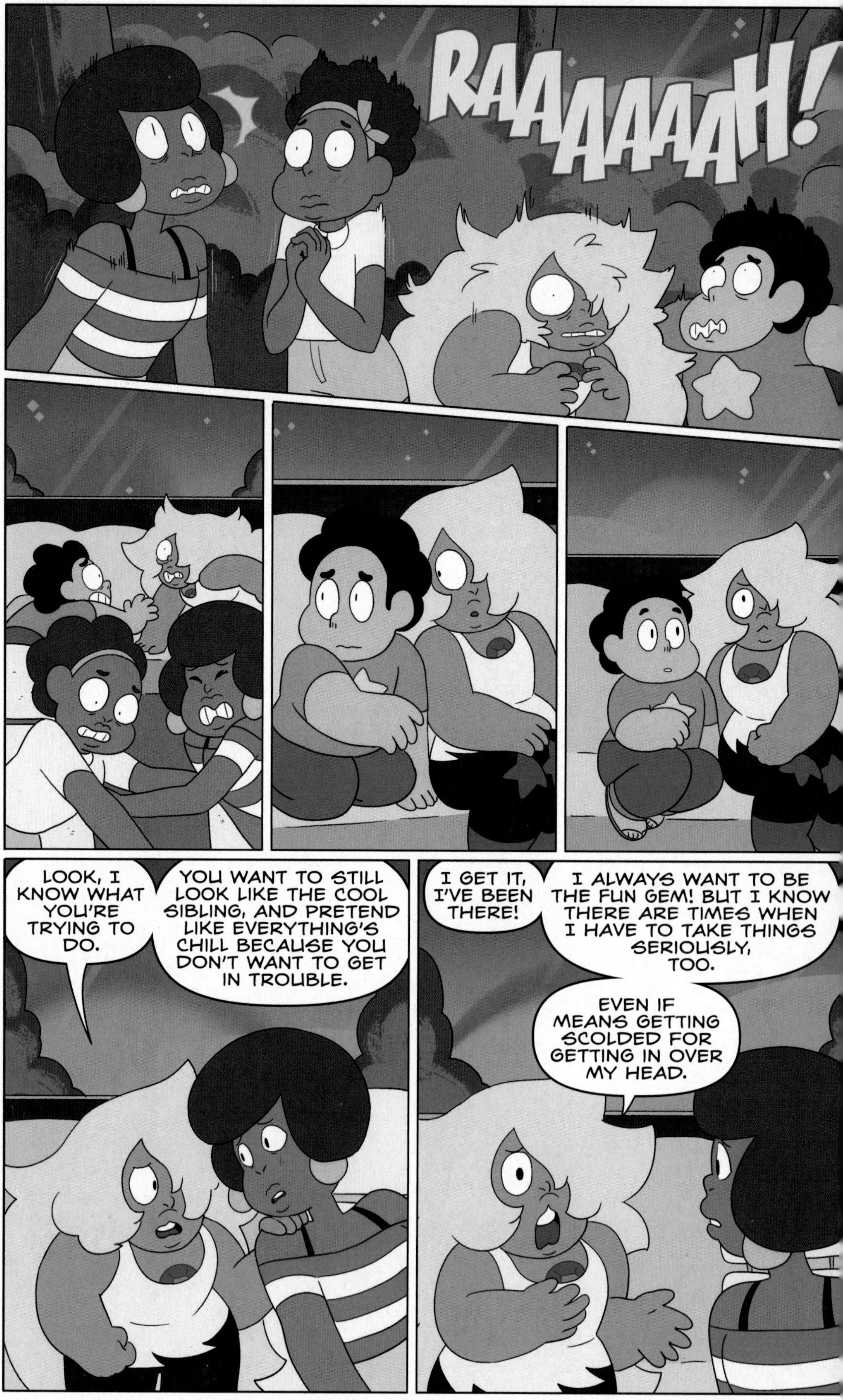
RAAAAAAAH!
LOOK, I KNOW WHAT YOU'RE TRYING TO DO.
YOU WANT TO STILL LOOK LIKE THE COOL SIBLING, AND PRETEND LIKE EVERYTHING'S CHILL BECAUSE YOU DON'T WANT TO GET IN TROUBLE.
I GET IT, I'VE BEEN THERE!
I ALWAYS WANT TO BE THE FUN GEM! BUT I KNOW THERE ARE TIMES WHEN I HAVE TO TAKE THINGS SERIOUSLY, TOO.
EVEN IF MEANS GETTING SCOLDED FOR GETTING IN OVER MY HEAD.

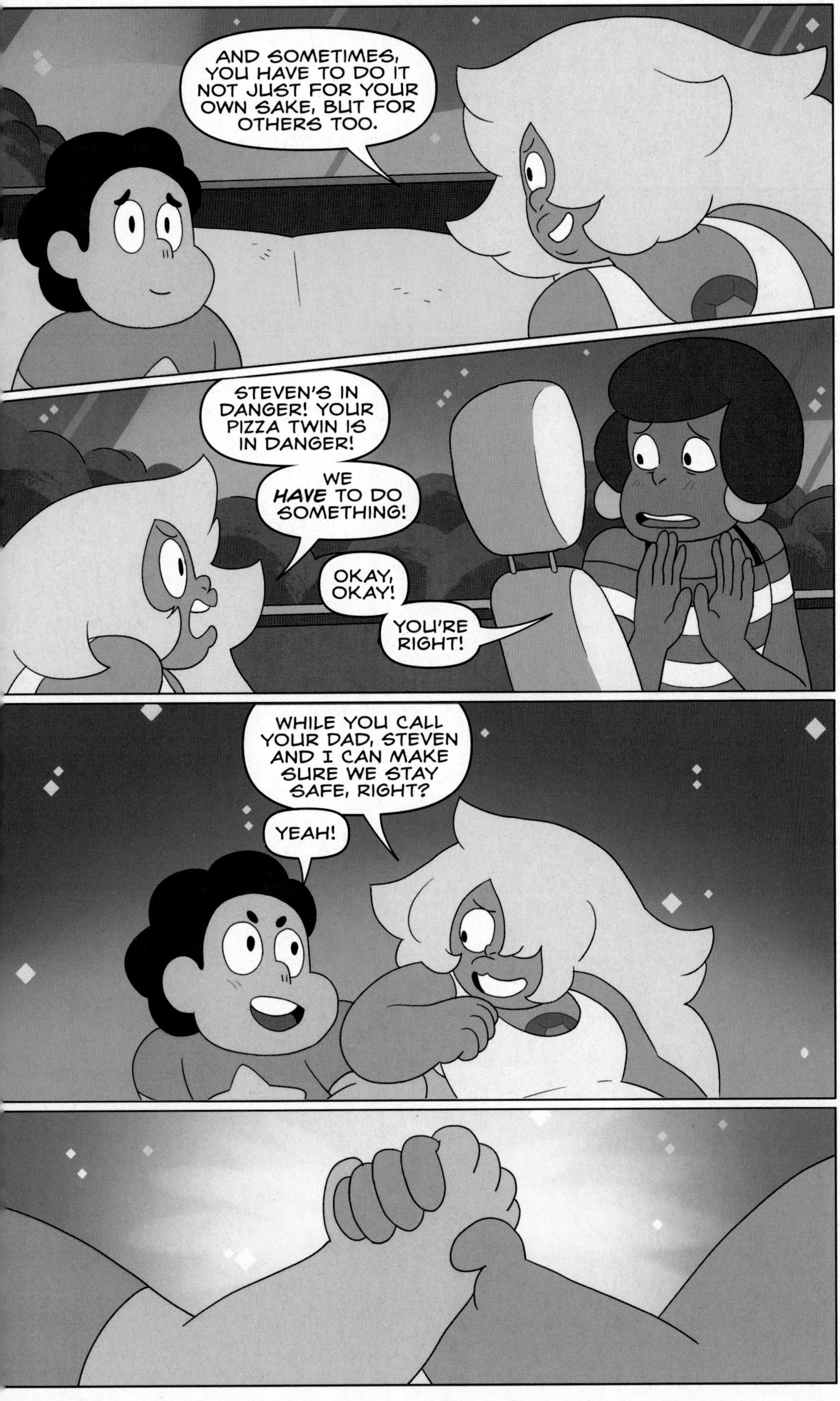
AND SOMETIMES, YOU HAVE TO DO IT NOT JUST FOR YOUR OWN SAKE, BUT FOR OTHERS TOO.
STEVEN'S IN DANGER! YOUR PIZZA TWIN IS IN DANGER!
WE *HAVE* TO DO SOMETHING!
OKAY, OKAY!
YOU'RE RIGHT!
WHILE YOU CALL YOUR DAD, STEVEN AND I CAN MAKE SURE WE STAY SAFE, RIGHT?
YEAH!

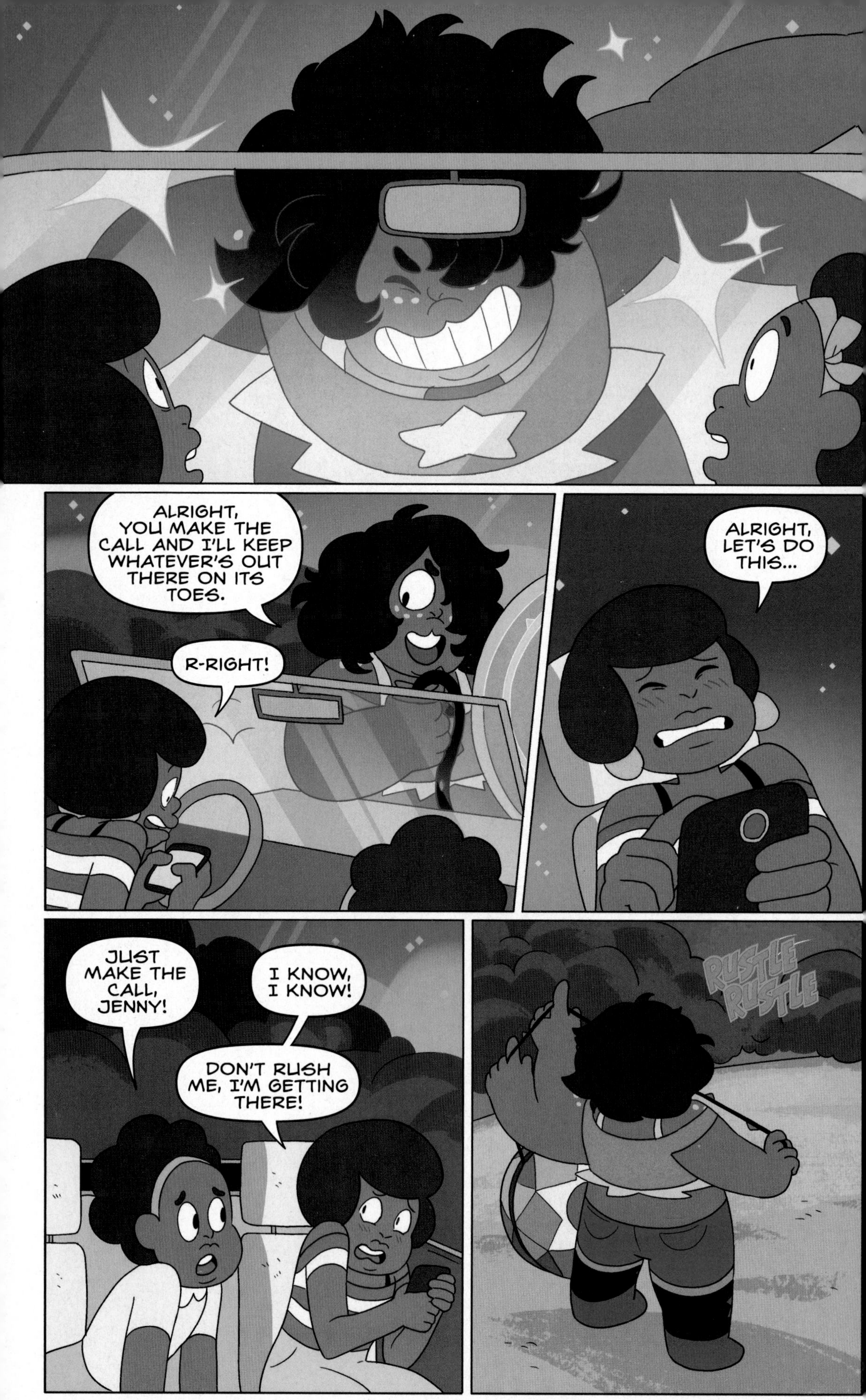
ALRIGHT, YOU MAKE THE CALL AND I'LL KEEP WHATEVER'S OUT THERE ON ITS TOES.
R-RIGHT!
ALRIGHT, LET'S DO THIS...
JUST MAKE THE CALL, JENNY!
I KNOW, I KNOW!
DON'T RUSH ME, I'M GETTING THERE!
RUSTLE RUSTLE

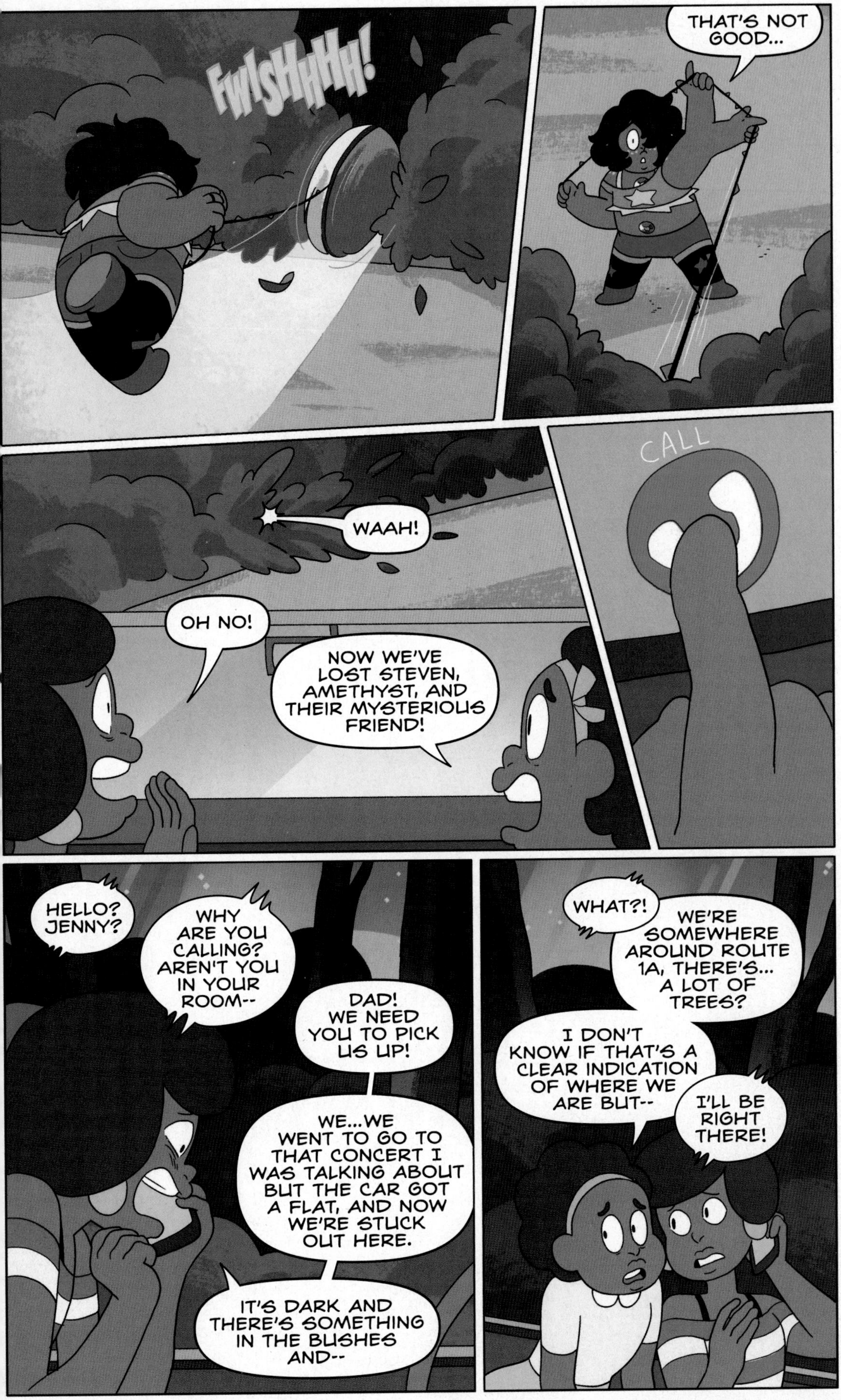
FWISHHHH!
THAT'S NOT GOOD...
WAAH!
OH NO!
NOW WE'VE LOST STEVEN, AMETHYST, AND THEIR MYSTERIOUS FRIEND!
CALL
HELLO? JENNY?
WHY ARE YOU CALLING? AREN'T YOU IN YOUR ROOM--
DAD! WE NEED YOU TO PICK US UP!
WE...WE WENT TO GO TO THAT CONCERT I WAS TALKING ABOUT BUT THE CAR GOT A FLAT, AND NOW WE'RE STUCK OUT HERE.
IT'S DARK AND THERE'S SOMETHING IN THE BUSHES AND--
WHAT?!
WE'RE SOMEWHERE AROUND ROUTE 1A, THERE'S... A LOT OF TREES?
I DON'T KNOW IF THAT'S A CLEAR INDICATION OF WHERE WE ARE BUT--
I'LL BE RIGHT THERE!

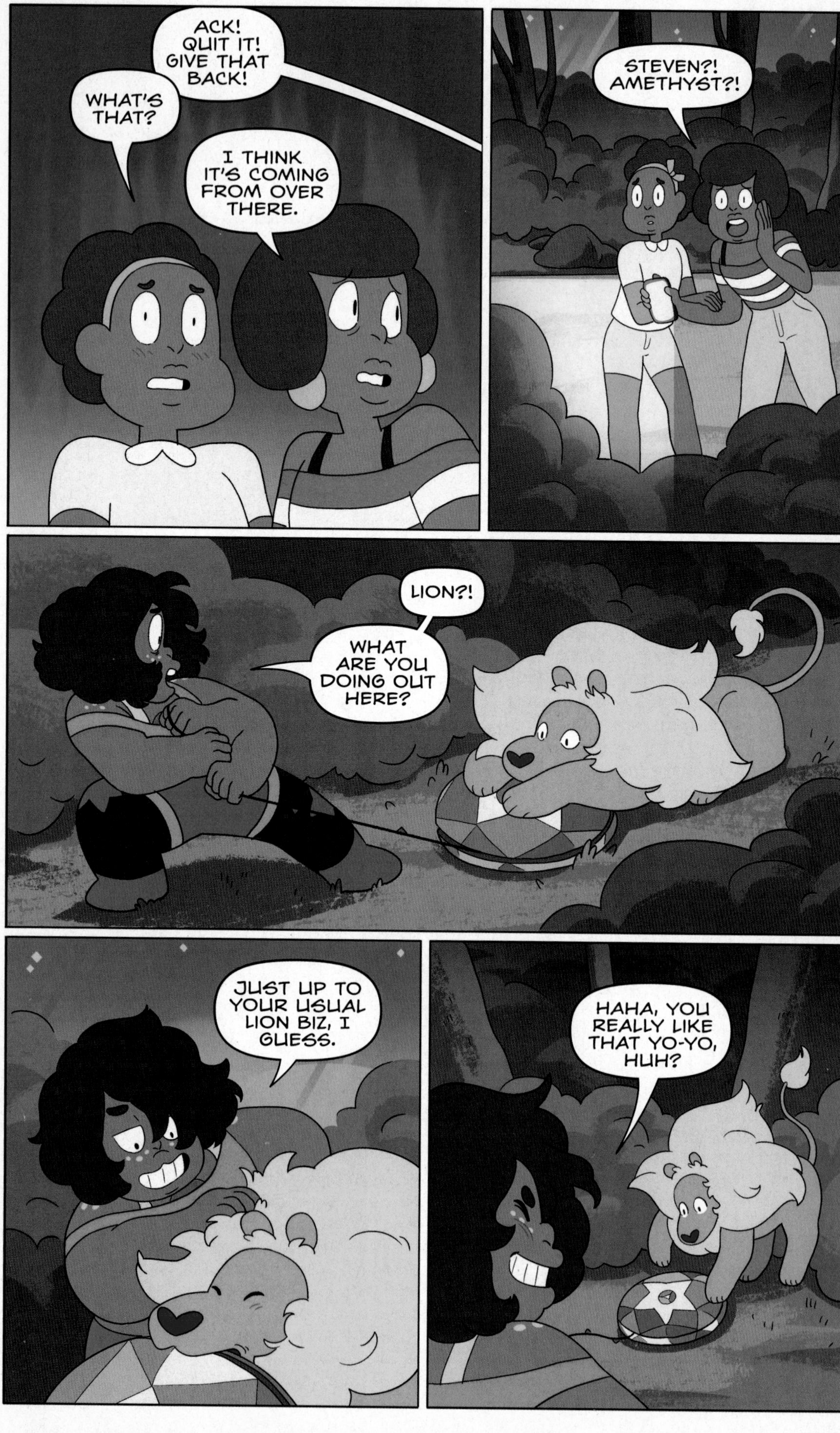
WHAT'S THAT?
ACK! QUIT IT! GIVE THAT BACK!
I THINK IT'S COMING FROM OVER THERE.
STEVEN?! AMETHYST?!
LION?!
WHAT ARE YOU DOING OUT HERE?
JUST UP TO YOUR USUAL LION BIZ, I GUESS.
HAHA, YOU REALLY LIKE THAT YO-YO, HUH?

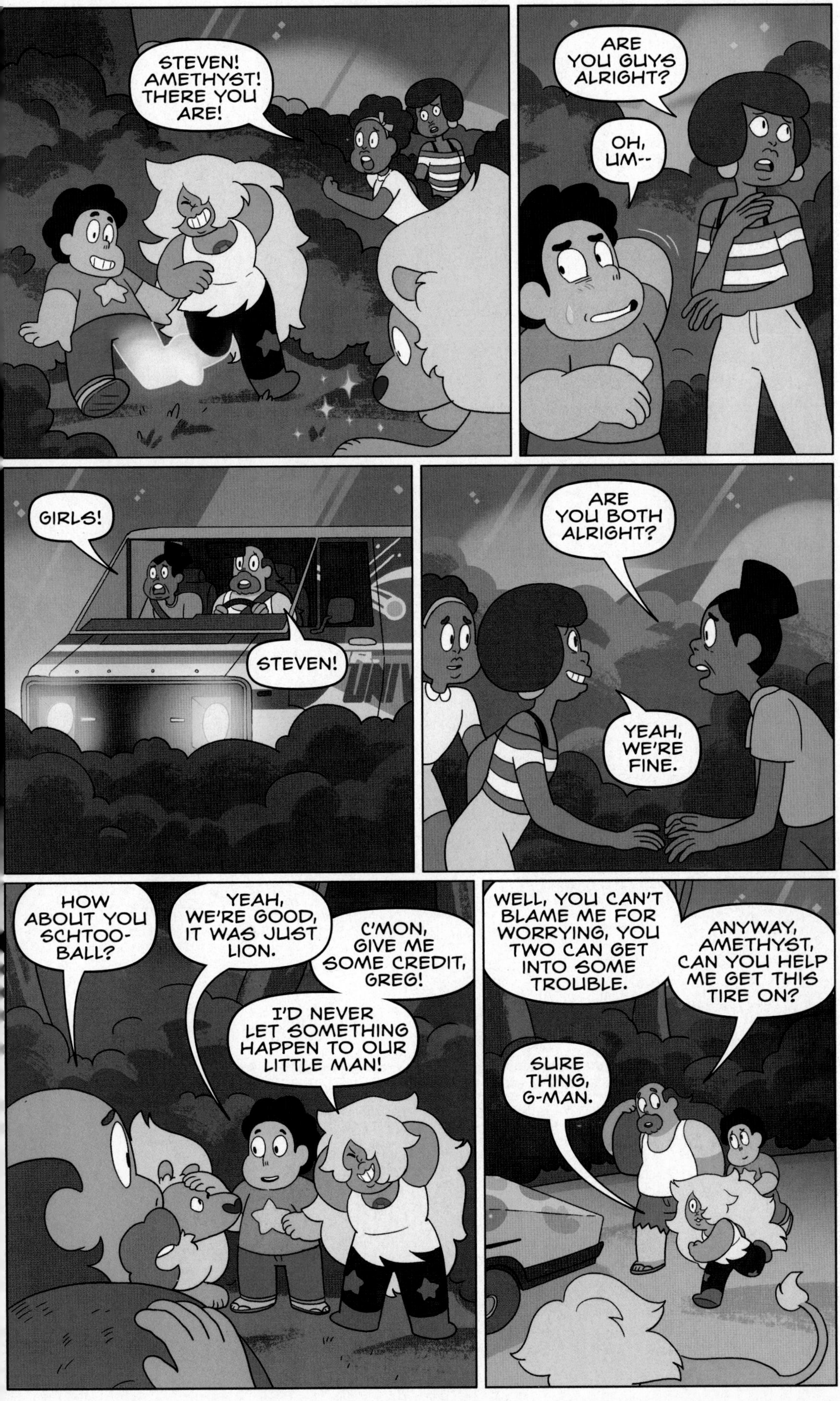
STEVEN! AMETHYST! THERE YOU ARE!
ARE YOU GUYS ALRIGHT?
OH, UM--
GIRLS!
STEVEN!
ARE YOU BOTH ALRIGHT?
YEAH, WE'RE FINE.
HOW ABOUT YOU SCHTOO-BALL?
YEAH, WE'RE GOOD, IT WAS JUST LION.
C'MON, GIVE ME SOME CREDIT, GREG!
I'D NEVER LET SOMETHING HAPPEN TO OUR LITTLE MAN!
WELL, YOU CAN'T BLAME ME FOR WORRYING, YOU TWO CAN GET INTO SOME TROUBLE.
ANYWAY, AMETHYST, CAN YOU HELP ME GET THIS TIRE ON?
SURE THING, G-MAN.

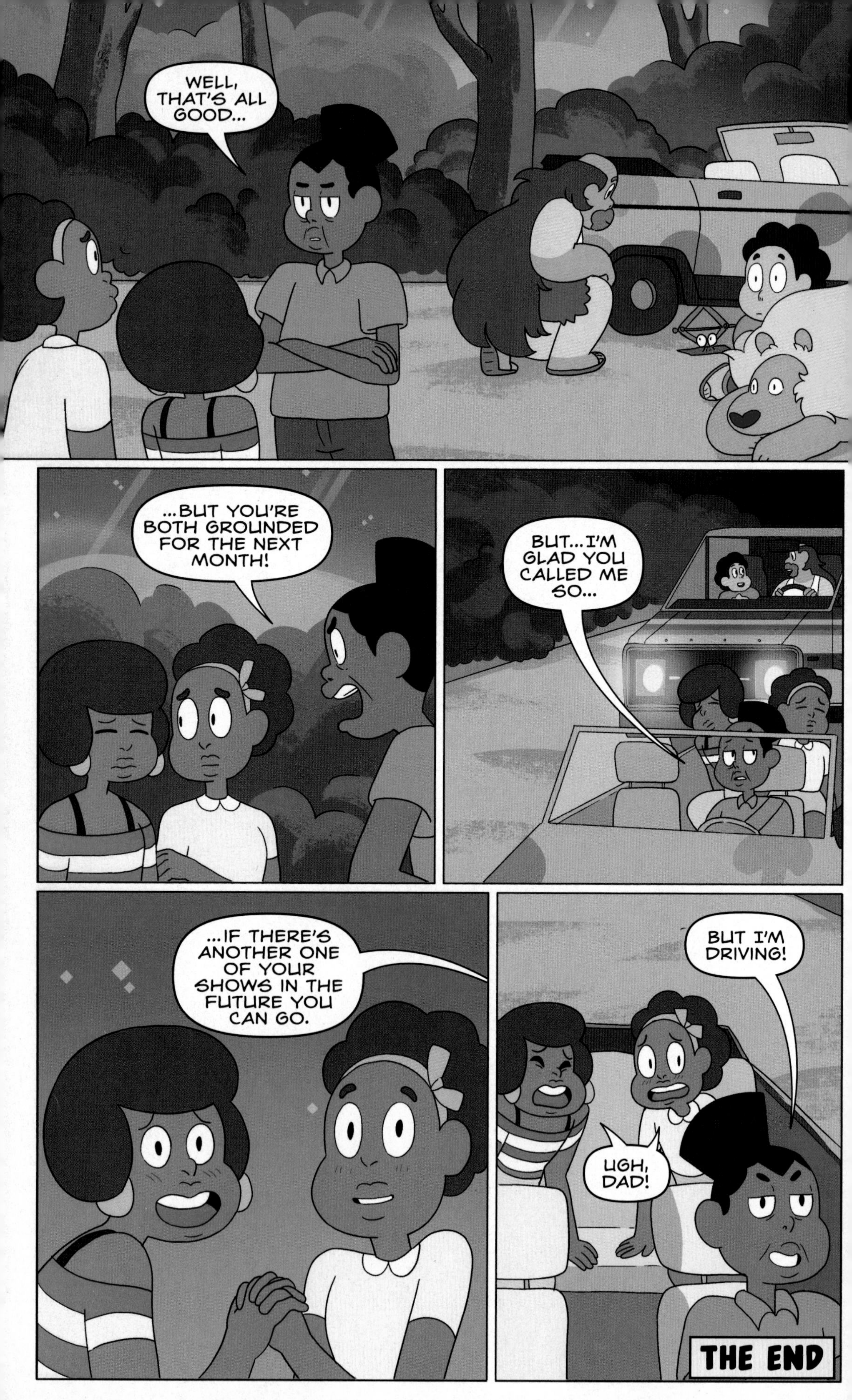
WELL, THAT'S ALL GOOD...
...BUT YOU'RE BOTH GROUNDED FOR THE NEXT MONTH!
BUT...I'M GLAD YOU CALLED ME SO...
...IF THERE'S ANOTHER ONE OF YOUR SHOWS IN THE FUTURE YOU CAN GO.
BUT I'M DRIVING!
UGH, DAD!
THE END

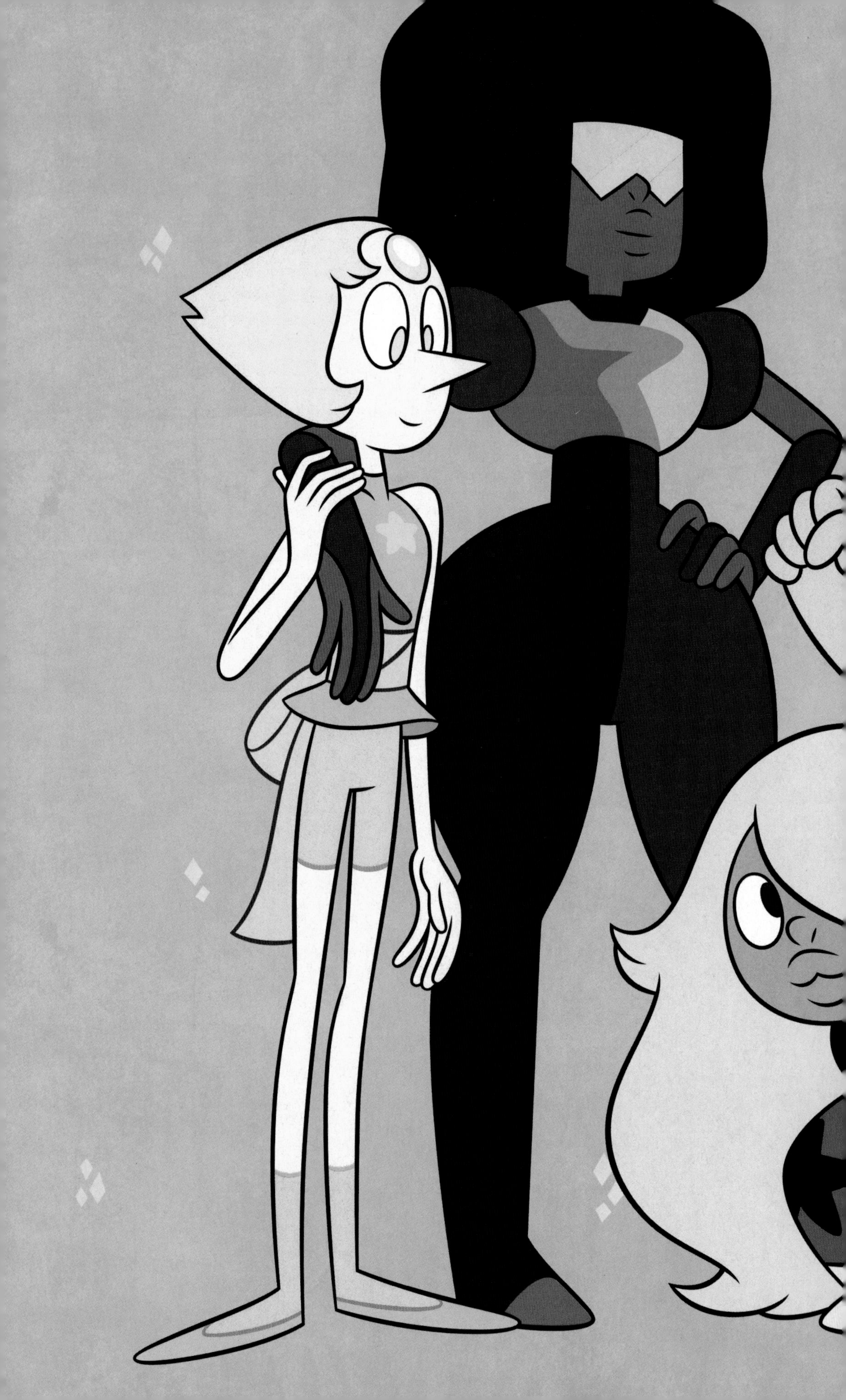

COVER GALLERY

issue thirteen main cover

MISSY PEÑA

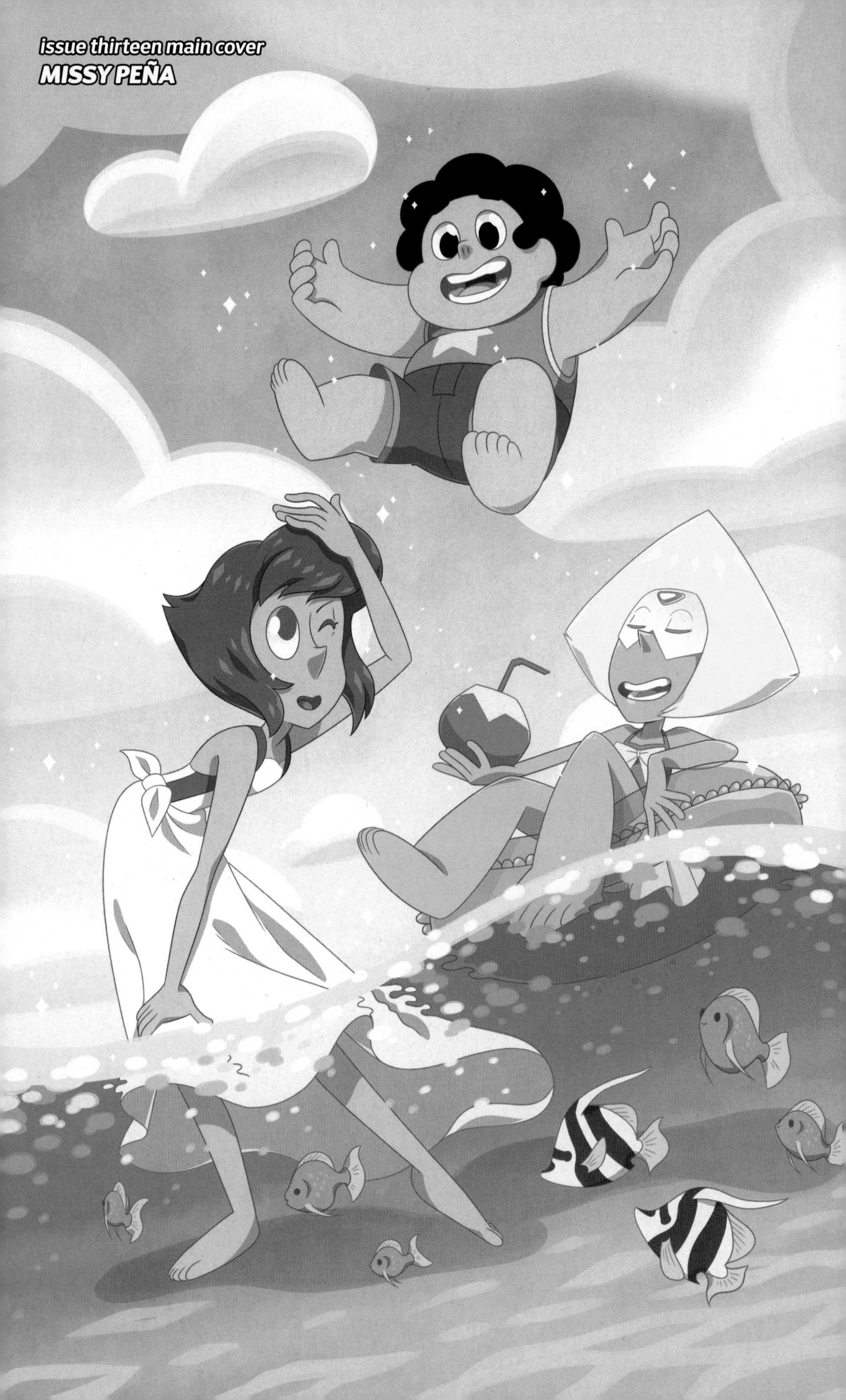

issue thirteen subscription cover

MIRACLE MOSLEY

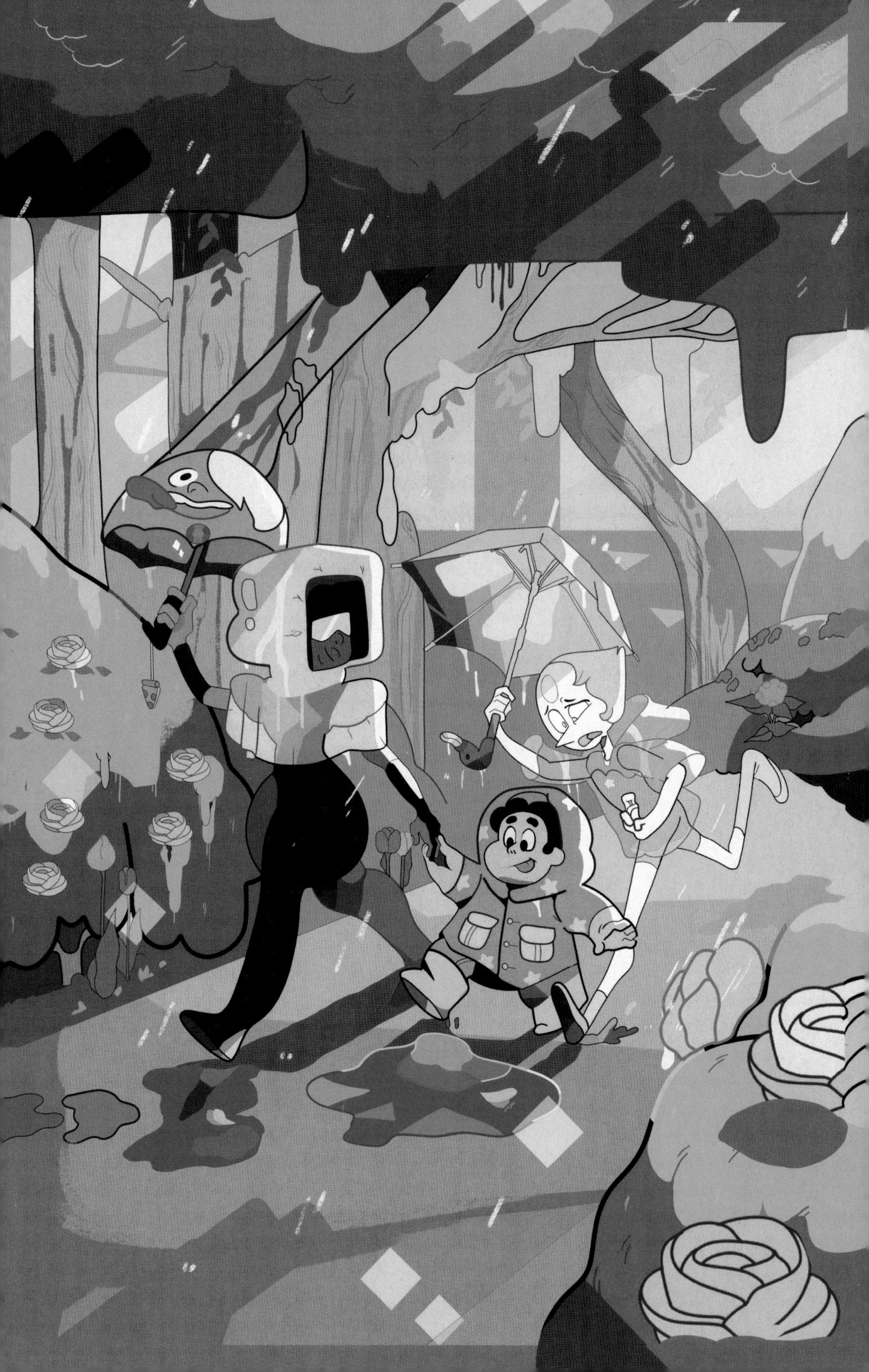

issue fourteen main cover

MISSY PEÑA

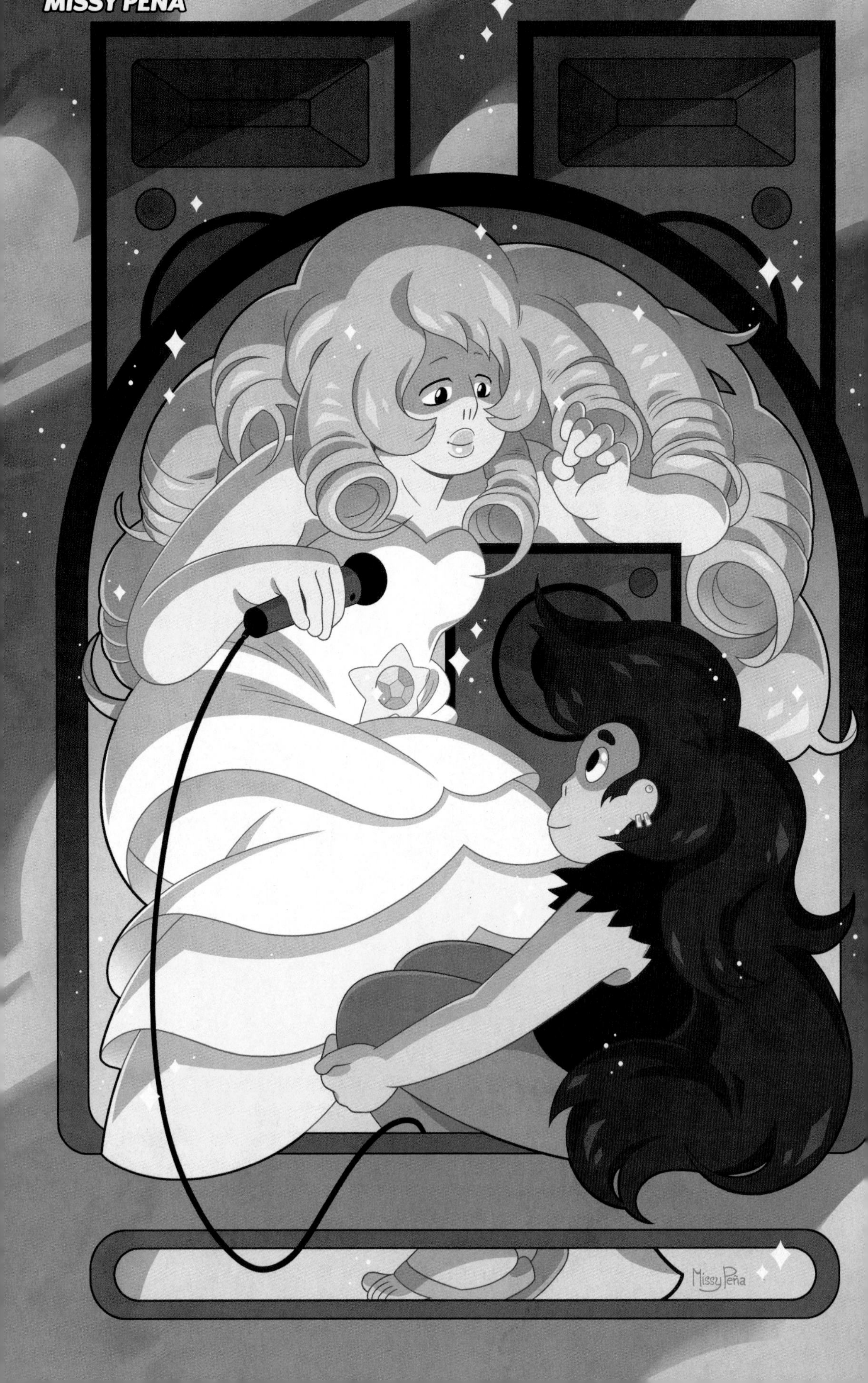

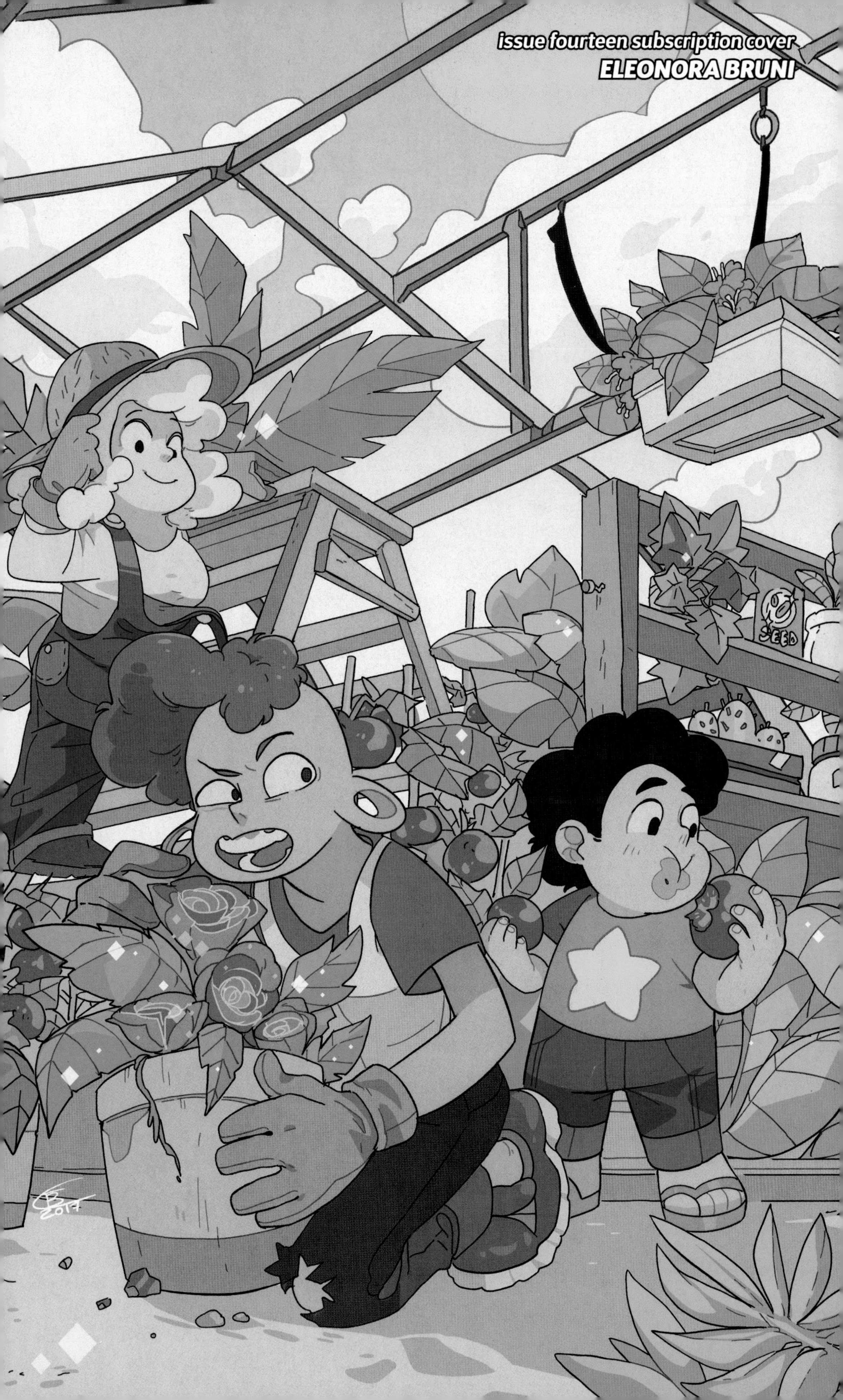
SEED

issue fourteen subscription cover
ELEONORA BRUNI

issue fifteen main cover

JOEY GRANGER

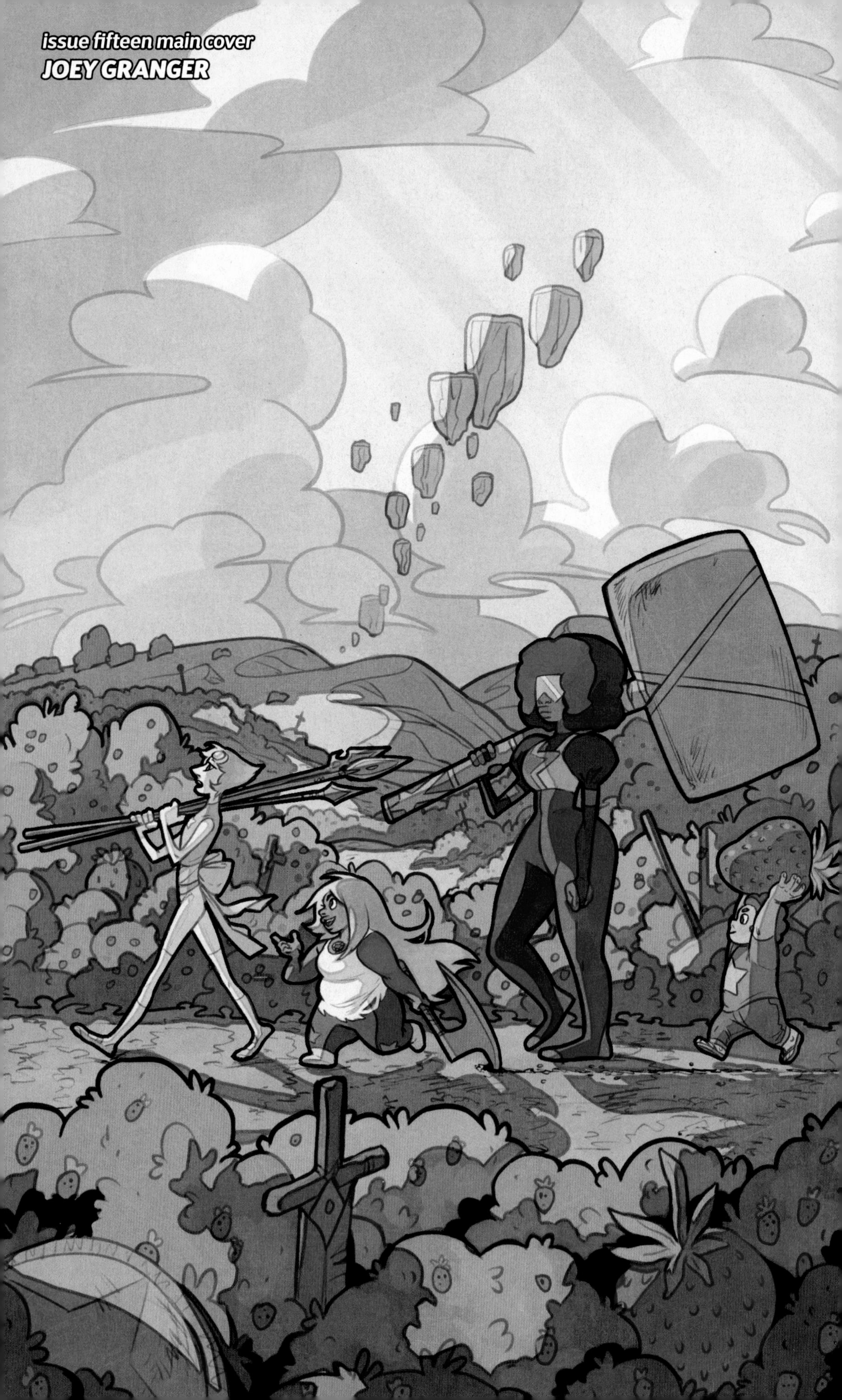

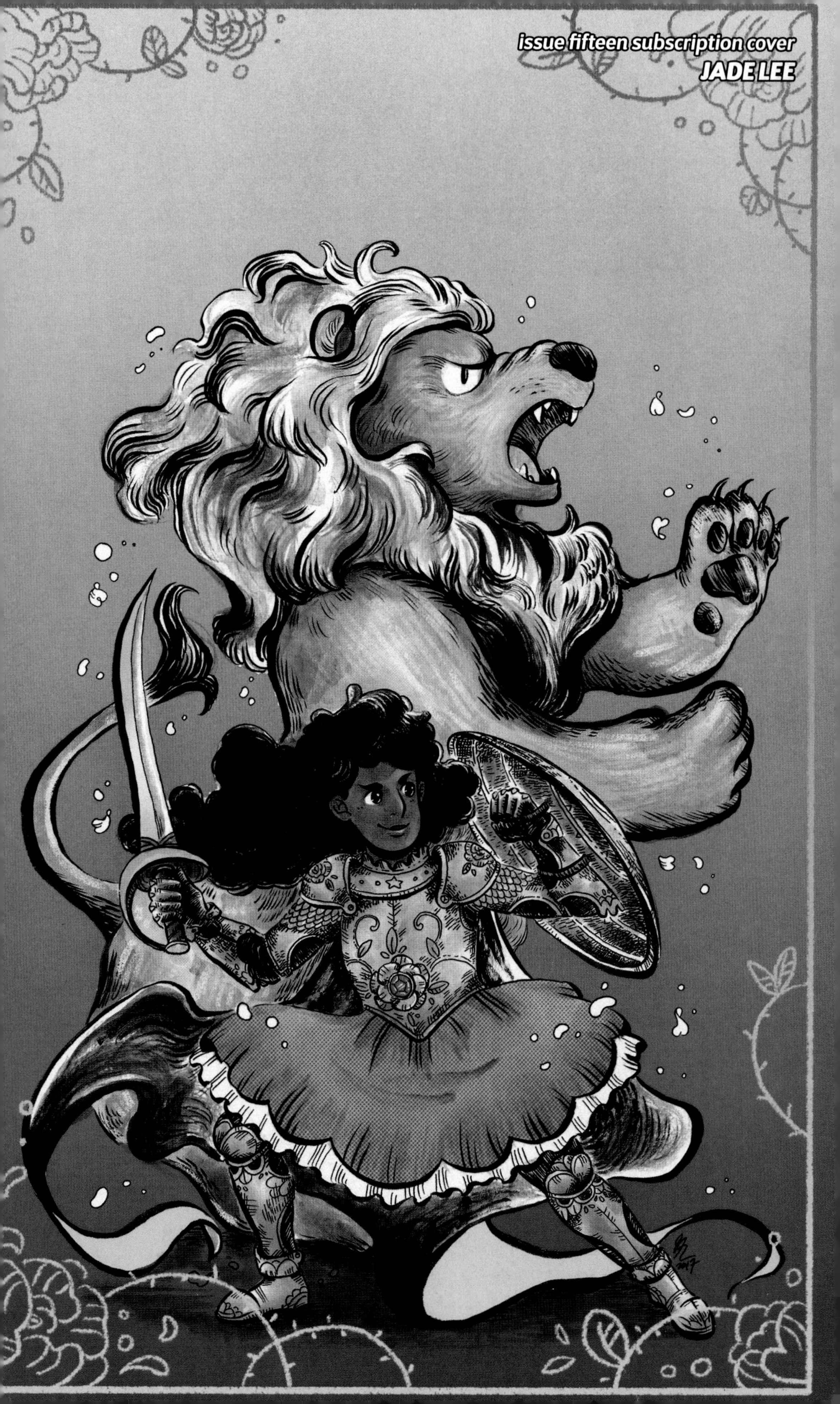

issue fifteen subscription cover
JADE LEE

issue sixteen main cover

GRACE KRAFT

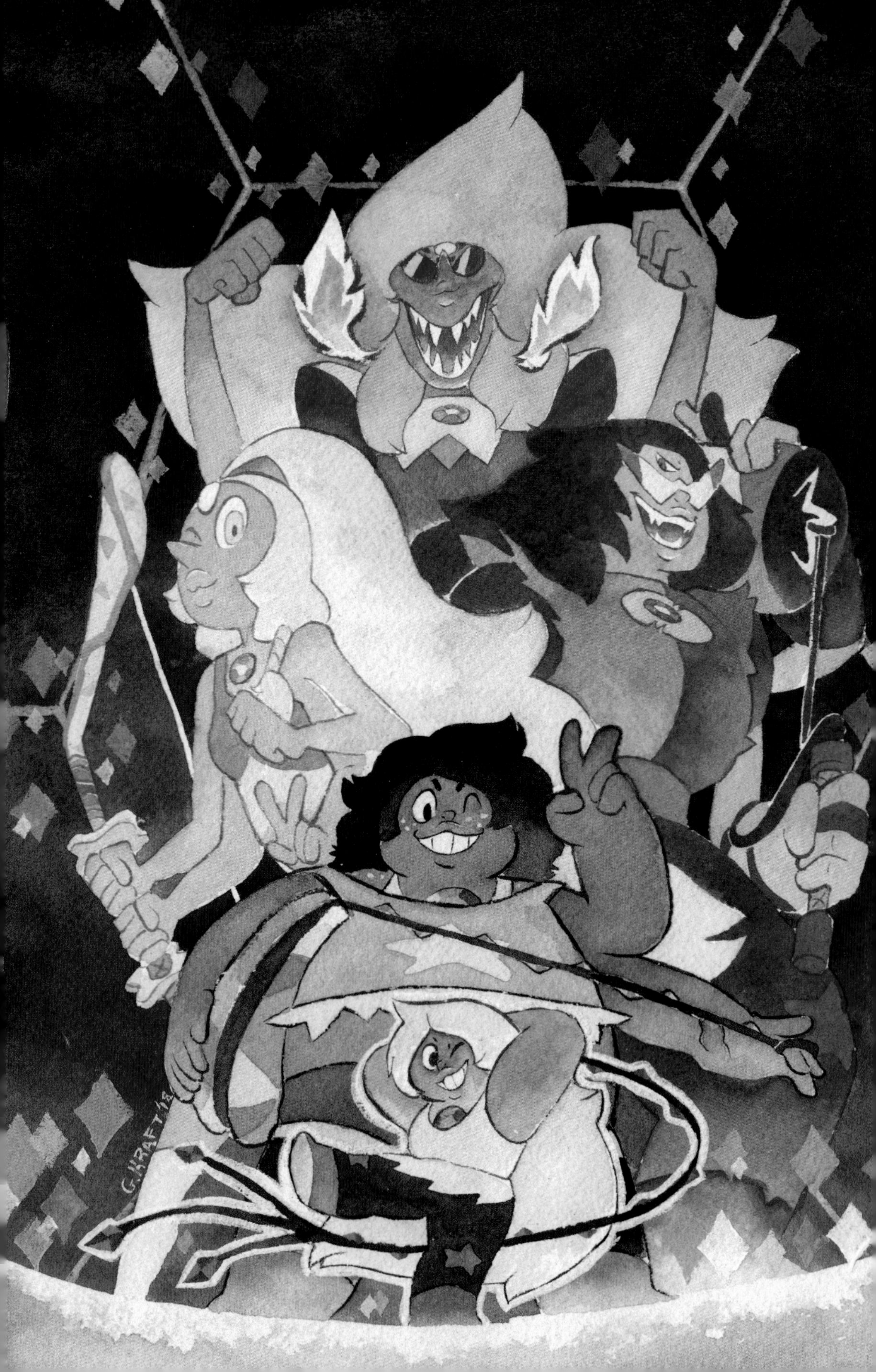
G.KRAFT'18

issue sixteen subscription cover
CASEY DIMOFF

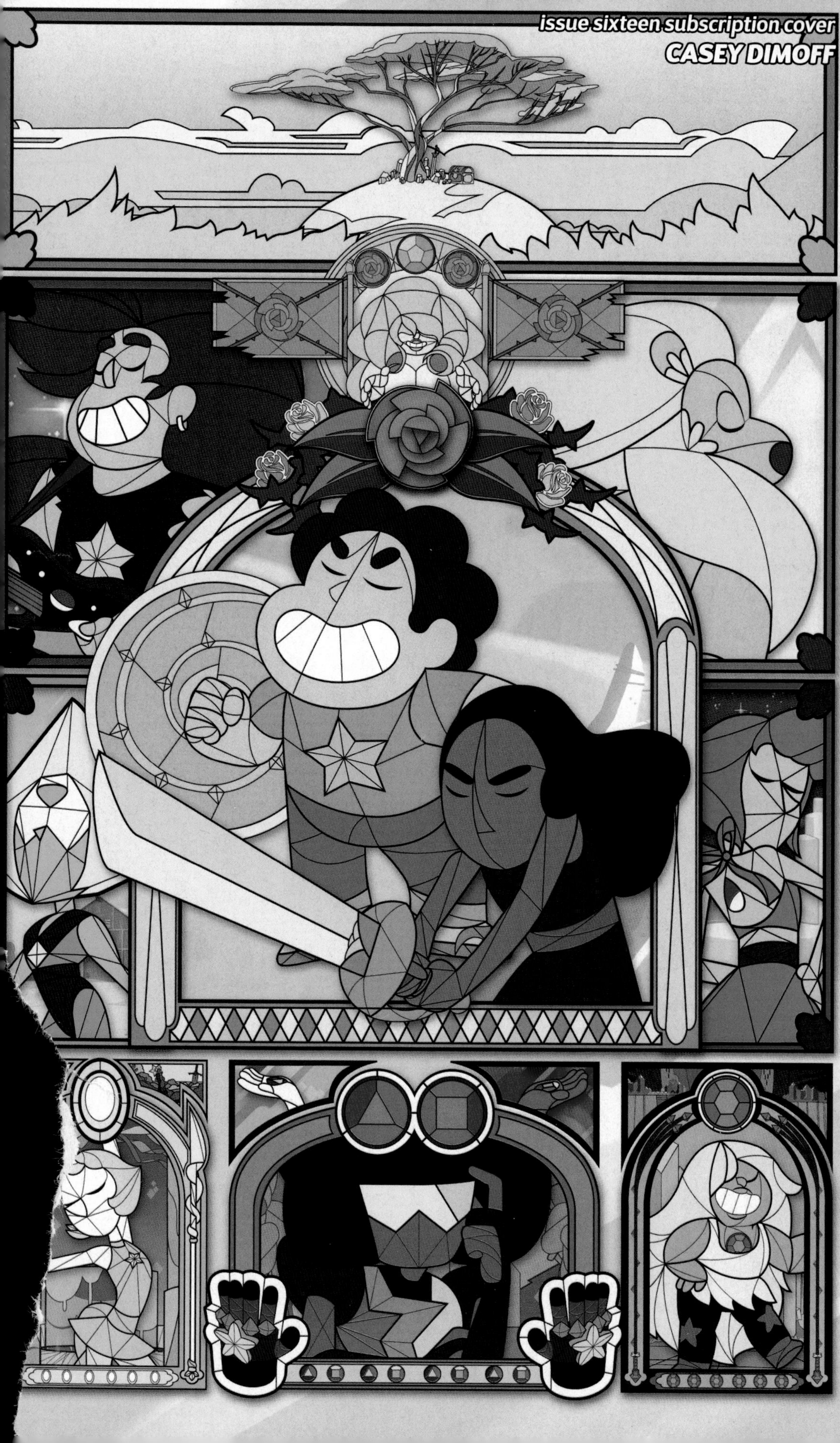

DISCOVER
EXPLOSIVE NEW WORLDS

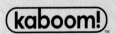

AVAILABLE AT YOUR LOCAL
COMICS SHOP AND BOOKSTORE
WWW.**BOOM-STUDIOS**.COM